WOLF

Barry squatted in the timber, trying to decide what to do now that he had located the underground complex. Perhaps the best thing to do was nothing at all, except alert the FBI and let them handle it. He shape-shifted and began his run through the woods.

He knelt above the bunker entrance and called for Van Brocklen. A moment later, the inspector stepped out, looking all around him.

A scratching sound above and behind him turned the FBI man around. He sucked in his breath at the sight before him. The biggest timber wolf he had ever seen stood above him, the yellow eyes glowing in the night. Van Brocklen didn't know much about wild animals, having been city born and bred, but he had seen enough wildlife documentaries to know better than to reach for a gun. He remained motionless, but his heart was beating so fast he thought it might explode.

Then, suddenly, the wolf was gone and Barry Cantrell was standing where the wolf had been, smiling at him. "Eight and a half miles due west of here, Inspector, there is a small valley. A tumbledown old house sits in the center of that valley. The entire area is honeycombed with underground bunkers. President Hutton is being held there. How you get him out is up to you."

Van Brocklen's mouth opened and closed silently a couple of times. He finally found his voice. "How did you . . . I mean . . . you were a *wolf*. How . . . ?"

But Barry was gone, melting silently into the night.

PREY

William W. Johnstone

PINNACLE BOOKS
KENSINGTON PUBLISHING CORP.

PINNACLE BOOKS are published by

Kensington Publishing Corp.
850 Third Avenue
New York, NY 10022

First Printing: October, 1996
10 9 8 7 6 5 4 3 2 1

Printed in the United States of America

BOOK ONE

The past is but the beginning of a beginning, and all that is and has been is but the twilight of the dawn.

—H.G. Wells

Prologue

He was born in the Transylvanian Alps in Romania and christened Vlad Dumitru Radu. On the night of his birth, the wolves came out of the dark woods and circled the village, howling until no other sound could be heard. When the first wavering notes of the wolves' song reached the infant's ears, his birth crying ceased and the baby's eyes became bright and attentive.

Holding the child to her breast, Vlad's mother sensed that this baby was special, very different from other babies.

She would soon find out just how different he was.

It was December 25, A.D. 1300.

One

The house was built of native stone and sat in the middle of two hundred and fifty acres of land, mostly in timber. It was not a large house, but was suitable for the new owner's needs. A spring-fed creek flowed through the center of the property. The nearest town was several miles away. A new chain link fence encircled the house and several acres around it. A satellite dish brought in dozens of TV stations.

This was an area of the country where people would be as friendly as you wanted them to be . . . and would leave you alone with no hard feelings if that was what you wished.

It did not take people long to learn that the new owner of the property, while not a bit unfriendly when encountered at the store or the gas station or the post office or the bank, wished to be left alone when he was home.

The sheriff of the county took note of the new resident and, out of curiosity, checked him out. Barry Cantrell had no criminal record. As a matter of fact, his past was very nearly blank. But he had passed the test for an Arkansas driver's license, and had new Arkansas plates on his pickup truck. He had opened a checking account at a local bank. Money was electronically deposited in his account every month, coming in from some attorney's office in San Francisco. The same attorney had handled the purchase of his home and acreage. His driver's license listed his age as thirty, height five-ten. The sheriff knew from observing Barry that he was very muscular, and moved with the grace of a dancer. He felt that Barry Cantrell would be damn hard to handle if angered.

The sheriff would occasionally go up into the high country with a lunch packet, a canteen of water, and binoculars. He had found a nice secluded place where he could watch Barry Cantrell. The very first thing Sheriff Don Salter noticed were the two dogs.

"Dogs, hell!" he muttered. "Those are *wolves.*"

He was part right. Pete and Repeat were hybrids: a cross between husky and wolf. But more wolf than husky. Each weighed over a hundred pounds, and they were fiercely loyal to Barry. They had linked up with him when he was living out in the Idaho wilderness.*

The sheriff watched from his hiding place for several hours each day, but the only thing out of the ordinary was that one day instead of two hybrid wolves, there were three.

"Now where the hell did that one come from?" the sheriff whispered.

The new hybrid was much larger than the other two. And Sheriff Salter noticed something else, too: the new and bigger hybrid seemed to be the boss.

That was the only time he saw the third wolf. At least in that form.

Barry knew he was being watched. He had sensed that the very first day. Barry could see and hear and

Hunted—Pinnacle

smell far beyond the capacity of a "normal" human being. He could sense danger before it could happen. He could smell fear in another human. His eyesight was far superior to any human's vision. For while Barry was certainly human, he was also several other things.

He was immortal. He could not die. He could not be killed. He could be hurt, but he healed rapidly. When he was fourteen years old, he discovered he could shape-shift at will, moving between human and animal form, although he did that only in moments of great danger and stress. Over the centuries, he had traveled the world. He had fought by the side of Joan of Arc, Napoleon, George Washington.

Barry Cantrell was the world's consummate and eternal warrior.

And he had been for seven centuries.

"He's in Arkansas."

Robert Roche, one of the five richest men in all the world, swiveled in his chair and smiled, his back to the man who stood before his desk. "Going under what name?"

"Barry Cantrell."

"I suspected he might do better than that," Robert muttered. "From Darry to Barry. Not very original."

A year past, in Idaho, when Robert Roche had sent a dozen mercenaries after him, Barry had been going under the name of Darry Ransom.

"Have you located the other one?"

"Yes. He's living in Ireland. Just outside of Cork. He is now using the name of John Ravenna."

"Has he been approached by others, and what was his reply to their offer?"

"Yes, sir. He has been approached, and he is mulling over their offer."

"Go to Ireland. Talk to this John Ravenna. Tell him whatever the others have offered him, I'll triple it if he'll come to work for me. I do not want Cliff Madison assassinated. Go!"

After the man had left, Robert Roche rose from his chair and paced the huge office. "Those idiots," he muttered. "Don't they have sense enough to know that if I thought political assassination was the route to go, I'd have taken it years ago?"

Sheriff Salter had slipped into his hiding place and had been watching Barry for about fifteen minutes, when suddenly he lost him from view.

"Where the hell did he go?" the sheriff muttered. "He was right there and now he's gone."

But the two big hybrid wolves were still on the porch, dozing, apparently unconcerned about their master's disappearance.

"I ought to be back in the office," the sheriff said. "I have a thousand things to do before the Speaker gets here next month."

The Speaker of the House of Representatives was coming to spend a week's vacation in North Arkansas, fishing, hiking, and river rafting along the Buffalo River.

Sheriff Salter lifted his binoculars and scanned the area below him. Barry Cantrell was not in sight.

The sheriff decided he was being just a little bit silly. After all, the man had done nothing. There certainly wasn't any law against minding one's own business and living a very quiet life.

Still . . . the guy was far too young to be retired. So how did he live? What had he done to earn this money he got every month? It wasn't a government pension. So . . . ?

Maybe he'd come here to join one of those damned survivalist groups that were all over the area. The sheriff shook his head. No, the survivalist groups were all right. He knew a lot of the men and women in those. But there were several very racist groups in the area, hard right-wing organizations that preached hate. And one neo-Nazi group.

Was this Barry Cantrell a part of those groups?

The sheriff almost stopped breathing when the voice spoke from behind him. "Something I can do for you?"

Sheriff Salter dropped his binoculars and knocked over his canteen getting to his feet. Barry Cantrell stood about two feet away, smiling at him.

"Jesus, man!" Salter blurted. "You move like a ghost."

"So I've been told. Sorry I startled you." Barry held out his hand. "Barry Cantrell."

The sheriff took the greeting, noticing that the hand was hard and callused. "Don Salter. I'm the sheriff of this county." God, he felt like a fool. He'd been caught on private property without a warrant.

"If you want to know all about me, Sheriff, why don't we go on down to the house and we'll have some iced tea and talk? I'll introduce you to my dogs. If you plan on coming out here often, it's best you get to know them."

"Might be a good idea."

"Come on."

At the gate, Barry said, "Let me go in first, Sheriff."

"I wouldn't have it any other way," Don said drily.

Barry laughed and stepped into the fenced area.

Don noticed that Barry spoke no words to the huge hybrids. He just looked at them. After a moment, he waved for the sheriff to come on in. Being careful to close the gate behind him, Don let the animals sniff him.

"Pet them," Barry said.

Don looked down at the two hybrids. Their teeth were about twice as long as those found on full-breed dogs. Don inwardly shuddered at the thought of how much damage they could do . . . in a very short time.

"That's Pete, and that's Repeat," Barry said, pointing out the dogs as he named them. "Come on in the house. Where is your car, by the way?"

Don pointed. "Other side of the ridge. On the south side of the county road."

"I'll drive you over there after we talk. That's a good hike and the day is getting warm."

Pete and Repeat slid under the high porch, and Don and Barry went into the house. The air conditioner was humming softly, cooling the air to a comfortable level. Barry waved the sheriff to a chair. "I'll get the tea. You take it plain or sugared?"

"Two sugars, please."

Barry disappeared into the kitchen, and Don looked around. The living room/den was clean and neat and sparsely furnished. One chair, a recliner. A couch, a coffee table. An end table by the chair. A new television against the wall. Two prints on the wall: a seaside print and one of the mountains. No pictures on the mantel above the fireplace. Don sat down on the couch.

Barry returned with two large glasses of iced tea. He put one glass on the coffee table, the other on the end table by the chair. He sat down in the recliner and looked at Don.

The sheriff sipped his tea. Good. "I should apologize for spying on you, Mr. Cantrell."

"Call me Barry. No apology necessary, Sheriff. I'm

a stranger in your community. No visible means of support. I live alone, except for two hybrid wolves. Don't socialize. I don't blame you for checking me out. What did you find out?" That was asked with a slight smile.

"To be honest, nothing. You don't have a past, Barry."

"Oh, everybody has a past, Sheriff. Mine just isn't very interesting, that's all. I'm a recluse. I like living alone. I really prefer the wilderness areas, but they're getting hard to find."

Sheriff Don Salter hesitated. He'd been a cop all his adult life. Started out as a deputy, then chief deputy, then ran for the office and to his surprise was elected. He was just starting his second term. Not bad for a man in his late thirties. Don was on very shaky legal ground with Barry Cantrell, and he knew it. He had no warrant to be here, had not apprised the man of his rights, and knew that anything he might learn, more than likely, could not be used in a court of law.

"I came here from out west, Sheriff," Barry said. "Idaho, to be precise. I was homesteading a piece of land in the wilderness area. You might recall there was a lot of trouble out there last year . . . ?"

Don nodded. "I sure remember seeing that on the TV and reading about it. You were there?"

"I was close enough to it to get real nervous. I could sure hear the gunfire, and there was a lot of it. I decided to move to a more peaceful area."

"I don't blame you for that. That was a real mess. But some good did come out of it."

"A lot of shake-ups in the FBI and ATF. And the IRS got its nose bloodied, too."

Don smiled. Like a very large percentage of Americans, he had absolutely no use for the IRS and the dictatorial way in which they operated. He looked at Barry. He couldn't push this much further, not without stepping off into a very chancy area.

"We have several survivalist groups in this area, too, Barry."

"They don't bother me. Most of them are Americans who just don't like the direction this nation is heading. And I sympathize with them. It's the hate groups that I try to avoid."

"We have a couple of those in this area, too," Don said softly.

"I didn't know that. But I am very sorry to hear it."

Don believed him. He didn't know why, but he did. Something in Barry's tone, he guessed. "Jim Beal is the leader of the larger, but not necessarily the more dangerous, of the two groups around here. Victor Radford ramrods the second bunch. They re much smaller, but much more dangerous. They're neo-Nazi. I'm surprised you haven't been approached to join one or the other."

"I don't get out much, Sheriff. Maybe they don't know I'm here."

"Oh, they know, Barry. Believe that. Beal has at least one man in my department, but I don't know who it is. It's the same in many, if not most, departments all over the nation." Don hesitated, picked up his glass of iced tea, and leaned back. He smiled. "You're a very easy man to talk with, Barry. Why am I telling you all this?"

Barry shrugged his shoulders. "Perhaps you don't have anyone else to talk with, Sheriff." He matched Don's smile. "I do know the feeling."

President Richard "Dick" Hutton had weathered many a firestorm in his relatively short political career.

He had been a lawyer, had run for state representative as a very young man, been elected, then after three terms, when he was just old enough to do so, had been elected to the United States Senate. Twelve years later, he was elected president, just squeaking by the sitting president.

He was starting the second year of his first term, and knew he was in big political trouble. To his mind, it all started with the opposition party gaining control of both houses, followed by scandals that he had not been involved in but took the blame for anyway. Then last year all that trouble out in Idaho with rogue federal agents running wild, killing innocent people. Then right on the heels of that, all that mess with IRS agents and the killings in Texas and New York. Then the Coyote Network started a news department and sank its teeth into the government and wouldn't let go. Now anytime the IRS froze a bank account or seized property, there they were, filming and interviewing people and in general making the entire government look like heartless bullies and bad guys.

His ratings were the lowest since he'd taken office. Some in his party were already talking about dumping him, and unless he did something to turn those ratings around, he was through. After the disastrous four years of his predecessor, his party was in trouble.

What President Richard "Dick" Hutton didn't know was that a few in his party were ready to take some rather drastic steps to be rid of him. Permanently.

The Coyote Network's news department was now recognized worldwide as being one of the most aggressive news-gathering organizations ever put together . . . as well as one of the most conservative. And their reports had irritated a lot of people . . . mostly politicians and hanky-stomping liberals. The former because Coyote constantly held their feet to the fire; the latter because Coyote laid the blame for criminal behavior directly on the criminal, not on a poor diet, or because the punk didn't get enough presents at Christmas, or because the kid next door had a fancier bicycle, or because the devil made them do it, or any of the other bullshit that the hard-working, law-abiding, tax-paying American citizens had been forced to endure from the mouths of liberals for forty years.

In other words, a rose was a rose was a rose.

As Stormy Knight, one of Coyote's ace field reporters, stated in an editorial, "It is past time for us all to accept that to a very large degree, the individual controls his or her own destiny. If we fail in one endeavor, the fault is ours; it is not the fault of society. People who turn to a life of crime do so knowingly and willingly. They are not forced into it. Criminals deserve our contempt, not our pity. Many great and successful men and women have risen from the grips of abject poverty without whining or turning to a life of crime or blaming society for their lot in life. This reporter is sick to the core of liberals attempting to explain away why this or that criminal behaves as he or she does. This commentator is tired of reporting about some no-good jerk being released from prison and then raping or assaulting or killing some innocent person seventy-two hours later. It is my opinion that there are only two kinds of people in the world, decent people and indecent people. And the sooner we find a way to either permanently contain or do away with the indecent, the better off society will be."

In North Arkansas, as Stormy's beautiful face faded from the TV screen, Barry leaned back in his chair and laughed. "That's my girl," he said.

Two

Stormy had entered what used to be called Idaho's Great Primitive Area just a year ago in search of a story. She had found her story, but instead of going on the air with it, she had fallen in love with the subject.

Vlad Dumitru Radu, known then as Darry Ransom, now going by the name of Barry Cantrell, had saved Stormy's life. The two of them were forced to hide out in the wilderness area for days while a battle between misinformed and poorly led federal agents and a band of innocent campers, hikers, river rafters, and militiamen raged all around them.

Long years before Stormy met "The Man Who Could Not Die," as the mysterious and elusive Vlad had been dubbed, Stormy had carefully put together Vlad's life story. It had been a pet project of hers since high school days. This time, Vlad knew he was caught.

But before Stormy could make up her mind about filing the story, the pristine wilderness had erupted in battle and they'd had to run for their lives.

Now, a year later, Vlad had once more changed his name and location, but with technology advancing at nearly mind-boggling speed, his running and hiding was becoming increasingly more difficult. He did not know how long he could continue evading not only the press, but also the relentless pursuit by the men and women hired by the billionaire industrialist, Robert Roche. Roche wanted Barry for study, in hopes of learning the secret of eternal life. That was a joke, as far as Barry was concerned, for there was no medical reason for his stroll through the centuries, no gene that gave him the powers to shape-shift, no gland that gave him the ability to never age. He and the others like him—and there were more than a few—were that way because a higher power so decreed it. If Robert Roche wanted the secret, he might consider prayer. That was the only response Barry could possibly give him.

Barry did not possess magical powers. He could not make articles disappear; he could not snap his fingers and produce wondrous things, all materializing in a puff of smoke. He simply did not age and could not die, and he could shape-shift at will. But the ability to shape-shift was nothing new. Indians had known of shape-shifters for thousands of years. Barry knew the white man could learn a lot from the American Indian; they had only to listen and believe. But while many listened, few believed. And therein was the hitch.

"You could call him and tell him you're on the way," Ki Nichols said to Stormy, sitting in her office in New York City.

"No phone," Stormy said with a grimace. "You know how he feels about phones."

Ki laughed at her friend's expression. Then she sobered. "Stormy? What are you two going to do? How are you going to work this out?"

Stormy, nicknamed the Ice Queen because of her sometimes standoffishness, but mostly because of her astonishing Scandinavian beauty, sighed and shook her head, a thick strand of very blond hair falling out of place, almost covering one eye. "We take it one day at a time, Ki. Or one visit at a time. Barry realizes that technology is rapidly catching up with him. But he's made up his mind to resist going public for as long as possible."

"Do you fault him for that?"

Stormy shook her head. "No. Not now. Maybe at first, but certainly not now."

Ki closed the door to the office and sat down. "He's really talked about going public?"

"In a roundabout way, yes."

Ki stared at her. Ki's hair, worn short, was as black as a raven's wing. While Stormy was tall, Ki was almost petite. But while Stormy was city born and reared, Ki had been raised on a working farm in Missouri, and could be as tough as wang leather. Ki was one of the top camera-persons in the business, and liked to work with Stormy. Both of them had been known to take incredible chances in getting a story. "Explain roundabout."

Stormy fiddled with a pencil, tapping it nervously on her desk. "Barry knows these two things to be fact: The military wants to study him. The CIA wants him as an agent. He knows but can't prove that the billionaire industrialist, Robert Roche, hired those mercenaries to come after us last year in Idaho. Roche wants to see if he can learn the secret of eternal life from Barry."

"I'll bite. Can he?"

Stormy shook her head. "No. All Barry knows is that it is a gift. He's firmly convinced, now, that the Almighty gives certain people that gift. As far as his ability to shape-change, he says that shape-shifters have been on the earth for thousands of years. He says it's all in the mind. He told me it took him years to finally learn how to control the shape-shifting."

Ki nodded her head. "Changing the subject only slightly, how do we get to this little town in Arkansas to watch the Speaker of the House glad-hand?"

"We can either fly into Springfield, Little Rock, or Memphis and rent a car."

"You ready?"

Stormy grinned. "I thought you'd never ask!"

The Speaker of the House, since he, or she, is next in line for the Oval Office should anything happen to the president and vice president, is provided security when he travels. They can be Secret Service, FBI, or Deputy U.S. Marshals. Local police, sheriff's deputies, and state police or highway patrol (and there is quite a difference between the two) are also used, at the discretion of the local, county, and state officials. If the police and sheriff's departments are small ones, the visit can put a hell of a strain on local authorities. And Sheriff Don Salter and Police Chief Russ Monroe did not have large departments.

"Hell, the Speaker travels all over the country," Don said to the police chief, the morning after his unexpected visit with Barry. "There's never been any trouble. At least not that I know of."

"Those other areas didn't have Jim Beal and Victor Radford," the chief reminded the sheriff.

Don leaned forward, putting his elbows on the desk. "Russ, we have one of the largest militias in the state located not twenty miles from here. We have about a hundred people who subscribe to the Tri-States' philosophy living just outside of town. They've never caused any trouble."

The police chief shook his head. "Oh, hell, Don! I'm

not talking about those people. Those are good, decent, law-abiding folks. I wish to hell we *could* follow the Tri-States' doctrine. We'd all be a lot better off. I can talk to Jim Beal, but Vic Radford is a hater." The chief sighed. "Don, I've known you since you were just a boy. You know how I feel about certain things. I don't have a lot of use for black folks. And we don't have to get into the reasons why I feel like I do. You know why . . ."

The sheriff nodded his head in agreement. Don felt pretty much the same way as the chief.

Russ said, "I also know that for every one bad black person, there are twenty-five good, decent black folks. And I'm not going to tolerate any good, decent person, regardless of color, getting hurt by the likes of Victor Radford and his neo-Nazi nuts."

Don smiled and waited. Russ would get to the point, maybe, in his own time. This part of Arkansas was almost one hundred percent white, and the citizens were determined to keep it that way. And Don understood why the citizens wanted that. It did not take a rocket scientist to interpret crime statistics.

Blacks did travel through this part of the state; but they did not stay long, and few ever attempted to buy property. The blacks who did stop for gas or food or lodging were not mistreated, but they were met with a solid wall of silence. If they visited a real estate agent and requested to see listed property, they were shown property, for there is a federal law against housing discrimination, but those blacks who did buy property didn't stay long. As of this writing, there is no federal law, yet, against not speaking to someone, regardless of color.

Sheriff Salter stirred restlessly in his chair. He decided to push the issue. "Russ, is there a point to all this?"

The chief looked at the sheriff. "Don, I don't entirely disagree with what Jim Beal has to say."

"I know. Neither do I. But Radford is an idiot."

"I'll certainly agree with that." The chief tapped the badge on his chest. "But you and me, we're wearing these."

"That's right. And because we do, we have to push personal feelings far into the background. Where is all this going, Russ?"

"I get word that both Radford and Beal are up to something no good."

"Russ, there are maybe ten black families in the whole damn county. They've been here for years and years. They're as law-abiding as anyone I could name. Are you saying that Beal and Radford are going to make some sort of move against them?"

The chief shook his head. "No." He smiled, then chuckled. "Do you recall the time, years back, when Radford first started his movement, and he went out and burned that damn cross on Lucas Wilson's front yard?"

Don laughed. "Yeah. Lucas shot him in the ass with a Sweet Sixteen. Took the doctor about half the night to pick out all the birdshot. Vic had to eat standing up for a month."

The chief's smile faded. "Well, it's a bit more serious than that now. According to what I hear, Beal and Radford are gearing up to pull something during the Speaker's visit."

"Pull what?"

"I don't know. I do know that I've got at least one of their men on my department, just like you do. But I don't know for sure who it is."

"They're not stupid enough to try to harm the Speaker. Hell, Cliff Madison is a conservative Republican. He believes in the right to own and bear arms. He wants to repeal the assault weapons ban. Why would Beal and Radford want to harm him?"

"I don't think Beal does. But Vic and his people are something else entirely. I've been trying to find out more, but I've hit a brick wall. Look, what do you know about this new fellow who just moved in, this Barry Cantrell?"

"He's all right. I checked him out and I had men tailing him for a time. He's clean."

"Awful young fellow to be keeping to himself the way he does." The chief rose from the chair with a grunt and a rueful smile. "I've had it after this term," he said. "I've been in law enforcement for damn near forty years. That's enough. I'll be sixty-five soon and I want to go fishing and relax some."

"You've earned it, Russ."

"Sure have. See you, Don." He tossed what Don felt was a very strange look, then walked to the door. Without looking around, he added, "Keep your powder dry, boy."

"Two more security people are being added for this trip," Congressman Madison's chief aide told him. "The Secret Service is providing them. They'll be out of the Little Rock office. Agents Warner Lenox and Susan Green."

Cliff Madison leaned back in his office chair and looked at the aide. "Why the added security?"

The aide shrugged. "No reasons given, sir. I would guess it's due to the current political climate."

Cliff smiled. "And what would that be, Ed?"

The younger man returned the smile. "The conservatives are on a roll."

"Yeah," the Speaker said. "And don't we just love it!"

The message light was flashing on Stormy's answering machine. She punched the play button and then walked to the closet for a suitcase. The first voice message was from a man who'd been trying to date her for months.

"I'll give him an *A* for persistence," Stormy muttered, ignoring the crux of the message.

The second message was from her stockbroker, telling her he'd just made her a nice chunk of change.

The third message was from her office, confirming travel reservations to Memphis and the confirmation number of a rental car.

But the fourth message stopped her in her tracks, the suitcase in her hand forgotten. The caller had disguised his voice, muffling it in some way. "Your life is in danger, Miss Knight. Don't go to Arkansas."

Stormy set the suitcase on the floor and replayed the messages. But after repeated playings, she still did not recognize the voice. She hesitated for a moment, then shrugged it off. Death threats were nothing new to people who were constantly in the public eye. They all received them, and usually the threats turned out to be nothing.

But still . . .

Stormy shook her head in irritation. She had covered everything from Desert Storm to Bosnia and was a seasoned veteran; no stranger to gunfire.

Besides, in Arkansas, she would be close to Barry. And the only thing she feared when close to him was her own emotions. No doubt about it: she was deeply in love.

With a man who was almost seven hundred years old.

Three

Barry's eyes popped open to the sounds of Pete and Repeat growling low in their throats. The clock radio read 5:10. Barry lay in his bed, every sense working overtime.

"Be quiet," he whispered to the hybrids.

They hushed immediately.

Barry slipped silently out of bed and pulled on jeans and moccasins. "Stay," he told the hybrids, buttoning up a dark shirt.

The day had been unusually hot, and the night was muggy, so the air conditioning was on. Despite the house being closed up, something had alerted the animals.

Barry silently walked the house, pausing to glance out of windows. He could spot nothing out of the ordinary. He opened the back door, which he never locked while he was home. It swung noiselessly on well-oiled hinges.

Barry stepped out into the warm night, staying close to the outside wall of the stone house. He sniffed the air and smiled as the odor of sweat came to him. Two distinctive smells. Males. So there were two men on his property, inside the chain link fence. He waited. The next move was theirs.

Then the two men made a very bad vocal mistake.

"If those big-assed dogs come out," one whispered, the words very audible to Barry. The man was just around the corner of the house. "I'll shoot both of them."

"Damn right," the second man whispered.

At that, Barry's darkness-shrouded smile was not pleasant.

Barry picked up a small piece of kindling that was stacked in a wooden box on the porch and tossed it out into the backyard. It landed with a thud.

Barry heard the sounds of both men bellying down on the ground beside the house. He picked up a more substantial piece of wood and waited.

"That wasn't nothing. Look, let's do it. You take the back door," the whisper reached Barry. "I'll take the front. Remember, we've got to take him alive."

Barry smiled at that.

"Right."

He heard the faint sounds of one man moving away; then the second man came into view, standing by the edge of the back porch. Barry counted to five, then whacked the man on the head with the piece of wood. The man sighed softly and collapsed to the ground. Barry left the porch and circled around to the front of the house, staying close to the exterior wall. The other man was on the porch. Barry dropped down and crawled around the porch, coming up behind him. Silently, he stood up and stepped onto the porch, moving up to within inches of the man standing in front of the screen, his left hand outstretched.

"Looking for me?" Barry spoke in a normal tone.

The man jumped in shock and whirled around, a pistol in his hand. Barry gave him a short and very brutal right fist to the jaw, then a left to the belly, then came up with an uppercut that dropped the intruder to the porch.

Using the man's belt, Barry quickly trussed him up, then did the same to the man in the back of the house. Then he took a leisurely stroll down the road to a neighbor's house to call the sheriff's department.

If this continues, I'm going to have to get a phone, Barry thought.

"Ah, Vlad," the man using the name of John Ravenna whispered. He was wide awake, lying on the bed in his New York City hotel room. "How long has it been since we last confronted one another?"

The answer was just over fifty years, during World War II, in occupied France. John Ravenna had been working for the Nazi Gestapo. Barry, going by the name of William Shipman, had been TDY'd over to the American OSS and was operating behind the lines in France, working with the French Resistance. It was just a few weeks after D-Day, and John Ravenna had captured a female member of the resistance and was doing what he loved best, inflicting torture upon a woman in a vain effort to make her talk.

Lying in his bed in the darkened hotel room, John Ravenna scowled at the memory of what had happened next . . . just as the woman was screaming in hideous pain.

The front door to the small house burst open. Ravenna whirled around, dropping the electrified wires he was using on the woman's naked body.

"Well, now, cousin," John said, a cruel smile playing on his lips. "What an unpleasant surprise."

"I'm not your cousin, Ravenna," Barry told him.

"Related in kind, then."

"Unfortunately, that is true."

"You always pick the wrong side, Vlad."

"A matter of opinion, John."

"I suppose you've burst in to save the fair maiden?"

"Something like that." Barry cut his eyes to the woman. She was not dead, but not far from that long sleep. She had been tortured for hours.

"You're too late, Vlad."

"A little matter of a German patrol that had to be dealt with."

"So what happens now?"

"It would be rather pointless for us to fight, would it not, John?"

"That would be fun, of course, but yes, it would be pointless."

"Then, goodbye, John Ravenna."

"Auf wiedersehen, Vlad Radu."

The two men stood staring at each other. John Ravenna was several centuries older than Vlad, and he had not ceased his aging until about age forty. He was dark-complexioned, with black hair, graying at the temples when the aging stopped. His eyes were black, usually holding a contemptuous light. He was handsome, in a cruel sort of way.

While the immortals could not kill each other, they could inflict great injury, and immortals felt pain just like anyone else. But the healing process was very swift. They could, however, use their minds to exert control over each other, and since John Ravenna was several centuries older than Vlad, he could project the greater control. Which he was now attempting to do.

"It won't work, John," Vlad told him, just as the woman tied to the table gasped and struggled to move her head, her pain-filled eyes searching Vlad's face. "You have never been able to overpower me with your mind."

"Perhaps it's because you are such a simpleton."

"You wish."

The woman on the table began moaning in pain. John Ravenna took a pistol from a belt holster, looked at Vlad for a moment, then shrugged his shoulders and unemotionally shot her in the head, stilling her cries. He holstered the pistol and smiled at Vlad. "I was hoping you would try to interfere, Vlad. It would be interesting to see how you tolerate a gunshot wound."

"She was perhaps an hour away from death. Why let her linger in pain? You did her a service."

"Naturally, you would look at it that way."

"This war is about won, John. The Nazi empire is just about over. A year at the most. What are your plans?"

"You think I would tell you?" He laughed. As Vlad recalled from years back, the laughter still sounded evil. "Oh, I'll get by, Vlad."

"I'm sure you will."

"Someday, cousin, you and I will fight. You know it's coming. As pointless as it is."

"Perhaps."

John Ravenna turned without another word and walked out the back door of the cottage.

That was the last time Vlad Dumitru Radu and John Ravenna had met.

But all that was about to change.

Soon.

"And you have never seen either of these men before, Barry?" Sheriff Salter asked, after taking a sip of coffee from a paper cup.

"No. Never."

A deputy walked up. "We found their car, Sheriff. It's a rental out of Memphis."

"Their DLs?" Salter asked.

"Fakes. But very good ones. They crossed state lines to commit a kidnapping. Does that bring the FBI into it?"

"I suppose," the sheriff replied. "If we want them."

"What kidnapping?" one of the men called from the rear seat of a deputy's car. He was sitting with his hands handcuffed behind his back. "I told you, we got lost and wanted to ask if we could use the phone here. This guy attacked us. I pulled a gun in self-defense."

The sheriff looked at Barry in the silver-gray of early dawn. "We probably won't be able to make any attempted kidnapping charges stick. Your word against theirs. About the best we can do is trespassing, carrying concealed weapons without a permit, and operating a motor vehicle with a fake driver's license."

"I'm gonna sue that guy for assault with a deadly weapon!" the man with a knot on his head shouted from the back of an emergency services vehicle.

"You're sure those two have been advised of their rights?" Don asked a deputy.

"Oh, yes, sir."

"Get them out of here." Don waited until the car carrying the two men had pulled away, then turned to Barry. "What's going on here, Barry?"

"I don't know, Sheriff. And that is the truth. I have no idea who those two men are. I heard them say they would shoot my dogs. That's when I got angry." Barry did not mention that he also heard them say they had to take him alive, and he was reasonably certain the two men in custody wouldn't bring it up.

One of the newly arrived deputies looked nervously around him. He had heard all about the two big hybrids living within the confines of the fence. "Where are those dogs of yours, Mr. Cantrell?"

Barry smiled. "In the house. If you'll keep your

hands away from your guns, I'll release them and introduce you. They are not vicious animals. I would have a fenced-in area if they were poodles. I don't believe in letting animals run unsupervised." For their safety, he silently added.

"Stand still and keep your hands away from your side arms," Sheriff Salter told the two remaining deputies. "You need to let the . . . ah, dogs, get to know you." Then he added, "I have a hunch this won't be the only visit we make out here."

"The president cannot be allowed to run for a second term," Gene Dawson opened the breakfast meeting in the back room of a Washington restaurant. The room was used frequently for highly secret and clandestine meetings. It was electronically "swept" before each meeting and was as secure as man could make it. "The sooner we start making plans to get him out of office, the better. I wish to hell he'd drop dead tonight."

"Wishful thinking," a United States senator spoke up. "But that would be nice. However, the Speaker is the man causing the trouble. If we could get him out of the way, it would rip the guts out of the opposition and put them into a panic."

"I personally think a terrorist attack is the way to go," a United States representative said. "We know the Republicans are planning a strategy meeting in a couple of months. Over in West Virginia. Get rid of the whole damn bunch. We could blame it on Libya or Syria or the Palestinians and be rid of those right-wing bastards once and for all."

"Oh, get real, Paul!" Senator Holden quickly spoke up. "Good Jesus Christ. I don't want to hear any more talk about such nonsense. Murder? Impeachment? You're all crazy!"

"If we don't do something and do it damn quickly, our party is going to be a thing of the past," Paul Patrick came right back. "And I for one am prepared to do anything, *anything*, to prevent that from happening."

"Murder, Paul?" another senator whispered. *"Murder?"*

"I agree with Paul," a woman spoke. "We've got to disarm the right-wing nuts in this country. We've got to disarm *everybody*. We're in a war for our party's very survival, and for the welfare of every good, decent American citizen. And in a war, anything goes."

"You would go that far, Madalaine?"

"Yes. I think the time has come for drastic steps."

"I wouldn't even know where to begin," Gene Dawson said in a subdued tone.

The woman smiled. "I do. I've already contacted a man."

Robert Roche hurled his coffee cup across the room and cursed at the news just delivered him. He turned to face the man. "Gone? Gone where?"

"He's here in the United States . . . somewhere. Our sources in the State Department say he entered the country just a few days ago. He may still be here in the city."

"Someone, some group, hired him?"

"From all indications, yes."

"Find out who hired him and why."

"I will do my best, sir."

The billionaire fixed the man with a cold stare. "Do better than that, Ray. Or hunt for another job."

After Ray had gone, Robert poured a fresh cup of

coffee and sat down behind his desk. Slowly, he calmed himself and began thinking rationally. He knew from years of quiet investigation—which had cost him several million dollars—that John Ravenna hated the man who was born Vlad Radu. John Ravenna was the pure personification of evil; Vlad Radu was just the opposite.

If John Ravenna was in the States, he had been hired to kill someone, or do something equally nefarious, for the man had been a killer for hire for nearly a thousand years. He had been killing for kings and queens and potentates and generals for all his adult life.

But who hired him, and why?

Robert felt sure that Ravenna would never take a contract on Vlad, for that would be pointless. No, something very big was about to go down here in America. Something earth-shaking in magnitude.

But Robert was certain of one thing: whatever it was, the man now living under the name of Barry Cantrell was somehow involved. He might not know it yet, but he had a part to play in this little drama.

Just how big a part Robert did not know.

Yet.

But he would.

And when Barry showed his hand, Robert's men would grab him.

Robert Roche chuckled, then laughed aloud. "The game is almost over, Vlad. And as usual, I win!"

Four

Barry picked up the mailgram from his post office box and waited until he was back in his truck before opening it. He knew it was from Stormy. He smiled as he read. Stormy would be landing at Memphis International Airport later on today, and would be in this area in the morning.

Barry drove to a filling station and topped off the tank, then drove down the street to a supermarket. Sheriff Salter drove up just as he was pulling into the parking lot.

"As soon as bail was set, those two goons made one call to a Little Rock lawyer," Don told him. "I had to cut them loose about an hour ago."

Barry nodded his head. "They'll be back in New Jersey by this afternoon. They won't be back here. You can bet on that."

"How'd you know they're from New Jersey? They never told me that."

"Accents. They're from the New York/New Jersey area. I have friends from there."

"Uh-huh," Don said very drily. He knew with a cop's instinct that Barry had been lying to him from the first moment they met. But he couldn't prove it . . . so far.

Problem was, he didn't believe Barry was a criminal. He didn't know why he believed that, he just did.

"Buy you a cup of coffee, Sheriff?" Barry asked, a sudden twinkle in his eyes. "There is something I want to talk to you about."

"Sure. Nellie's all right with you?"

"It's close enough." Right across the street.

Over coffee, the sheriff asked, "What's on your mind?"

"When is the Speaker of the House due to arrive in town?"

Sudden suspicion flared in Don's eyes. "Why do you ask?"

Barry chuckled. "Sheriff, relax. It's just that a New York-based reporter from the Coyote Network is coming in to cover the story. As a matter of fact, she'll be here tomorrow, for a few days' vacation. She'll be staying out at my place. I just want to know how much time we'll have together before she has to go to work, that's all."

"What reporter?"

"Stormy Knight."

The sheriff's eyes widened in disbelief. "Are you lyin' to me, Barry?"

"No. We've been seeing each other socially for about a year now. Let me check with Stormy to see if she wants company, and if it's all right with her, why don't you and your wife come out for supper?"

The sheriff was incredulous. He sat for a moment, his mouth hanging open, his coffee forgotten. "I, ah . . ." He shook his head. "Okay, Barry. My wife never misses a Stormy Knight report. She would love to meet her."

"I'm sure it will be all right with Stormy. Just keep all this under your hat, if you don't mind." He smiled. "Not that I wouldn't like for the whole world to know."

Barry took out his wallet, removing a snapshot that Ki had taken in Idaho the past year. He held out the picture. "This is us last year."

The sheriff studied the picture, then looked across the table and grinned. "Well, I'll just be damned." He quickly revised his thinking about Barry. If he was dating a reporter of Stormy's status, he sure as hell had nothing to hide from the law.

Which was exactly why Barry had brought up the subject and showed him the picture.

"You understand, then, what you are to do, Mr. Ravenna?"

John looked at the senator's intermediary with much the same expression he would use if gazing at a large roach. He did not reply vocally, just let his countenance speak for him.

"Then I'll be leaving," the go-between said.

John arched an eyebrow in reply.

The spokesman was only too glad to get the hell away from John Ravenna. Even though he'd been dealing with thugs and muscle and professional hit men for years, this man scared him—reached down into his soul and touched some primitive part.

John waited for a moment, then followed the man. John always covered his bets.

"My people in New York tell me that Stormy Knight, of the Coyote Network, is going to cover the Speaker's trip," Jim Beal told a gathering of his cell leaders. "I have got to get to her . . . somehow. Our side of the story has to be told, and told to someone who will report it fairly and accurately. Miss Knight will do that without liberal bias."

"What about Victor Radford?"

"Vic is an idiot. Struts around in that damn Nazi uniform and spouts the writings of Hitler. He and that whacky bunch of his have given all of us a bad name."

After the short meeting was over, Jim Beal sat down in a recliner-lounger and sipped his bourbon and water. He had to find a way to meet with this reporter; had to impress upon her that he and his followers presented no threat to the government or to any person, regardless of color. Jim Beal simply did not believe in race mixing. He did not wish any harm to come to black people, but he did not wish to live around them or to have his children go to school with black children. He believed that he had a right to refuse people service in his place of business. He used his own money to start his business, used his own money to see the business through the rough times, and the government had no right to tell him how to run his business.

Unlike Victor Radford, Jim Beal was very careful about who he allowed in his group. There were no cross burners in his association, no radical haters, no wild-eyed revolutionaries. The weapons they practiced with were all legal.

Furthermore, Jim Beal knew that the majority of people living in this area supported his views, to one degree or another, but most were reluctant to speak out openly for fear of government retaliation. Privately, the majority of people agreed with him, and he understood why they could not go public with their sentiments. While not a fanatic about religion, Jim was a religious person, and he tried to live a decent life, in accordance with his views of right and wrong.

The few black families who lived in the county would not trade in any of the several businesses owned by Jim Beal or in any business owned by members of

Beal's organization. That was a silent understanding
that went back years.

Jim would have laughed if someone had told him
he was a very complex man. But he most certainly was.

Stormy had no trouble locating Barry's house, for
he had drawn her a detailed map of the area. After
visiting briefly with Barry, Ki had driven on up into
Missouri to visit her family for a few days.

After getting reacquainted in the privacy of the bedroom, Barry and Stormy went for a leisurely walk
around the property, Pete and Repeat with them. Because of who he was and what he could become, the
hybrids obeyed every command from Barry and always
stayed close.

Pausing to sit by the bank of the little creek that ran
through the property, Stormy told Barry about the
warning she had received on her answering machine.

"You've gotten these before?"

"Oh, sure." She flipped a pebble into the cold waters of the spring-fed creek. "Probably everyone in the
public eye gets threats sometime in his or her life. But
this one was, well, different in a way that is hard to
explain. Most of the others, if they were delivered vocally, were screaming threats from obvious nuts. If they
came by letter, depending on what report set them off,
they would be something like, 'Die, you fag-loving
bitch,' or 'God will punish you for your sins.' But this
one, this one was calmly given, as if the man was trying
to warn me of impending danger not of his doing or
liking."

"Could you tell if it was long distance?"

She shook her head. "Not really. But I got the impression it was."

"Why?"

"The voice spoke with an accent not from the North-east. Much softer than that."

"Southern accent?"

"Probably. But not deep south. Not syrupy. Mid-south."

"This area would be called mid-south."

"Yes."

"I wonder if it might have something to do with the Speaker's visit next month."

"Which is next week, by the way. I don't know. Maybe."

Barry told her about the sheriff's visit, his suspicions, and of inviting Don and his wife over for supper. "If that's all right with you."

"Sure. It'll be fun. Talking informally with the sheriff will also save me a lot of legwork."

Then he told her about his early morning visitors.

She was silent for a moment, then cut her eyes to him. "Robert Roche?"

"Probably." He sighed and shook his head. "Perhaps it's time for me to go public and put an end to this long run of mine. I have been giving it a lot of thought." He held up a hand for silence. "But . . . there are others like me in the world, Stormy. A lot more than I suspected even a short time ago." He smiled. "Well, a short time for me."

She ignored that, knowing that Barry's sense of humor could be very weird at times. "How many more, Barry?"

"Several hundred. Maybe a lot more than that. And they have to be considered in any decision I make. If I go public, what happens to them?"

"Nothing. If you don't mention it."

"Don't be too sure of that, Stormy. Many other governments around the world have suspected there are people like me. Many have married and produced offspring. Although that is something most of us try not to do."

"The children, are they immortal?"

"Rarely. And both partners have to be the same."

"Then there might be . . . ?"

"A lot more of us? Yes. It's certainly possible. I've had to revise my thinking as to why we are what we are several times."

"I see now why this is not an easy decision for you to make."

"We'd be treated like freaks, Stormy. This government, all governments worldwide, might came up with some obscure law that would make it legal to imprison us indefinitely for study. And if they don't have it on the books already, they'll pass legislation. I know first-hand how governments work."

She studied his face for a moment, that handsome and ageless face that had witnessed so much during his long march through history. "You really despise big government, don't you, Barry?" she asked softly.

Barry picked up and rattled a couple of pebbles in his hand. "Yes, I do. Oh, most start out with good intentions. But that doesn't last long, once the men and women in control realize that they have absolute power. You recall that line about absolute power and what it leads to?"

"Corruption."

"Yes. And once they taste the heady wine of absolute power, most are very reluctant to give it up. They think of themselves as gods, looking down on all the little people and thinking, 'I know what is best for you. You might not like the legislation I'm introducing, but trust me, it's for your own good.' It doesn't take long for the men and women in power to lose touch with the people, the masses, if you will. And it makes no difference what political party is in power. They still think they know what is best for everyone else. Bear this one small example in mind, Stormy: I helped build the first T-model automobiles to roll off the assembly line, the engine and the body. A simple, highly functional mode of transportation. And for years it remained basically the same. Then, some years ago, when the balance of power shifted in Washington the automobile changed . . ."

"What the hell are you talking about, Barry?" Stormy asked with a frown.

"Just listen for a moment. The men and women in power, the liberals, instead of demanding that the punishment for stealing a car be made more severe, demanded that the car itself be made more theft-proof. At whose expense? The consumer—the long-suffering taxpayer—who must foot the bill for all the nonsense that comes out of Washington. Remember, Stormy," Barry's tone was sarcastic, "don't let a good boy go bad. Always take the keys out of the ignition. Stormy, good boys don't steal cars, punks do."

Stormy looked at him, an exasperated expression on her face. "Barry, you can come up with the damndest analogies I have ever heard." Then she laughed. "But I see your point. Okay, all right. You don't have to convince me that big government is out of control. I agree with you. And I know you have a very difficult decision to make. I also know you don't think much of the press. But in this case, we can help you."

Pete's and Repeat's heads suddenly rose as one, their ears pricked up, eyes looking in the same direction.

Barry sniffed the air. The odor of nervous human sweat filled his olfactory sense.

"What is it?" Stormy asked.

The hybrids growled low in their throats.

Barry threw himself against her and pinned her to

the ground just as a bullet whined over their heads, the crack of the rifle a split second behind it.

"I feel like I'm back in Bosnia," Stormy muttered.

Five

Barry shoved Stormy behind the bank of the creek into a slight depression in the earth. Pete and Repeat were already there, belly down on the ground. "All of you, stay! And don't move!" he ordered, and then was gone, slipping through the brush and timber.

Stormy looked into the eyes of the big hybrids, their snouts about three inches from her face. "Life with your friend is certainly not lacking in excitement," she muttered.

Pete licked her on the nose.

Barry ran for about fifty yards, then cut to his left, jumping over the creek and bellying down on the other side. He got his bearings, then began slipping toward where the shot had come from. He rose to his feet and began running just as the rifle banged again, then once more. Barry burst out of the brush and jumped, landing on the man, feet first, both his hiking boots impacting against the man's chest and knocking him backward, the rifle falling from his hands.

The sniper recovered very quickly and rolled to his feet, coming up with a knife. In the sunlight that managed to filter through the thick timber, dappling the ground with shards of illumination, Barry could see the blade was honed down to a razor sharpness.

Barry could also see that the man was not an experienced knife fighter. He held the weapon all wrong. Instead of moving his free hand to distract his opponent, the man was moving only the blade. Barry did not think he had ever seen the man before.

The man lunged at him, and Barry easily parried the move, sidestepping with the grace of a dancer—a vocation he had worked at in the seventeenth century in Italy.

The man cursed him. Barry's only response was a smile.

The assailant tried to fake Barry out, and that got him a hard right fist to the mouth that crossed his eyes and brought a bright stain of blood to his lips. Before he could fully recover, Barry whirled and kicked high in a classic savate move, the sole of his boot slamming into the side of the man's face and knocking him to the ground. The knife slipped from suddenly numbed fingers. Barry moved in quickly and applied a pressure hold to the man's neck. In a few seconds, the man was asleep and softly snoring.

Barry used the man's belt and strips of his shirt to truss him up securely; then he ripped down thick vines and tied the man to a tree.

Barry walked back to the creek. "It's all right," he announced. "Let's go find a phone and call the sheriff."

Stormy rose from the ground and brushed the dirt and twigs from her clothing. "Where is the nearest phone, Barry?"

"Oh, about a mile down the road. Come on. We'll drive."

"One of these days, Barry, you're going to have to accept the fact that you are in the twentieth century."

"Soon to be the twenty-first."

"And you might get a phone then?"

"We'll see."

* * *

One of Salter's younger deputies took a misstep and fell off the front porch while staring at Stormy. Salter gave the deputy a look that promised this was not the end of it.

"We'd better go get this guy before you lose all your troops," Barry remarked innocently.

Salter sighed with a patience that was somehow bestowed to all sheriffs and chiefs of police.

The trussed-up man glared ribbons of silent hate at the sheriff, the deputies who were still able to walk, and at Barry. Stormy had elected to stay in the house, with Pete and Repeat. The signs of his thrashing about, trying to free himself, were evident, but Barry had tied him securely.

"Bag the rifle, the knife, and this guy's hands for residue testing," Salter ordered. He looked at the deputy who had fallen off the porch. "You go find the slugs that were fired at Miss Knight and Mr. Cantrell. And don't come back until you have them in an evidence bag."

"But that's liable to take me a week!" the young deputy protested.

"The elementary school at Chestnut and Poplar still needs a crossing guard for this next term," Salter told him. "Would you like that position?"

The deputy quickly headed into the timber.

"You don't know this guy?" Don asked Barry.

"Never saw him before, and neither has Stormy. And I don't know if he was shooting at me or Stormy."

"Abortionists must die!" shouted the man, who was now on his feet and handcuffed, startling everyone. "Those who support abortion are murderers. Praise be to the Lord. Give me strength to kill that harlot."

"Now we know," Barry said. "Stormy did an editorial last month on a woman's right to choose."

"Get this nut out of here," Don ordered. "Book him on two counts of attempted murder."

"I hope the events of the past couple of days are not any indication of things to come when the Speaker gets here," Barry remarked.

"Don't even think it," Don replied, taking off his cowboy hat and wiping his forehead and face with a handkerchief. The woods were deep and no breeze touched them.

Barry told him about the warning Stormy had received before she left New York City.

The sheriff nodded. "This is probably what the caller meant. Someone in that nut's group got cold feet and tried to warn her away."

Barry said nothing, but in the back of his mind, he did not believe the shooter had anything at all to do with the warning Stormy had received. "Don, I talked it over with Stormy. How about you and your wife coming out tomorrow evening for steaks and beer?"

"Sounds good to me. I told Jeanne, and she's real excited about it."

"Okay, then. That's settled. I'd better get back to the house and see about Stormy."

"We'll finish up out here and get out of your hair. See you tomorrow, Barry."

"Going to report this, Stormy?" Barry asked, when the outside world was hushed by closed doors and the soft hum of the central air-conditioning.

"You know I have to, Barry." She smiled. "I'm going to drive into town, find a pay phone, and call it in. But your name won't be mentioned. I'll just say, 'While visiting a friend.' "

"I told the sheriff about your warning call. He thinks the call was about the abortion report you did."

"And you don't?"

"No. Let me change clothes and I'll drive you in." He glanced at a wall clock. "And if we hurry, I can put in a rush order for a telephone. I'll talk to the sheriff. He can probably expedite the request."

"Welcome to the twentieth century, Barry."

"The last one was better."

Don Salter certainly did expedite matters. The phone company installation man was knocking on the front door of the house at eight o'clock the next morning. Since the lines were already in place, it took him only moments to get the phone (which Barry had bought at a local Wal-Mart the afternoon before) up and humming. He would be charged a small fee each month to have his number unlisted and unpublished.

Ki had heard Stormy's phoned-in report on the evening news and had left her parents early. By mid-morning she was sitting in Barry's living room.

"How have you been, Ki?" Barry asked, smiling at the petite woman with the shining black hair.

The award-winning camera-person waggled her right hand in a so-so gesture. "This shoot going to be as exciting as Idaho, gang?"*

"I hope not," Stormy replied. "But it's certainly starting off with a bang."

Ki cut her dark eyes to the newly installed telephone, then to Barry, and grinned. "Progress slowly closing in on you, huh?"

Hunted—Pinnacle

"It seems that way."

"Don't like it, though, do you?"

"No. But progress is inevitable. The alternative would be much worse."

The phone rang and Barry glared at it. "Shit!" he muttered, getting up to answer it while Stormy and Ki laughed at the disgusted expression on his face. "What?" Barry spoke into the phone. "What are you talking about? No, I don't want to listen. Goodbye." He hung up and sat down. He pointed to the phone. "I haven't been with this phone service for two hours and already another company is calling trying to get me to switch. I thought my number was unlisted."

Stormy laughed at him. "Modern technology, love. Isn't it grand?"

"That's one word for it. I can think of a number of others that would be more appropriate."

"You were right about us hammering away on government excesses against private citizens, Barry," Ki said. "The other networks have even changed their formats—to some degree—but nothing like we're doing."

"They never will, either," Barry told her. "They don't have the stomach for it."

The phone rang.

Barry looked at it and sighed.

"Why not buy an answering machine?" Ki suggested. "That way you can screen each call and let the recorder take the ones you don't want."

"Good idea." Barry rose from the chair and walked across the room and stilled the ringing. He listened for a moment. "No," he said, then hung up and sat back down. "I had a telephone in 1910," he said. "It was a very simple device. You lifted one part, stuck it to your ear, and turned the crank. When the operator came on, you spoke into the mouthpiece and gave her the number. I don't recall anyone ever trying to sell me anything over the telephone."

Stormy was having a difficult time keeping a straight face. "What was that last call?"

"Some long distance service." He looked at Ki. "You armed, Ki?"

"Not for this trip, Barry. This is a resort area. I wasn't anticipating any trouble."

"That's when it always comes at you. I have a pistol you can use. It's an old Chief's Special."

The phone rang. Barry gave the instrument a very dark look.

Stormy quickly stood up. "I think we'll drive around a bit. Get a feel for the area."

Just as the two women were walking out the front door, Barry grabbed up the phone and started speaking in what sounded to the women very much like Chinese . . . sort of.

"Ma Bell will never be the same," Stormy muttered.

Most conservatives and moderates of all political parties loved the news format of the Coyote Network. Liberals hated it. The Coyote news staff never let up on government excesses, be they national, state, county, or local. But it wasn't just the government who felt the bite of Coyote. The Coyote reporters went after welfare cheats with a vengeance, asking questions that the viewers had never heard a reporter ask before. They went after rich farmers who received massive farm subsidies they didn't need. They went in depth on every subject they probed, from crime to religion. But more than anything else, Coyote loved to tweak the nose of government . . . and especially loved to bloody the nose of liberals. But conservatives quickly learned that Coyote had no intention of treating them with kid gloves. Coyote went after military waste and all sorts of pork with the tenacity of a pit bulldog. Members of Congress—republican or democrat, liberal or conservative—discovered early on that when they spent taxpayer money, there had better be a damn good reason for doing so.

The Coyote Network had eyes and ears everywhere across the nation. And most citizens wouldn't take a dime for their efforts: they just wanted to see corruption on all levels ferreted out, placing strong emphasis on getting repeat drunk driving offenders off the road (Coyote publicly humiliated them and the judges who kept turning them loose and the sheriffs and chiefs of police who showed favoritism toward them).

Coyote went after men who battered women, showing their faces to the world in public service announcements. They went after deadbeat dads, punks, gangs.

Coyote grabbed the IRS by the butt and wouldn't turn loose. Since the Internal Revenue Service was, without question, the most loathed of all federal agencies, the weary-of-taxes public loved the reports. But Coyote didn't just hammer at the IRS; they reported on the taxes imposed upon the citizens by states and cities and counties, where the money was going and more importantly, why.

Coyote questioned, loud and frequently, why the government had to have certain departments.

Coyote was, in the words of one bureaucratic twit, "A great big pain in the ass!"

But the public loved it and clamored for more.

Coyote didn't do any reporting on the personal hygiene problems confronting the Glopawho-pamopapoopoo tribe in Lower Boomgawha, or the political problems of the prime minster of England, or the sexual escapades of the prince of Romania, or homosexuals in Denmark, but they sure as hell caused many a sleepless night for elected and appointed officials in the United States in all levels of local, state, and federal government.

Six

After Stormy and Ki left, Barry checked the freezer to see if he had enough steaks for tonight's cookout. He did. But since he seldom drank, he had no beer in the house. He drove into town and bought several six-packs, then drove to a local bakery that baked some of the finest breads and pastries he had ever tasted, and purchased bread and two freshly baked apple pies. Back at his house, he put the beer in the refrigerator and stowed the rest of his purchases away. He tidied up the house a bit, then looked around for something else to do. The house was neat and orderly and spotless.

"Charcoal," he muttered. "Do I have enough?" He checked on the back porch and found he had plenty.

Barry was not accustomed to having company. Not since technology had begun taking giant steps. It had been so different in the old days. That brought a smile to his lips. The old days. Which old days in particular are you referring to, Barry? he silently questioned. He shook his head, attempting to clear away those thoughts. He did not often dwell on the far past, for that usually left him with a feeling of depression.

Possessing the ability to live forever was not all wine and roses, he sourly mused. Barry stepped out on the porch and stood for a moment, recalling a few good and close friends he'd had in the past. Jean Laffite did not deserve the bad reputation that had been hung on him . . . at least that was the impression Barry had gotten during the few years he'd known the man. He was a gentleman pirate. Indeed, just after the battle of New Orleans, General Andrew Jackson had called Jean one of the ablest men he'd ever met. Jean had died a relatively young man, only forty-five years old. However, it was certainly true that Jean had burned Galveston to the ground just a few years before his untimely death. Barry didn't know what had happened to Jean's brother, Pierre. The last time he'd seen Pierre, the man was running a blacksmith shop in New Orleans. That was . . . oh, around 1814, as Barry could best recall.

Barry had returned to the western mountains after the Battle of New Orleans, resuming his lonely life as a mountain man and living with a pack of timber wolves in the Rocky Mountains. When he desired human company, he would visit an Indian village. The Indians knew who he was and greatly respected him. Barry knew that even today, Indians still sang songs about him.

He could only stay a few years in any one spot, for since he did not age, suspicions would quickly grow. That was why Barry seldom allowed people to get very close to him, or he to them.

Then Stormy came along and his life had not been the same since.

Standing on the porch, Barry smiled at that last thought. He had to admit that that particular change had been, for the most part, for the better.

A sudden feeling of great danger seized Barry, and he quickly stepped off the porch, moving to his left. He stood by the corner of the house wondering what had caused that moment of alarm. Pete and Repeat were in the living room, behind stone walls, out of harm's way.

Barry moved to the rear of the house and squatted down behind a stack of firewood in the backyard. Something had triggered his inner alarm system, but what?

Barry left the neatly stacked pile of wood and headed for the woods, after securing the back gate. He was unconsciously sniffing the air, tracking head up instead of nose down, so his vision would not be impaired. He slowly began his circling of the property. Very faintly, a scent came to him, a familiar scent. Barry smiled, but it was not a pleasant curving of the lips. It was more like a snarl. A low growl left his throat, a menacing rumbling that he was not cognizant of emitting.

John Ravenna was here!

Jim Beal sat in his office at the rear of the huge building that was the headquarters of his lumber yard and experienced waves of doubt and confusion. He just did not know what to do. He had no solid proof that what his informants in Washington, D.C. were telling him was anything other than rumor.

But if it was fact . . . ?

Therein lay the kicker.

Both informants, whom his movement had years ago planted very deep and who had worked their way high into government circles, had told him that Congressman Cliff Madison's life was in danger during this vacation trip. The informants both agreed that a plot to assassinate the Speaker was in the works. But if Beal went to the feds with this rumor, they would want to know where he had learned of it. He certainly couldn't tell them about his people in Washington, one on a senator's staff and another placed high in the Justice Department.

Jim knew he had been under federal investigation for a long time. Off and on for years, actually. He knew the feds had an informant within the ranks of his organization, and Jim knew the identity of the man. Nothing of any importance was ever discussed in the presence of the government informer.

Jim didn't blame Wesley Parren for what he was doing; the feds had the poor guy over a barrel because of an unintentional foul-up on his personal income tax returns for several years. Wesley had taken some deductions that he had honestly believed were legal and the IRS caught it, but only after about five years, and that left the guy owing the goddamn government about fifty thousand dollars, most of that in penalties and interest. So the feds worked a deal: inform on Jim Beal and his survivalist group, and we will, eventually, forgive the money.

Wesley really didn't have much choice in the matter. He had two kids in college and a hypochondriac for a wife who rushed off to the doctor every time she experienced an ache or a pain. He was in debt up to his butt with no way out. Then the feds moved in on him.

Jim Beal knew personally what kind of a bind Wesley was in, for the feds had been auditing him for years . . . on a regular basis. Auditing him, investigating him, spying on him. There was not one area of his life the feds had not scrutinized, from the cradle to the present.

And Jim Beal hated them for it.

He rose from his chair to pace the office. If he could, he would see the reporter, Stormy Knight, and tell her about the planned assassination, on the condition that he remain anonymous. It was a big story, and Jim felt that she would go for it. He hoped she would, for he knew he had to do something. Congressman Madison was a good man.

Then Jim pondered for a few moments over this: if the visiting dignitary being lined up in cross hairs was a very liberal senator or representative, would he make any effort to save his life?

After a moment, he decided he would not.

Victor Radford closed the book and put it aside. He never tired of reading the writings of his hero, Adolf Hitler. Such a great man. A man with vision. And really, a peace-seeking man. It was all nonsense about the concentration camps and the killing of millions of Jews. That was just Jew propaganda. Lies to sully the memory of a man with a wonderful vision of a master race and a society free of inferiors.

But the dream did not die with the führer. Oh, no. Not at all. Hitler's vision was very much alive and doing quite well, thank you. And not just in this area. Oh, no. There were cells all over America. Men and women who shared the dreams of the great man.

Victor looked at the wall of his den, covered from floor to ceiling with Nazi memorabilia. And right in the center of the wall, hanging above the fireplace, a huge portrait of Victor's idol: Adolf Hitler.

"I am really looking forward to this vacation," Congressman Madison said to several of his colleagues. The legislature's summer break had rolled around, and members of Congress were anxious to get back to their home base. "I've never been river rafting before."

A representative from Idaho smiled. "Well, you can

practice on that little river in Arkansas, Cliff. When you get ready for the big time, come on out to my state and run our wild rivers."

The men and woman gathered around laughed, then shook hands and said their goodbyes for the upcoming month's vacation.

Cliff Madison's aide said, "You'll be met at the lodge by two Secret Service agents out of the Little Rock office, Mr. Speaker. You and your wife will be accompanied on the plane to Memphis by two deputy federal marshals."

"Any word on why the beefed-up security, Ed?"

"No, sir. I think it's just a precaution, that's all."

"I'm sure that's it. You and Emily all packed and ready to go?"

Ed smiled. "Rarin' to go, sir. We're leaving several days ahead of you and Jane. We're going to drive and enjoy the scenery."

Cliff sighed and returned the smile. He looked tired and was tired. This session of Congress had been grueling on everybody in both parties in both houses. "I sure wish we could. I'd like to just disappear into the woodwork for the entire month."

"That is never going to happen, Cliff," the chief aide said in low tones. Even though they were good and close friends, Ed never used the Speaker's first name unless they were alone together. "Not until you retire, and that is years away."

"Hopefully, Ed," the Speaker said with a smile. "Years away, hopefully."

Laughing, the two men walked away.

Seconds after he picked up the scent of his old adversary, John Ravenna, Barry ducked behind some thick underbrush and dropped to a crouch.

He did some fast thinking. If Ravenna was here—
and there was no doubt about that; Barry's nose didn't
lie—trouble was sure to be hanging around the man
like a shroud . . . a very deadly shroud. But what type
of trouble? Directed against whom? Not against Barry,
for the two men would accomplish nothing by fighting.
Stormy? Maybe. But somehow Barry didn't think she
was Ravenna's target. Then . . . who was it?

It had to be Speaker of the House, Cliff Madison.

Barry knew that John Ravenna's deadly services were
very expensive. Indeed, Ravenna was a wealthy man,
amassing a fortune over the bloody centuries. He certainly did not have to work. Ravenna killed because he
liked to kill.

Barry sniffed the air again. The scent was quickly
fading. Ravenna was gone.

But Barry was certain of one thing: Ravenna would
be back.

Sheriff Don Salter sat in his office and looked at the
information he had just received by fax. The shooter
behind the rifle out at Cantrell's property did indeed
belong to a very radical antiabortion group; a group
that was suspected of several abortion clinic bombings
and burnings. The guy was wanted up in Michigan for
arson and attempted murder. So that cleared up the
warning Miss Knight had received before leaving New
York City.

Don looked up as Chief Monroe tapped on the door-
jamb. "Come on in and take a load off, Russ. Coffee?"

The chief sat down. "No, thanks, Don. I cut myself
back to two cups a day. Both of them in the morning.
Feel better. You seen Jim Beal today?"

"I haven't seen Jim in, oh, a week or better. Why?"

"That's a mighty worried man. Something is gnawin' on him, big-time."

Don looked at his empty coffee cup, started to get up, then thought better of it. Maybe he should cut back on caffeine, too. And cigarettes. "You still think Jim and his bunch are up to something, don't you?"

Russ shook his gray head. "No. But I think they, or at least Jim, know something that we ought to know. By the by, I just saw a lady that is the spittin' image of that reporter, Stormy Knight. Damn near run my car off the road lookin' at her."

"Well, I guess it's no secret anymore, Russ. That was Stormy. She's stayin' out at the Cantrell place. She and Barry have this little thing goin'."

"No kidding! The man must have hidden talents."

"And good taste."

"Damn right. And that was no woofer with Stormy."

"That was probably her camera operator. Barry told me about her. Ki Nichols. She was jerked up just north of here, little town in Missouri. Anyway, Stormy said that in about three/four days, we can expect this area to be flooded with reporters."

"Wonderful," the chief said, no small amount of sarcasm in his tone. "I just can't express how much I love those liberal bastards and bitches. And since we're not exactly overrun with black folks, you can bet the networks and newspapers will send black reporters in to cover the Speaker's vacation. That's the way they operate."

Don could not contain his laughter at the expression on the chief's face. Don remembered all too well when several very racist and antigovernment groups settled not too many miles away from town. Several reporters had insinuated, not too subtly, that Russ and Don were protecting those groups, and just maybe were actually a part of them. Nothing could have been farther from the truth, but both men had been very unfairly tainted nonetheless.

Don's feelings toward the national press were not as virulent as Russ Monroe's, but they weren't too far behind the chief's views. As millions of Americans had done, when the Coyote Network's news department came to be, he had switched over to them for any and all news broadcasts. The Coyote Network people told it straight with no frills, and they gave Americans news about America.

Don tapped a pencil on his desk, then lifted his eyes to look at Chief Monroe. "You've known Jim Beal for a good many years, right, Russ?"

"All his life. I know everybody in his organization. Jim is really not a bad person. When it comes to race, he is a separatist, but not a supremacist. Hell, I'm not tellin' you anything you don't already know." The chief stood up. "I think I'll just go have a little chat with Jim. He knows I'm not his enemy, and he just might level with me . . . or at least give me a clue."

"Russ?"

The chief looked at the sheriff.

"What about that bunch of so-called skinheads that have formed up north of here?"

"Oh, yeah. I must be gettin' old. I was gonna tell you about that. The word I get is that they're about to link up with Victor Radford's group. Vic is gonna give us some grief, I'm thinkin'."

"And you can bet he's got it timed for Speaker Madison's visit."

"Yeah. That's the way I have it figured."

"Are you going to call up your reserves?"

"All of them." He smiled. "All eight of them."

Don laughed. "I've got about ten reserves that I know I can count on. I guess I'd better give them a call. They can handle traffic and crowd control and free up my people for everything else."

"It's about to get real interestin' around here, Don."

"I hope that's all it gets."

"I might know more after talkin' to Jim. I'll let you know what, if anything, I find out."

"I'll either be here or in my unit."

"I'll give you a bump whichever way it goes."

Russ closed the door behind him. The only sound in the office was the hum of the air conditioner, the window unit turned down low. Don felt jumpy, as if he'd been up a long time and was on a caffeine jag. But he knew that wasn't it, for he'd gotten a good night's sleep and hadn't consumed that much coffee.

He felt as though something, well, just plain *awful* was about to happen.

A deputy tapped on the door and pushed it open. "You got a minute, Sheriff?"

"Sure, Al. Come on in and have a seat." The young deputy seated, Don said, "What's on your mind?"

"It's probably nothing, Sheriff. But . . . well, I was over on the lake early this morning. Got called out of bed to answer a prowler call—turned out to be a raccoon—and I stopped by Will's Grocery just as he was opening up and had a cup of coffee. He was telling me about this man who rented the old Hawkins camp. Said that man was spooky-lookin'. No sooner had the words left Will's mouth when the guy in question walked in. Sheriff, you remember when you were a kid and went to see a real scary movie? You knew who the bad guys were right off the bat. They were, well, sinister-lookin'. Well, this man made chill bumps rise up on my arms. He's about forty, dark complexion, real black hair graying at the temples, 'bout six feet tall, muscular build, and in tip-top shape. You could tell that by the way he moved. Will told me before the guy walked in that he

was scared of him, and the man hadn't been nothin'
but polite. Sheriff, that man had the coldest eyes I ever
seen in my life. I swear to you, and you're going to think
me a damn fool, but lookin' into that man's eyes was
like lookin' into an open grave."

"For a fact, Al, he's got you spooked. Does this man
have a name?"

"Yes, sir. He stuck out his hand and shook and how-
died soon as he walked in. Said his name was Ravenna.
John Ravenna."

Seven

Sitting on his front porch, Barry thought of and immediately rejected a dozen plans, and in the end, knew there was nothing he could do except wait for John Ravenna to show his hand.

Chief Russ Monroe went to see Jim Beal, but the man was gone. The manager of the lumber yard and hardware store did not know where he had gone or when he would return, or even if he would return this day.

Sheriff Don Salter, on an impulse, drove out into the country to the headquarters of Victor Radford's whacky bunch of neo-Nazis. Victor was standing by the rural mail box when Don drove past. Victor gave him the middle finger, and Don returned the gesture, feeling just a little bit foolish as he did so. Flipping the bird to someone was not against the law (at least not in this area), not since a local judge had ruled it was freedom of expression.

Don could see no one else on the property as he slowly cruised past. But he knew that didn't mean a thing, for Victor had underground bunkers dug all over the place. Victor was certain that a revolution was just around the corner, and he intended to be ready.

And that was the one and only issue that put Sheriff

Don Salter and Victor Radford in agreement, for Don firmly believed that if the government of the United States didn't get off the backs of Americans, some sort of violent upheaval was right around the corner.

Don knew that many of the people in his county, and in the surrounding counties, were heavily armed, with many stockpiling ammunition and keeping a thirty-day supply of food and water at all times. Don also was well aware of how the majority of people in his county felt about the ever-growing power of big government and the government's snooping around in citizens' lives. Don knew that all across America, there was a growing feeling of resentment against the government. Something had to pop this festering boil, and Don was very much afraid that when it happened, the result would be violent. And he also knew, from talking with law enforcement officers around the nation, that the mood was the same all over America.

And the sad thing was, Don firmly believed that most elected officials in Washington did not have a clue as to what was really happening.

For politicians to be so far out of touch with the citizenry was a disgrace, to Don's way of thinking.

Don came to a crossroads and turned left, heading for the lake. Maybe he'd get lucky and meet this mystery man that had spooked his deputy.

"It's beautiful country," Stormy said, after sitting down and thanking Barry for a tall glass of iced tea. "And the people are so friendly."

Ki had insisted upon checking into a motel. She wanted to give Barry and Stormy as much time alone as possible.

"They'll be friendly and helpful to you and the other Coyote reporters," Barry replied. "The majority won't be all that friendly to correspondents from the other networks."

Many Americans held the belief, whether it was true or not, that the big three networks and the all-news networks held decidedly liberal views and slanted the news to the left. It was a hard fact that Coyote was the only network whose news reporting nearly always took the conservative side (some dissenters called it right-wing news reporting). Coyote field reporters asked the hard and often inflammatory questions. One Coyote reporter actually went out and found jobs for half a dozen people, white and black, in an attempt to get them off public assistance; then when five of the six refused to accept the positions (it was demeaning and humiliating work, so they said), did a five-minute story about their refusal to take gainful employment and choosing instead to remain at the public trough, slopping like hogs and breeding like rabbits (or words to that effect). Coyote was still being sued over that one.

But the majority of viewers loved it.

Including Sheriff Don Salter, who grew up in a family where there was never enough money to go around and everybody worked, before school, after school, and on weekends, in an oftentimes vain attempt to make ends meet. He had worked too hard and struggled for too long to believe in free rides. And he had absolutely no use whatsoever for cry-baby liberals.

Don and Barry had a lot more in common than either man realized.

"How did you enjoy our county, Miss Knight?" Don asked.

Everyone was settled in the den with a beer or cocktail and the mood was relaxed. The late afternoon was hot, and the air-conditioning softly hummed, keeping the house at a comfortable level. Pete and Repeat were asleep on the floor of Barry's bedroom.

"It's Stormy, Sheriff. And in answer to your question: I think this is beautiful country. We"—she cut her eyes to Ki—"drove over a hundred miles today, sightseeing and talking with people." She frowned for a second. "Almost everyone was very nice and friendly. Except for one man. We got lost a couple of times and stopped at a house to ask directions. That man was very unfriendly . . ."

"That's not all," Ki picked it up. "We could see into his living room. He had a huge picture of Hitler hanging on the wall. It was grotesque."

Don chuckled. "Just north of town on a county road?"

"Yes," Stormy replied.

"Describe him." After Stormy had painted a vocal picture of the man, Don said, "You met Victor Radford. He's the leader of a neo-Nazi group. A bunch of kooks and flakes. They look silly parading around in their Nazi uniforms, but they're dangerous. And that's off the record, Stormy."

"All right. Any other off-the-wall groups around here I need to know about?"

"Well, yes, sort of. Jim Beal fronts a large group of people, men and women, who call themselves the AFB. The Arkansas Freedom Brigade. They believe in the complete separation of the races, but they are not white supremacists. Jim doesn't preach hate toward other races; he doesn't advocate violence toward other races. Actually, except for his strong views about separation, Jim is a nice guy and a reasonable man."

"Sounds as though you genuinely like the man, Sheriff. And I'm not interviewing you, and none of this will go on the air, I assure you."

"Yeah, I like the man. He's never been in trouble

with the law. I don't think Jim Beal has ever so much as received a traffic ticket. And in a lot of ways, he makes sense. He's a very intelligent man. And on the plus side, he's never belonged to the Klan, or any group like it. He's very selective about the people he allows into his organization."

"I'd like to interview this man, Don."

"I can arrange that, I think. Jim has said a number of times that the reporters for the Coyote Network are about the only ones he trusts not to do a hatchet job on people who believe as he does."

"I'd also like to interview this Victor Radford. Is that possible?"

"I don't know about that. I don't even like to get around the guy. He's a flamin' screwball. But I'll see what I can do. I can't make any promises."

"That's fair enough. Now then, at your convenience, I would like to interview you and get your views on the Speaker's visit here."

Don suddenly looked nervous. "On camera?"

"Sure."

His wife, Jeanne, grinned and tickled his ribs. "Oh, go on, Don. Do it."

The sheriff's grin wiped years from his face. "Oh, okay, Stormy. I guess it won't kill me."

Barry fixed fresh drinks and cold beer for everyone—except himself, he rarely drank—and sat down in time to catch the last of Don's remarks.

". . . and this man really spooked one of my deputies. And Al is a steady sort of fellow."

"Did the man do anything to bring this on?" Jeanne asked.

The sheriff shook his head. "No. Al said he was really quite friendly. But something about the man caused the short hairs to stand up on Al's neck. He was still spooked when he talked to me, hours later."

"This man live around here?" Barry asked, after taking a sip of iced tea and carefully placing the moisture-covered glass on a coaster.

"No. Well, for a while, I guess. I checked and found that he's leased some property for a couple of months. Ah, he's all right, I'm sure. Probably a nice guy just here to do some fishing and relaxing."

"Does he have a name?" Stormy asked.

"Yes," Don replied. "Ravenna. John Ravenna."

"Those idiots," Robert Roche muttered, still irritated about the hired thugs' failure to grab Barry. Then he calmed himself. He had known all along that they would fail. The man who was born Vlad Radu was too smart, too wary, to allow himself to be captured by garden variety thugs.

Perhaps he'd been taking the wrong tack with the man who now called himself Barry Cantrell. Robert hated to think he could ever be wrong, but sometimes one simply had to reassess matters and take one's losses and change, if change was needed.

And in this case, it was needed.

"Yes," Robert muttered. "Yes, indeed."

President Dick Hutton stared out the window of the Oval Office, watching the rain splatter against the bullet-proof panes. Congress had gone home for a month, and Dick and his family were scheduled to take a two-week vacation. But getting out of Washington's pressure cooker was not foremost on the president's mind. No, something was all out of focus; something very unhealthy was growing like a cancer. Dick was a good politician, with a politician's knack for sniffing out trouble, and he could sense that something was terribly wrong.

But he didn't have a clue as to what it was.

Yet.

Dick glanced at the clock. He had thirty free minutes before his next appointment. He picked up the phone and punched a button. "Max? Come in here, will you?"

Max Montgomery had been with Dick Hutton since he was first elected to the senate. The first thing Dick did after becoming president was to name Max his chief of staff. It was one of Dick's better moves.

The door opened and Dick pointed to a chair. "Sit down, Max. Something's been bugging me . . ."

"Bad choice of words, Dick," Max said with a smile. "Let's hope not."

Dick grinned. "Right." He sat down in the chair next to Max. "Max, what's going on?"

"I beg your pardon, sir?"

"Something smells bad, Max. And it ain't cabbage cookin' in the kitchen. So what are you holding back from me?"

Max didn't hesitate. He knew his friend and boss could pick up on a lie as easily as any streetwise cop. "Totally unsubstantiated rumors, Mr. President. Concerning Speaker of the House Madison."

"What rumors, Max?"

The chief of staff sighed heavily. "That a contract has been placed on his life."

"Good God!" The president's reply was filled with genuine concern. While Dick Hutton and Cliff Madison were on opposite sides of nearly every issue, the two men had been friends for years. Indeed, they were the same age and had actually played football against each other in high school. Both were from Tennessee. Dick's family had moved to Ohio in his junior year, and he had called the Buckeye State home ever since. Dick Hutton was the ninth man from the state of Ohio to be elected to the presidency.

Congressman Cliff Madison still called the Volunteer State home.

"Both the FBI and the Secret Service are trying to track down the source of the rumor—"

The phone rang, interrupting Max. The secretary's voice pushed through the speaker. "For you, Mr. Montgomery."

Max listened, his face paled. "Oh, dear God!" he said, then hung up. He turned to face the president. "Sir, Senator Holden's body has just been found. He apparently shot himself in the head. The cleaning lady found the body on the bedroom floor."

Dick Hutton slumped back in his chair, a stunned expression on his face. He was speechless.

"Mr. President," Max began, "I'll get right on this. I—"

"Cancel all my appointments for the rest of the day, Max. I don't have anything urgent on the agenda."

"Yes, sir."

Max left the Oval Office, and Dick rose and walked to his desk, sitting down. His mind was racing, his thoughts dark. He did not believe for one second that Senator Holden had committed suicide.

He buzzed his secretary. "I don't want to be disturbed, Ruth."

"Yes, sir."

All presidents, if they expected to last in Washington, had their personal cadre of spies. Such was the nature of modern-day politics. Dick knew all about the secret meetings held by the ultraliberal left of his party. He knew who met with whom, where they met and how often. While he did not know for sure what they discussed behind those closed doors, he had a very good idea.

Senator Holden had been a moderate, a voice of reason among the liberal left. Gene Dawson was a big-money man here in Washington, a philanthropist who loved even the most hopeless of liberal causes. He had inherited a fortune from his father and mother and, as far as Dick knew, had never worked a day in his life. Gene also disliked Republicans. No, dislike was too mild a word. Loathe was a better choice of words. Senator Paul Patrick hated anything and anybody of the right-wing persuasion. Senator Sam Stevens was another ultraleft liberal. Just like Dawson, Sam had inherited a huge fortune from his parents. But Madalaine Bowman was quite another story. Possessing the disposition of a pit viper, Madalaine was the most dangerous of those who attended the private meetings in that room behind the restaurant. Dick had always felt Madalaine was capable of anything . . . even murder. The others who attended, even though they wielded great power, were tagalongs, sheep. They would follow the Judas Goat blindly and without question.

Dick scribbled on the legal pad. It was all beginning to add up, at least in his mind. And what it was adding up to both disgusted and frightened the president. It was unthinkable.

Dick knew Madalaine hated him. He could read it in her eyes each time they met, and Gene Dawson and Paul Patrick shared her feelings. Dick was a moderate liberal, just as Holden had been.

The kicker in this hypothesis was Vice President Adam Thomas, a very good friend of Madalaine Bowman, and a man Dick Hutton could just barely tolerate. For the sake of the party, in public, they were buddy-

buddy, but in private, they loathed one another with equal fervor.

Dick's spies had informed him that Madalaine had called for some sort of emergency meeting just a few nights past. Of course, VP Thomas could never attend those gatherings, but he would be kept abreast of anything that was discussed. Dick's spies had told him that when Senator Holden left the meeting, he appeared to be badly shaken.

Dick was now certain that the "rumor" about a contract on Congressman Madison's life was no rumor. And he felt sure he knew why Senator Holden had been killed.

Dick pulled out a drawer of his desk and paused for a moment before using his private line to place a call. Meeting secretly with Speaker Madison would be chancy, but his Secret Service people could work it out. They'd *have* to work it out. And they wouldn't have much time in which to do it. The call concluded, Dick summoned the head of the White House Secret Service detail. Moments later, the man was standing in front of the president's desk.

"Let's do it, Walt," the president of the United States said.

Eight

"John Ravenna is not here to relax and fish," Barry told Stormy and Ki, after the sheriff and his wife had left. "Ravenna has been a hired assassin for nearly a thousand years. And he despises me."

"When did you last see him?" Ki asked.

"1944. In France. I was with the OSS, working with the French Resistance."

Stormy and Ki knew all about the man who was christened Vlad Dumitru Radu. They were the first mortals Barry had leveled with in more than half a century.

"You think Robert Roche hired him?" Stormy asked.

"I don't know. But I suspect not. That would not be Ravenna's first choice of assignment. He's a hunter, a torturer, a killer. He lives to kill. He talks of us fighting, but for obvious reasons, it would be a useless physical confrontation. No, John is here for someone other than me."

"Pete and Repeat?" Ki asked, looking at the huge hybrids, sprawled in sleep on the floor of the living room.

Barry shook his head. "No. John knows I would track him until the end of time if he harmed something I loved. I would never let him rest; I would expose him wherever he went. So that means he isn't after either of you." Barry went into the kitchen, poured a mug of coffee, sugared it, and returned to the living room. "So that leaves only one other possibility as John's target."

"Who?" Both women asked.

Barry told them.

It was possible for the president of the United States to slip out of the White House undetected by the press. It wasn't easy, but it was possible. Over the years, sitting presidents had used doubles, disguises, secret passageways, tunnels running under the White House, and other techniques of evading the press and the public. Usually they didn't work. This night, the president was successful.

The president's wife was back at their home in Ohio, where they had planned to spend a few days of their upcoming two-week vacation. Both their children were in college. Dick had canceled all White House functions. So on this night, Dick Hutton slipped out the back way, got into a nondescript Secret Service vehicle, and left the grounds undetected, even though actions such as these made the Secret Service awfully nervous.

At the same time, Speaker of the House Cliff Madison was being picked up by another unmarked government vehicle. The president and the Speaker met in the underground parking area of a government office building. Present at the meeting were selected agents of the Secret Service, U.S. Marshals, and the FBI.

Dick Hutton pointed a finger at the FBI. "Just listen, don't talk. Not yet. I want your best people working on the death of Senator Holden. It was not a suicide. I strongly suspect it was a contract killing." The president told the gathering who he suspected was behind the killing, and that shook the men and

women right down to the soles of their shoes. Dick
looked at Cliff Madison. "I believe there is an assassin
already in place in Arkansas waiting to kill you, Cliff.
I believe an accident has been planned for you while
boating." He looked at the gathering of federal law
enforcement personnel. "Get undercover people into
that area ASAP. The very best you have, no fuck-ups.
This country cannot take another Waco, or Ruby
Ridge, or, God help us all, another fiasco such as the
one in Idaho last spring. I want no large display of
force. You've got five days to set this up." He looked
at Cliff. "Unless you want to cancel, and I hope you
do."

"No," the Speaker said. "No way. You know as well
as I do that if we're targets, they'll get us, one way or
the other. It goes with the job. But what do I tell my
wife?"

"The truth, Cliff. And won't that be refreshing?"

Cliff smiled.

Dick turned his attention to the federal enforcement agents. "I have alerted certain people at NSA
and CIA. And I accept full responsibility for using
the CIA domestically. But if some people have to be
taken out, and you know what I mean, the Company
does it better than anyone else. All right, get your
people in there as fishermen, hikers, tourists, people
looking for investment property, retirement homes. I
want around-the-clock surveillance on Gene Dawson,
Senators Stevens and Patrick, and especially on that
venomous bitch Madalaine Bowman. Phones bugged;
the whole nine yards. I've already spoken with a federal judge who is a close friend of mine. Everything
is legal and above-board—more or less—but we're
ready to go. I don't want young agents in on this.
No cowboys or hot dogs. I want highly experienced

men and women who won't panic and jump the gun. Understood?"

Perfectly.

"That bitch reporter, Stormy Knight, is in the area," Alex, the boss of this particularly odious bunch of shaved heads, told his equally shiny-domed gang. "Vic Radford just confirmed it. She's gonna do a number on us."

"Maybe we better lay low," a gang member suggested. "We don't need no more heat on us."

"We ain't done nothin' wrong," Alex countered. "We got a right to our opinions same as anyone else. Fuck 'er."

"I'd like that," another shaved head said with a dirty laugh.

"You wouldn't when you come down with AIDS or some other fag disease," Alex said. He frowned at all the members gathered around. "She's like all reporters: in love with niggers and queers and Jews. Liberals think it's fashionable to fuck niggers and kiss queers. If our race is gonna survive, we gotta be more careful than ever before. You boys and girls keep that in mind."

Alex gave his following a slow visual once-over. They were small in number, but they would grow with time. Alex knew that, for he had met with the leaders of other chapters around the country before deciding upon this location for a cell. And in only a few months five new members had been added. It did not take long to convince a certain type of person that Hitler was a great and wise man. You just had to know what to look for. Alex had been carefully coached in that and was not nearly as dumb as he appeared to be.

Which certainly could not be said for most of his followers.

Stormy and Ki were prowling around the country, would be gone most of the day. Barry made certain Pete and Repeat had plenty of fresh water, secured his place, and took a drive out to Will's store on the lake. Barry was more aware than any other living person that when it came to men of John Ravenna's caliber, there was no point in pussy-footing around: they had to be met head-on. He was also well aware that moments after he stopped at the store and asked directions to Ravenna's place, Will would be on the phone to Sheriff Salter. Couldn't be helped. This was something that had to be done.

Barry had a soft drink and chatted with the old man who had established the store and operated it for almost half a century.

"I bet you've seen some changes in this country since you first opened your store, right, Mr. Will?" Barry asked.

"Son," the old man replied, "I could sit here for the rest of the day and tell you stories about this area of the state. And I wouldn't even scratch the surface. Not just this little part of the country, but the whole nation. We're headed straight down the toilet, we are. And I don't see no way it can be stopped. Sit down, boy, sit down." He pointed to a chair. "Make yourself comfortable. You ain't in no hurry, are you? Good. I don't take to many folks, but you got an honest face. Manners, too. That's rare nowadays." Will poured himself another cup of coffee and sat down. "I was raised right here in this country. Born in 1918, I was. On the day the big war ended. The war to end all wars, they said. Twenty-four years later my ass was in North Africa in the infantry. Two years later I waded ashore on D-Day. I was the only man in my squad to survive that bloody day. When the Krauts finally surrendered, I was the only man out of the original platoon left alive. I come back here and by God I ain't left the state since then."

Will took a sip of coffee. "I got married a year after I come back. Had four kids. Two of 'em turned out all right; last two ain't worth a sack of shit. Haven't seen them in years; don't wanna see 'em. Last time I seen the youngest was back in the late sixties. He come wanderin' in here drivin' a van had flowers painted all over it. He was dressed up so's he looked like he oughta be a part of a freak show. Had a girl with him—I think it was female, I ain't sure to this day—had a conversational ability about like a concrete block. The boy told me the war in Vietnam was wrong and anybody who fought over there was a criminal and should be put in prison. I knocked him down right over there by the front door, kicked his ass off the porch and ain't seen him since. After I kicked him off the porch that girl-thing with him said something like, 'Oh, wow, man, I mean, that's truly heavy, like, you know?' I ain't figured out yet exactly what the hell she was talkin' about."

Will got up to wait on a customer wanting minnows and worms and then returned to his chair. "This part of the country used to be a nice place to live. Folks got along. Now we got Nazis, skinheads, hippies, so-called survivalists, big militia group, and God only knows what else. These new-Nazis say that Hitler was a great man. The son of a bitch was a ravin', murderin' lunatic, that's what he was. Wasn't nothin' great about him. I don't know what them damned shaved heads believe in; nothin', probably. Don't know where they get their money to live like they do. I get along pretty well with the few hippies left around here. They work hard and mind their own business. The survivalists make me laugh . . . but I think they're harmless, for the most part. They gather together one weekend a month and dress up like they was in the army and run around in the woods, shootin' and hollerin' and carryin' on. I been knowin' most of 'em since they shit yeller. But them militia folks is serious now . . . and I tend to agree with most of what they espouse . . ."

Barry noticed that the old man would occasionally slip out of his folksy, backwoods way of speaking. He'd noticed the stack of newspapers and magazines behind the counter, and accurately guessed that Will was well read and highly literate—when he wanted to let it show. Barry had also seen the book, *Lost Rights,* authored by James Bovard, on a bookshelf behind the counter. One of the finest books about the destruction of American liberty to be published in years. Barry suspected that Will might play well the part of backwoods philosopher, but the still waters that flowed throughout the man ran deep with knowledge.

Barry accepted Will's offer of coffee and poured a cup and sugared it. "How about this nation, Mr. Will. America. Where are we heading?"

Will shook his head. "Country's in trouble, boy. Bad trouble. Folks are unhappy. Thousands of 'em joinin' this group or that group or the other group. But all the groups have one thing in common: they don't like the federal government. Government's got too big and too bossy. Stickin' their noses into a person's personal business. They got no right to do that. None at all."

"You think we're looking at revolution, Mr. Will?"

"Maybe," the older man said solemnly. "It wouldn't surprise me none to see it happen. Hard-workin' folks get pushed long enough, they'll push back. Feds know that, too. That's why those goddamn egg-suckin' liberals up in Washington are tryin' so hard to disarm us all. They're scared, boy. And they ain't scared of criminals like they say is behind the move. They're scared of me and you and folks like us all over America."

"Would you turn in your guns to the government, Mr. Will? If that legislation were to pass both houses and get signed into law?"

The man smiled, and it was not a pleasant smile. "Hell, no. Would you?"

"No."

"Didn't think so. You don't look the type. But"—Will smiled widely—"you might be another one of those snoopin' Feds that come around here ever' so often askin' all sorts of damn fool questions 'bout things that ain't none of their goddamn business."

Barry laughed. "No, sir. I can assure you I am not a federal agent. I bought a piece of property on the other side of town, about five miles out. I think it's called the old Pearson place. Something like that."

"Yeah. I know where you live. I just wanted to see any reaction you might have when I mentioned the feds."

"Mr. Will, I live a good ten miles from this store. How would you know about me?"

"Oh, people stop by and keep me up to date, son. I like to know when strangers move into our area."

"Any strangers moved out this way recently?"

"I wondered when you'd get around to that, son."

Barry smiled. "I suppose you know all about the trouble out at my place."

"I think I've heard something about it, yeah. That good-lookin' lady reporter is stayin' out there with you, right?"

"That's right."

"Sure can't fault you for that. We've had a stranger or two move in around here lately, for a fact. One of 'em's gonna be comin' through the front door in about half a minute. He might be a nice enough feller, but I just can't cotton to him. After he leaves, you gimme your impression, boy."

Barry twisted in his chair. John Ravenna was opening the front door to the country store and bait shop.

Nine

"We'll fly into Little Rock," Robert Roche told a gathering of his people, including the pilot of his personal Lear. "I've called our offices there, and cars will be waiting. No limos. I want this low key all the way. We'll drive to the area. Cabins have been rented along a lake that is close to the town. We leave in the morning. That's all."

His staff dismissed and out of the room, Roche sat down and again studied a map of Arkansas, occasionally glancing at a tourist guide. After a time, he leaned back in his chair, a wry smile curving his lips. Actually, he did enjoy fishing; it was very relaxing. But staying on top of and manipulating billions of dollars did not leave much time for relaxing of any sort. Consequently, Robert had not fished in years. So, this little trip might turn out to be fun after all.

In more ways than one. Ten billion dollars could buy a lot of amusement. Fun being relative to one's particular sense of humor, of course.

Federal agents had already begun moving quietly into the area. They came in as salespeople, vacationers, folks looking for investment property, or for a vacation home. Several federal agents rode motorcycles in; they would frequent the rougher honky tonks in the area. They rode Harleys that had been confiscated during a drug raid in California several years back. One of the men had his "old lady" with him, riding her own chopper.

One of the few things the government could do well was get people into a designated area in a hurry.

During the summer months the area was filled with tourists constantly coming and going; therefore the locals paid no attention to the new people. But the cops did.

John Ravenna's face was expressionless as he stepped into the store and spotted Barry. But his dark eyes glinted with savage amusement for a few seconds. He walked to the counter and spoke first to Mr. Will, then turned to Barry and held out his hand. "John Ravenna, sir. And you are . . . ?"

Barry shook the hard hand and said, "Barry Cantrell."

"So very pleased to meet you, Mr. Cantrell."

"Likewise, I'm sure." Barry looked at the owner. "See you, Mr. Will."

"Come back anytime, boy. You're good company."

Barry drove down the road for a short distance, just far enough to put him out of sight of Mr. Will's window which faced the road, and waited. He felt certain that John would be along very shortly.

It was not a long wait. John pulled up beside Barry's pickup and lowered the passenger side window. "Let's drive over to my cabin, cousin."

"As I have repeatedly told you over the centuries, John, I am not your cousin."

Ravenna smiled his cruel movement of the lips. "Yes.

I know. But if merely the thought of our being related irritates you, I shall certainly continue the practice. Follow me . . . cousin."

Barry followed the evil immortal to his rented cabin, about a ten-minute drive along the shores of the lake. In the yard, Ravenna said, "Come on inside. I'll get us something cool to drink. It's very warm out this day." John read the wariness in Barry's eyes and laughed. "Relax, cousin. I won't try to drug you. I am not after you. And you have my word on that."

"Your . . . *word*, John?"

"My word, cousin. Whether you care to believe it or not, I do have some honor." He frowned. "If you are going to rebuff my offer of hospitality, then you can go right straight to hell." Ravenna turned and walked up the steps and into the cabin by the lake.

Barry smiled and followed the man inside. He could always count on ruffling Ravenna's feathers by questioning his peculiar code of honor. But Barry also knew that once John Ravenna gave his word, it was a bond he would not break. However, he usually gave his word to some malefactor of evil.

The window unit in the living room/den was humming, filling the air with coolness. John walked out of the small kitchen carrying two glasses of ice water. He set one down on a coaster beside Barry, on the table, and took a seat across the room. He smiled and lifted his glass in a sarcastic toast.

Barry raised his glass and returned the gesture.

"Fifty years, isn't it, Vlad?" John asked.

"Fifty-two to be exact."

"You're looking well."

"We both look the same and you know it."

"How long has it been since you've visited that miserable little village where you were whelped?"

Barry ignored the insult. "I went back just after

World War I. I really don't know why I did. I have never been able to locate the graves of my parents."

"They were both burned at the stake for performing witchcraft, and their ashes scattered. I thought you knew that."

"No. I did not. Only that they were killed shortly after I was forced to flee."

John grunted. "My parents were impaled and left to die much more slowly."

"I was always under the impression your parents were immortals."

Ravenna shook his head. "No. One day while I was practicing shape changing—I was about ten years old—a priest witnessed the metamorphosis. It frightened the fool half out of his rather shallow wits. He scurried off to tell his superior, and my parents were imprisoned within the hour. Then the two priests came after me." Ravenna shrugged his muscular shoulders. "Naturally I killed them both. The legend goes that from that moment on, I was cursed by God. Ridiculous, of course. But for years it made a nice story to scare children into behaving."

"Why are you telling me all this, John? We're not exactly old buddies."

"To be quite honest, cousin, you intrigue me. While you are certainly not a poor man—I have followed your niggardly life through the years—you have not, as I have, accumulated great wealth over the centuries. You choose instead to live as a peasant. You involve yourself for the most paltry of sums in wars and causes that really don't concern you. I simply cannot understand why we are so different."

"Because you were born evil, John, and I was not. It's that simple."

"Perhaps you're right. Oh, well. It's all moot anyway. We are what we are and nothing of this earth can

change it. I suppose you are curious as to why I am
here in the land of hillbillies and incomprehensible
speech?"

"I think I know, John."

"Do you, now? Assuming that you do know, what are
you going to do about it? Expose me? I doubt it. When
you expose me, you also expose yourself. If you went
to the police, they would want to know how *you* know
so much about *me.*"

"I realize that."

A frown clouded John's features. "You're not seriously considering going public, are you, Vlad?"

Barry maintained a poker face and did not reply.

"You really are considering doing just that," John
muttered. "Well, that throws everything under a different light. You do remember what happened to Basil
a few years ago, don't you?"

"It was a hundred and fifty years ago, John," Barry
corrected. "In London. Of course I remember. After
he told the authorities what he was, they locked him
away in a lunatic asylum. He finally managed to escape,
and no one has heard from him since."

"He was living up in Canada," John mused. "Of
course that was a hundred years ago. No telling where
he is now. You realize that if you attempt to go public,
there is a way for us to stop you?"

Barry took a sip of ice water. "Yes. I have given that
some thought."

Mind control. If several "older" immortals gathered
and directed thoughts toward another, they could overpower him with their minds. But there was only one
hitch in that, and Barry reminded him of it. "I can't
think of a single one of us who would assist you in
doing anything, John."

"You do have a point," John conceded. "I suppose
I am not the best liked among our kind."

"That's putting it mildly."

John began staring intently at Barry. Barry met the man's glare and instantly threw up mental defenses. Sweat began to glisten on Ravenna's brow. Several minutes ticked by. Finally, John threw himself out of the chair. "Goddammit!" he shouted the oath. "You've grown much stronger, Vlad."

"I'm no kid," Barry replied.

John pointed a finger at the immortal. "This is none of your affair, Vlad. My business does not concern you. You have no right to interfere."

"Being a citizen of this country gives me that right, John."

"*Citizen?*" John shouted. "We're citizens of the world, you idiot."

"Give up this assassination plot, John. If you even make an attempt, the U.S. government will never stop looking for you. You won't be able to rest for years. I'll personally see to that. Go on back to Ireland and enjoy your wealth. Haven't you done enough killing over the centuries?"

Ravenna glared hate at Barry. "I've only just begun, cousin. If you get in my way, I'll destroy you."

"How?" Barry laughed the question. "How can either of us die? You took a musket ball through the heart in Russia in the early days of the Romanov dynasty. You were up and going all out in three days. I was shot through the brain during the final days of this country's revolutionary war, and while I suffered some discomfort, the wound only slowed me down for a few days. Of course, I had to disappear after that, but that's beside the point. Are we going to fight, John? Fists? Guns? Swords? Or perhaps in our animal form? And what will it accomplish? Oh, we'll maim each other; but then we'll quickly recover, and nothing will have changed. I hope you won't shape-shift, John.

Just the sight of your Other makes me want to vomit."
Barry laughed. "God certainly played a very cruel trick
on you, didn't He, John. I suppose that proves He does
have a sense of humor."

Ravenna whirled around, his face colored darkly
with sudden rage. "Shut up, you bastard!" he shouted.
"Shut your mouth. Or we will fight, here and now and
the devil take the consequences. You hear me?"

Barry held up a hand. "All right, John. A momentary truce." He rose from the chair to face the man.
John accurately read the expression on Barry's face.
"If you continue with this assassination plot, I'll expose
you, John. And as you say, let the devil take the consequences."

"Why are you so concerned about the life of one
miserable windbag politician?"

"Because what you are planning is wrong. You have
time before the Speaker arrives to change your mind,
and I hope you do. Because I will not let you go
through with this. I will stop you."

Barry walked out the door, got into his truck, and
drove away. Several hundred yards away, his personal
car tucked in a driveway and obscured by a thick stand
of trees, Sheriff Salter lowered his binoculars and muttered, "Now, isn't that interesting? Barry Cantrell, just
who the hell are you? And what the hell are you really
up to?"

"Cliff?" Jane Madison called from the window of
their suburban Washington home.

"Yes, dear." Cliff looked up from the book he was
reading. He knew what his wife was looking at through
the rain, and he had dreaded this moment since meeting with President Hutton.

She turned to face him. "Would you care to tell me what is going on?"

Cliff laid aside his book and stood up, walking over to put a gentle hand on his wife's shoulder. "Jane, there are risks that go with this job."

She fixed him with a very direct stare. "Don't sugarcoat it, Cliff. Cars have been parked at each end of this street ever since you returned from last night's meeting. I had agents following me this morning. So what's going on?"

"I don't want you to go to Arkansas with me, Jane."

"Forget it. I'm going."

"It might turn into something very dangerous. And I stress might."

"Another death threat, Cliff?"

"Yes." He took a deep breath. The only issues Cliff ever held back from his wife were matters dealing with national security, and he was sworn by law not to discuss those. "Jane, I was on the phone with the president today for about half an hour. Since our meeting, he's learned a great deal more. Now, it's theory, so far, but there may be people planning some sort of coup. We don't believe Senator Holden committed suicide; we think he was murdered."

"A coup, Cliff? Here in America? A *coup?*"

"Yes. The president believes, and so does the FBI, that I am to be killed first, then the president. That will move Adam Thomas into the White House. Congressman Calvin Lowe will take over the Speaker's job."

"You have got to be kidding! Cal is weak."

"That's part of the plan. We think. We know that Cal is easily swayed. We also suspect that he has some dirt behind him and certain people inside the beltway have learned of it and will use that to force him to go along with them—"

"Madalaine Bowman," Jane interrupted.

"Probably. She's certainly a major player in this plot; we're sure of that."

"Who else, Cliff?"

"Gene Dawson, Sam Stevens, Paul Patrick . . . others, we're sure."

"Men who are on record as openly despising you."

"Yes."

"Our children?"

"Being protected. Very covertly. But we don't believe any of our children are in danger. Americans wouldn't stand for attacks against our kids."

"You mean it's all right to kill a politician but leave his or her kids alone?" Jane asked with the hint of a smile.

"That's about it."

She placed the palm of her hand on his chest. "Did the president ask you to call off the Arkansas trip?"

"Yes."

"And you refused?"

"Yes."

"Good for you, Cliff." She kissed him on the cheek. "I'm proud of you."

"Are you sure you want to come along, Jane? I believe this threat is very real. And if this plot is successful, the kids would be without parents."

She smiled. "Our kids are grown, Cliff. Their future is as secure as we could possibly make it. We've been equal-sharing partners for twenty-three years. I have no intention of changing that now." She stepped back and took his hand. "Let's go start laying out some things for our trip. But I need to add two more articles and have no idea where to get them."

"What?"

She grinned. "Bulletproof vests!"

Ten

Stormy looked around the building that was head-quarters of the Arkansas Freedom Brigade. She had expected to see a huge replica of the Confederate battle flag hanging prominently, but the only visible banner was the American flag. There were a number of very intriguing titles housed in the long bookcase, but they were mostly books on and about America and the Constitution and Bill of Rights, including the Federalist Papers. There were volumes of the tax code.

Stormy pointed to the thousands of pages of gobbledygook from the IRS. "You have actually read those things?"

"I have tried, Ms. Knight," Jim Beal replied. "But to a layperson, it's incomprehensible. And it's ridiculous when one considers that when the first tax code was written in 1914, it was fourteen pages long."

Ki was filming the interior of the long building while Stormy talked with Jim, trying to put the commander of the Arkansas Freedom Brigade at ease. "How many pages now?" Stormy asked, pointing to the volumes.

"Over nine thousand."

Stormy grimaced and shook her head in disgust. Barry should be the one interviewing Jim Beal about

that. She had never met a person who so despised the
IRS.

Jim had made a pot of coffee and set out cups. The
reporter and the man with the so-called controversial
views drank coffee, and Stormy watched as Jim slowly
relaxed and grew accustomed to the camera, now
standing stationary on a tripod.

"I'm not here to do a hatchet job on you, Mr. Beal,"
Stormy said. "Your views may be quite different from
the majority—and that hasn't as yet been established—
but you are entitled to your opinions under the First
Amendment."

"More or less," Jim said with a smile.

Stormy returned the smile. "Yes. Well. Mr. Beal, exactly what is the Arkansas Freedom Brigade?"

"It's a group of men and women that came together
as a unit about five years ago. And yes, it is a paramili-
tary group. However, we are strictly defensive in nature
and pose no threat to any government, local, county,
state, or federal."

"Why was the Arkansas Freedom Brigade formed,
Mr. Beal?"

"We believe this nation, the United States of America, is on the verge of collapse. As a nation, spiritually
and morally we have already collapsed. We believe that
economic collapse is sure to follow."

"Why, sir?"

"Because the nation is broke. Bankrupt. As a country, we have a tough time just paying the interest on
the national debt. We're unable to pay anything on
the principal. Yet, all we do is keep borrowing more
money and raising the debt limit. Really, our money
is worthless because it isn't backed by anything except
government promises. One of these days, probably
sooner than later, the American people will realize
that. Then the bottom is going to fall out."

"Do you believe your Freedom Brigade can prevent that from occurring?"

"Oh, no, ma'am. That's not why we formed. But when economic collapse does happen, we can assist in keeping order—at least in our small section of the nation. You see, ma'am, this collapse won't be like the stock market crash in the late twenties and the depression that followed. This collapse will be immediately followed by riots, looting, and a crime wave unlike anything this nation has ever experienced."

"Why do you believe that, Mr. Beal?"

"Because unlike conditions in the thirties, we now have millions of people, of all colors. People who, thanks to the liberals, expect the working taxpayers to provide housing for them, pay their utility bills, give them food stamps and pick up the tab for having children, and provide medical care for them . . . all without the recipients expected to hit a lick at anything to earn that help. I'm not singling out or blaming those folks on welfare; many of them really need our help. Rich folks receive welfare, too. It's just in a different form with a different name. But when the collapse comes, public assistance will stop. Then the rioting and the crime wave will start."

"Mr. Beal, I have to admit, publicly, that you are not what I expected. I expected some wild-eyed fanatic dressed in military field clothes, with guns and knives hanging all about you. You speak as a very educated man."

"I read a lot, Ms. Knight. I have some college. After my hitch in the army I was planning to return and get my degree. But . . ." He shrugged his shoulders and smiled. "I got married and we started a family."

"Are their any African Americans in your group, Mr. Beal?"

"No. There are very few Negroes living in this area."

"Would you allow an African American in your organization if one applied?"

"That would be up to the members. We vote on each applicant. I vote only in case of a tie. We have rejected many white people who have tried to join us."

"Can you tell me why they were rejected?"

"Many reasons, Ms. Knight. Some had criminal backgrounds. Others wanted to overthrow the government. Still others held views that were repugnant to us. There are all sorts of reasons why applicants can be rejected."

"Do you believe that if an African American applied for membership he or she would be allowed in?"

"No. They would be rejected."

"Because of their race?"

"That would play a very large part in the decision, yes."

"Why is that, Mr. Beal?"

"Because the Negro race is quite different from us, Ms. Knight. I believe, rightly or wrongly, that a large percentage of the Negro population is, educationally speaking, about a hundred years behind the white race. And that may be our fault. Probably is our fault. Until quite recently, we kept the Negro race under the hard boot of oppression. But in our eagerness to correct two hundred years of being wrong, we went too far in attempting to do what is right. Our educational system started deteriorating back in the sixties, when full integration began. Our schools were flooded with Negro children who just did not have the educational background to keep up. And I don't know whose fault that is. I do know that if a person wants an education badly enough, they'll get it, one way or the other. If they want to improve themselves, they can do it, but it's a tough row to hoe. I realize that. I do not come from a wealthy background, Ms. Knight. Quite the opposite. But I had a very deep driving, burning desire to improve myself. To learn all I possibly could about everything. I still do. But in our schools, the lowering of educational standards to accommodate one group is very unfair to the majority. Social promotion is wrong. It actually hurts the very people we are trying to help."

"You're speaking of black children, right?"

"Children of *any* color, Ms. Knight. Carrying it further, our schools are failing our kids. They're graduating kids who can't read, can't do simple math, don't know history, don't know geography. Our educational system is a mess."

"And the fault lies . . . where?"

"As far as I'm concerned, just about any problem facing this nation originated from the federal government. The government has managed to worm its way into all aspects of our lives. Sheriffs and chiefs of police don't run their departments and jails, federal judges do. If a wet spot appears out in some farmer's pasture, the government can declare it wetlands and forbid the farmer to use it or sell it. The EEOC, that's the equal employment opportunity commission, can fine a businessman thousands of dollars if he or she doesn't have a certain number of minorities on the payroll. The federal government tells the farmers what they can grow and how much. If a parent takes a picture of their baby having a bath, they can be arrested and jailed for pornography. Government snoops in all aspects of the citizens' lives. They can listen in on private phone conversations; they monitor electronic bulletin boards. The list of how the government is encroaching into citizens' lives is depressingly long and seemingly without end."

Stormy didn't agree with Jim Beal on many issues, but she did agree with him about government encroachment into the lives of American citizens. She signaled for Ki to cut the camera and asked Jim if he would like to take a break and have some coffee before they picked up the interview.

"Fine," Jim said. "I need a break." Coffee poured, Jim sat down at the table and said, "Ms. Knight, I need to tell you something, and I don't know how. This has got to be off the record. I can't take any more heat from the feds. But what I've learned has to be acted on . . . quickly."

"Does it deal with assassination, Mr. Beal?" Stormy asked, immediately recalling Barry's words about John Ravenna.

Jim Beal's hands were shaking so badly he had to set his coffee cup on the table before he spilled the contents. "You . . . you *know* about it?"

"I have a friend who suspected that was why a certain man suddenly appeared in this area." She smiled sadly. "Now I must ask you not to repeat that I know anything about it."

"Oh, I won't, Ms. Knight. You have my word on that. But what are we going to do about it?"

Stormy sighed. She and Barry had talked about what course of action to take. Barry was going to see Ravenna, to try to talk him out of the attempted hit. If that failed, then the plot must be exposed.

"I'm glad I'm out of it," Jim said, relief evident on his face.

"One more question, Mr. Beal," Stormy said. "And I give you my word, the camera is not recording and your reply is strictly off the record."

"Go ahead. I trust you."

"If the person coming under an assassin's gun was an ultraliberal senator or representative, would you have told me about it or gone to the authorities?"

Jim looked down at his coffee cup, sighed heavily,

almost painfully, then lifted his eyes to meet Stormy's gaze. "No," he said softly.

Don was waiting for Barry when he pulled into the driveway. He got out of his unit and waited until Barry had unlocked the gates and opened them wide.

"I suppose Ms. Knight has a key in case she gets back before you do?"

"Naturally," Barry replied.

"We have to talk, Barry. You've got to clear up some things for me. So call this visit official."

"Sounds serious."

"Not really. More mysterious, I suppose."

"I'm intrigued. Come on."

The vehicles parked inside the fenced area, the men entered the coolness of the home, and Barry waved the sheriff to a chair and poured them glasses of iced tea, then sat down on the couch.

"Go ahead, Don."

"This is the computer age, Barry," Don said. "Instant access to just about anything a cop would like to know about a person."

Barry nodded his head in agreement. "I noticed that all your units are equipped with small computers."

"Yes. That saves the dispatcher a lot of work and the office a lot of time. All the deputy has to do is punch in his request and usually it comes back in a matter of seconds."

Barry waited.

The sheriff stared at him.

Thunder rumbled in the heat of the afternoon, the sound very faintly reaching the men sitting inside the house. A summer storm was building.

"Barry, you don't know many people in this area, do you?"

"Very few people." Either Mr. Will had called the sheriff's department, or Don had been following him, and doing a very good job of tailing.

"Barry, I had a very interesting chat with the U.S. State Department about half an hour ago."

"Really?"

"Really. You know a man name of John Ravenna?"

Barry knew the sheriff had him on that one, and there was no need to lie about it. "Yes, I do. We've known each other for . . ." Barry smiled. "A few years."

"He's an Irishman, right?"

"I don't think so. But he does live in Ireland."

"What's he doing here, Barry?"

"Touring America. Stopped off here for a little rest, I suppose."

"Things are not adding up."

"What do you mean, Don?"

"All of a sudden, this area is filling up with feds. They're coming in here posing as all sorts of people, but they're feds."

"The Speaker of the House is coming in for a vacation. Maybe it's security for him."

"The Speaker doesn't get *that* much security. I checked. Now, I'm on good terms with the feds whose offices serve this area. First name basis with most of them. But they've clammed up tight. They're not unfriendly; they're just not giving me truthful answers to my questions. I'm a good cop, Barry. I can usually tell when someone is either outright lying or evading the truth."

"And you think I know what's going on, if anything, right?"

"I sure do, Barry."

"And you're going to dig into my background until you come up with something, right?"

"That's right. Unless you want to level with me now. Barry, I don't think you're a criminal. I don't believe you're running from the law. But I do believe you're hiding from something. Probably your past. Level with me, Barry, and whatever you tell me stays right here. That's a promise."

"You think you could handle it, Don?"

"I've been a cop for most of my adult life. I've seen it all."

"Have you now?" Barry said with a smile. "All right, Don. I'll just show you a little something you haven't seen."

An instant later, Barry became his Other.

Don dropped his glass of iced tea to the floor, the glass shattering and the liquid splattering.

Barry was gone. In his place, a huge gray timber wolf sat on the floor, snarling at Don.

The sheriff fainted.

Eleven

The thunderstorm rolled into the area just as Stormy and Ki were leaving the headquarters of the Arkansas Freedom Brigade. It began with a wicked, jagged slash of lightning followed by an earthshaking roar of thunder. Then the rains came, so hard and heavy Stormy could not see to drive. She pulled off onto the shoulder of the road, turned on the emergency flashers, and sat it out.

"What do you think about Jim Beal?" Ki asked, raising her voice to be heard over the fat, drumming raindrops on the roof of the car.

"Well, he's no raving nut," Stormy cautiously replied. Ki was superconservative on most issues, the exception being her belief in a woman's right to choose and animal rights. Even after working together as long as they had, Stormy really did not know Ki's feelings on the race issue. She did know that Ki was opposed to welfare except for the very old and the very young, felt that the Department of Housing and Urban Development, among others, should be done away with, and did not believe in affirmative action.

"Nice safe reply, Stormy," Ki said with a grin. "I'm anxious to go back for the second part of the interview."

"You don't agree with Jim Beal, do you?"

Ki shook her head. "Not entirely. But he makes just enough sense about some issues to be viable."

The rain slacked off just as suddenly as the deluge had begun and Stormy pulled back out onto the road.

"Where are we heading now?" Ki asked.

"Nellie's cafe for a sandwich. Both Don and Barry said the food was good."

"What was Barry going to do today? Did he say?"

"He was going out to see John Ravenna. After that, I don't know."

"How are we going to handle what Beal said about the assassination?"

"Just like porcupines make love—carefully!"

Barry stretched the sheriff out on the couch and dampened a cloth, then placed it on his forehead, though he knew there was no medical evidence that that action did any good. Then he cleaned up the broken glass, and a couple of swipes with a mop cleared away the spilled iced tea. Barry filled another glass with ice and water, set it on the coffee table for Don to drink when he woke up, then sat down in his chair and waited until Don opened his eyes.

The sheriff was out for only a few moments. He groaned, opened his eyes, and sat up. He stared at Barry through totally confused eyes. "That was the damndest trick I've ever seen, Barry," Don croaked. He picked up the glass of ice water and drank half of it.

"No trick, Don."

The sheriff stared at Barry for a moment, then drained his glass. He set the glass down carefully on a coaster. "What the hell do you mean, no trick? Of course it was a trick. An illusion."

"No trick," Barry repeated. "What you saw was real."

Don opened his mouth, but no words came out. He cleared his throat, shook his head, and whispered, "What are you trying to tell me?"

"The Indians call it shape-shifting. And I am not alone in the ability to do that. But that's only a part of it. I'm immortal, Don. And I am not alone on this earth. John Ravenna is an immortal, too. He's here to kill the Speaker of the House."

"Shape-shifter!" the sheriff blurted out the word. "Immortal? What you are is crazy, man! You're nuts!"

Barry smiled and said nothing.

Don rose from the couch, swayed unsteadily for a few seconds, then sat down. "I'm dreaming all this. It's just a dream. It isn't real."

"It's real, Don. I can assure you of that. I've been living it for nearly seven hundred years."

Don stared at him. He was unable to speak.

"How quaint," Robert Roche remarked drily, standing in the den of the house he had rented on the lake. His bodyguards, aides, and other staff members were housed in the cabins on either side of the larger house. The sudden storm had blown on east, the sky clear.

"It's the best rental property on the lake, sir," one of the aides said.

"It will do just fine," Robert replied in a civil tone, which was rare for him when dealing with subordinates. He turned to another aide. "Lay out my rustic clothing and get the boat ready. I want to go fishing for a time. It's been years."

"Ah, sir?"

Roche cut his eyes. "What is it?"

"Do you have a fishing license, sir?"

Robert pursed his lips in momentary anger. His fault. He could not blame others for his oversight.

"No. I do not. Thank you for reminding me. After I have changed clothes we'll drive down to that little country store we passed on the way in. Will's Grocery and Bait Shop I believe the sign read."

"Then we'll go fishing," the aide said.

Robert looked at him. "No . . . then I shall go fishing."

"I don't know if this means anything or not," the chief of the White House detail of Secret Service said to the president. "But Robert Roche has rented a lake house about a mile from where Congressman Madison and his wife will be staying."

President Hutton leaned back in his chair and thought for a few seconds. "The richest man in the world, practically a recluse for years, suddenly decides to break out of his protected ivory tower and go fishing at the same time Cliff is in the area. What do you think?"

"I think it is no coincidence, Mr. President."

"Neither do I. Check it out very closely."

"Yes, sir. I've got people standing by right now. Sir?"

"What?"

"You recall a couple of years ago, all that trouble out in Idaho?"

"Which incident?" the president asked only slightly sarcastically.

"The survivalists, the hippies, the press."

"How could I ever possibly forget it? It cost my predecessor his job, spawned the Coyote Network, and almost caused a damn armed revolt in this nation. Yes, I remember it well."

"The man who would not die."

"The what?"

"The man who would not die. That was the story Stormy Knight was chasing in the wilderness."

"What about it?"

"Well, I have information that, ah, the Company has placed a person high up in the Coyote Network . . ."

"Shit!" President Hutton blurted. "Goddammit, they *know* better than that! Are those goddamn people ever going to learn?" He slowly shook his head. "Go on."

"The story is true."

"Well, I don't doubt it. I wouldn't put anything past the Pickle Factory."

"No, sir. I'm talking about the man who would not die. He's real."

The president fixed the man with a very jaundiced look. "Walt, have you been drinking?"

"No, sir. The Bureau turned the CIA plant. He'll be through at Coyote the next time he's polygraphed. But the Bureau has him until then. He confirms the story is true. The man going by the name of Darry Ransom is about seven hundred years old. He's an immortal and a shape-shifter."

President Hutton opened a desk drawer and took out a bottle of Tylenol®, shaking out a couple of caplets. "I have suddenly developed a headache." He popped the caplets into his mouth, drank half a glass of water, then rose from his chair, placed both hands on his desk and shouted, "Are you fucking *serious?*"

"Yes," the Secret Service man replied.

The president sat down heavily. "I'm afraid to ask where you think this man might be living, hiding out, whatever."

"In North Arkansas."

"Why does that not come as any surprise to me?" He sighed. "Let's assume for the moment that this man who would not die is real, which I strongly doubt.

Does *he* have something to do with this planned assassination?"

"No, sir. The Bureau doesn't think so. They think he's screwing Stormy Knight."

The president muttered something inaudible. He lifted his eyes. "Walt, I am not interested in a seven-hundred-year-old man's sexual escapades. Jesus H. Christ! What am I saying! All right, all right. What do you propose to do about this rumor of a"—he grimaced—"man who would not die?"

"Check it out, sir."

"I assume you already have people in there doing just that?"

"Yes, sir. Well, they'll be in place in a matter of hours."

"You be sure and keep me informed about this . . . ancient paramour."

"Yes, sir. I'll do that."

The Secret Service man left the Oval Office, quietly closing the door behind him. President Hutton shook his head, cleared his throat, and drummed his fingers on the desk. "Shit!" he said.

Sheriff Don Salter was still badly shaken, but gradually growing calmer as Barry spoke to him. At Don's request, Barry had made a pot of coffee. When the hard rain started, the hybrids had come into the house and were now stretched out on the floor.

Don pointed to the pair of husky-wolf mix. "Do they know about . . . ah, you? I mean . . . ?"

"I know what you mean. Yes. You know anything about wolves?"

"Only what I see on the TV. Are you the alpha male?"

"Yes."

"Jesus!"

Barry smiled. "I never met Him. I'm not that old."

Don did not see the humor in the remark. "I don't know whether to believe any of this, or not. Part of me still thinks you are one hell of an illusionist."

"Then believe this, Don: John Ravenna is here to kill Cliff Madison."

"You told me that. But you don't have any proof. I can't go out and arrest somebody without some evidence to back it up."

"You could put him under surveillance."

"I plan on doing that. Tell me, if I went to the FBI with what you've told me, would you back me up?"

"You think they would believe me?"

The sheriff sighed, picked up his coffee cup and took a sip. "Hell, I'm not sure I believe it!"

"There you have it."

"Does Ms. Knight know about, ah, your age and ability to, ah, do what you do?"

"Yes. And so does Ki."

"Jesus & George Washington!"

"The latter I did know. Very nice gentleman. Contrary to what many historians have written about him, he had a fine sense of humor. Did you know that John Hancock was very jealous of George? It's true. Hancock was furious when George was elected commander in chief of the colonies' military. There were rumors that Hancock even thought of a duel between them. Of course, that never came to be."

Don sighed. "Thank you for the history lesson, Barry."

"You're welcome."

Don stood up to pace the room for a moment, then walked to the phone and punched out his office number. He spoke with his chief deputy and ordered a tight twenty-four-hour surveillance put on John Ravenna.

"Of course, John will immediately pick up on the tail," Barry said. "And when he wants to, he'll lose your people. He's also a shape-changer."

"Into a wolf?"

"Something like that." Barry spoke through a small smile.

"How long has the man been an assassin?"

"About a thousand years."

"I'm sorry I asked," Don muttered. He cleared his throat. "I suppose Ravenna has been responsible for the deaths of many heads of state?"

"Most of them."

"Did he kill John Kennedy?"

"No."

"Do you know who did?"

"Yes."

"Was it Oswald?"

But Barry would only smile.

"Doesn't matter," Don said, once more rising to pace the room. "I've got to alert Chief Monroe, and I have to tell the FBI and the Secret Service about Ravenna. So I'll tell them it was an anonymous tip. Phone call. How carefully built is Ravenna's background; how much digging could it stand?"

"John has been using a variation of Ravanna for over a hundred years. I know he was living in England before moving to Ireland. He worked for the Nazis during World War II. He was in Spain prior to that. He is a brilliant man. His background could probably stand any check Interpol might give it."

Don sat down on the couch and drank what was left of his cooling coffee. "The State Department could kick him out of the country."

"On what charge? He hasn't done anything."

"Well, dammit, Barry, somebody has to do *something!*

The man is here to assassinate a member of Congress; the Speaker of the House."

"When the time comes, I'll stop him, Don."

"How? If the man is, ah, like you, how will you stop him?"

"I'll think of something."

The sheriff shook his head. "I can't risk it, Barry. I have to go to the Bureau with this information."

Barry shrugged his shoulders. "Fine. Go tell them. John is expecting a crowd. It will just be more of a challenge to him, and he loves a challenge."

"Where will you be?"

"Around. Here and there."

"This area is already filling up with feds. By this time tomorrow, every other person will be a fed. Aren't you worried about that?"

"No. I'm used to being hunted. I've lived with it for a very long time."

"Don't you get tired of it all?"

For just a quick moment, Barry's face showed the strain of centuries past; then it was gone. "After seven hundred years, Don? Why in the world would you ask that?"

Twelve

"I think all hell is about to pop around here, Barry," Stormy said. She and Ki had pulled in a few minutes after the sheriff left and told Barry what Jim Beal had said, after getting his promise that Beal's name would not be mentioned in connection with it. "We passed the sheriff on the way in, and he had a very grim expression on his face."

"I leveled with him. Told him everything." Barry smiled. "And showed him."

Ki laughed. "What was his reaction?"

"He fainted. But I'm still not sure he believes what I told him about my life. A part of him still thinks I'm some sort of master illusionist."

"I can certainly understand that," Stormy said.

"I have an idea," Ki said, a wide grin on her face.

Stormy and Barry looked at her.

"Let's interview John Ravenna!"

Stormy smiled. "Sure. Get a foreigner's impression of America." She looked at Barry. "What do you think?"

"You can try. But I doubt that John will grant you an interview."

"But we'd still have his face on film," Ki said.

"It's dangerous, Stormy. John knows that we're a bit more than friends."

"Oh, we wouldn't go to his house. We could wait at that little country store out by the lake."

Barry nodded his head. "That would be much safer. And Mr. Will would get a kick out of it. I'll drive out tomorrow and talk to him. But I'm sure he'll go along with it."

"What do we do now?" Ki asked.

"Wait," Barry said.

There were still motel rooms to be had in the town by the lake, but not many. Federal agents had flooded into the area: FBI, Secret Service, federal marshals, and BATF. Undercover agents from the Arkansas State Police had converged on the town. Unknown to the others, agents from the National Security Agency and Central Intelligence Agency had also quietly arrived in the area.

It would be only a matter of hours before they would start falling all over each other.

Ed Simmons, the Speaker's chief aide, and his wife, Emily, were on the road and just a day away from the resort area.

Alex Tarver, leader of the local gang of skinheads, had applied to the city for a march permit and had been turned down. "Screw you, too," Alex said to the woman at the front desk, flipping her the bird.

"I'll have you put in jail, you freak!" she shouted at him.

"Yeah? And you'll shit if you eat regular," Alex popped right back, quickly moving out the door before the cops arrived to haul him off to the pokey. Permit or no permit, Alex planned to lead his people on a march when Congressman Madison arrived in town.

Vic Radford also applied for a march and rally permit, and he, too, was turned down.

"By God!" Vic shouted to the mayor. "It's a free country and we'll march whether you like it or not."

"Go to hell, Vic," the mayor told him.

"Asshole!" Vic replied.

Leroy Jim Bob "Bubba" Bordelon, chief klucker of the local branch of the Ku Klux Klan and all-around jerk, appeared at city hall for a permit to march.

"Good God, no!" the town council said.

"We'll march anyways," Bubba said. "Hell with you people. I got to get my robe out of the cleaners."

Shortly after Bubba had departed, Mohammed Abudu X (known to most as Willie Washington), self-appointed spiritual leader of the local chapter of the Back to Africa movement, also showed up at city hall for a parade and rally permit.

"You have got to be kidding!" the mayor blurted, eyeballing Mohammed.

Mohammed aka Willie was dressed in an orange, ankle-length robe, funky little round neat hat that absolutely defied description, and sandals. He was toting a large staff.

"We are the children of the sun," Mohammed proclaimed. "We shall march." He whirled around and stomped regally out of the meeting room, dragging his staff, which weighed about fifteen pounds.

"There's gonna be a goddamn riot," one of the town council predicted. "We've got the skinheads, Vic Radford's goofy bunch, the KKK, and now Willie."

No one really wanted to mention Jim Beal's Arkansas Freedom Brigade because two of the city council members belonged to it. But a city councilwoman finally, reluctantly, did bring it up before the board.

"No," the council president said. "Jim and his bunch won't march. I spoke with Jim soon after we learned of the Speakers visit, and Jim said his people would keep a very low profile. Jim will keep his word."

"It isn't Jim that worries me," another council member said. "Jim has strong views, but he isn't a hater. It's Vic and Willie, I mean Mohammed, whatever the hell his name is, and those damn skinheads. I heard that Willie is bringing in a whole bus load of Black Muslims from Little Rock. There is going to be trouble, people. Bet on it."

"Mohammed won't start it." Another council member spoke. "I don't like him, but I have to say he's not a troublemaker."

"That's not the point. Why did he ever come back here and bring those others with him?" the question was tossed out. "He was about fifteen years old when his family moved away to Little Rock. Why come back here?"

"Because he wasn't treated very nicely when he did live here." Sheriff Don Salter spoke from the open door to the meeting room.

Chief Monroe stood beside the sheriff. "As a matter of fact, he was treated real crappy, as I recall," the chief said. "Vic Radford sicced his boy on Willie. Whipped him bad."

"While a number of other boys stood around and cheered young Carl Radford on," Don added.

"I remember that," a woman council member said. "Willie got hurt pretty bad, didn't he?"

"Busted jaw, several broken ribs, broken arm and hand," Chief Monroe said, as he and Don walked up the center aisle and took seats in front of the council bench.

"Well, I seem to recall that this town took up a collection to pay the boy's hospital expenses," a councilman said. "That should have squared accounts. But no. Ten years later he comes back here dressed up like some African chief and starts stirrin' up trouble with the county's nigras."

Don smiled. "What does he have, Pete? Eight or ten members of that mosque. No more than that. And what trouble has he caused?"

"Mosque?" one woman blurted. "That's an old filling station."

Chief Monroe chuckled. "I recall when I was a boy there was a circuit ridin' preacher made an altar out of an old stump. If Willie wants to call old man Jensen's fillin' station a mosque, I reckon it's a mosque."

"You gone nigra-lover on us now, Chief?"

Russ Monroe laughed. "That's sort of a stupid question, Mathilda. But I'll answer it. No, I haven't gone nigra-lover. My feelin's toward blacks haven't changed . . . at least not much, they haven't. I just don't want trouble in this town. But trouble is what we're gonna get when all these factions come together: So we'd better brace for it."

"Town is fillin' up, for a fact," another member spoke. "Unusually so. I don't know if anyone else has noticed it, but I have. What's goin' on, Chief, Sheriff?"

"What's going on is a matter of national security." The voice spoke from the door to the chambers.

Don and Russ twisted in their seats. The council members looked up. Four people stood just inside the council room. Three men and one woman. They held up ID cases.

"FBI," two said.

"Secret Service," the other two said.

"And away we go," Sheriff Salter muttered.

Barry sat up in bed, alert, all senses working hard. Stormy slept peacefully beside him. Pete and Repeat were asleep on the floor. It was 4:30 A.M. Barry slipped from bed and tugged on jeans, moccasins, and shirt, and padded silently from the bedroom, letting Stormy sleep. The hybrids rose and followed Barry. He closed the door behind him so whatever slight noise he might make would not disturb Stormy.

He let the hybrids out to relieve themselves, and while they were out, he made a pot of coffee. While the coffee was dripping, Barry stepped out the back door to stand for a moment in the warm early morning air. He did not know what had awakened him, except that it was not caused by danger. Pete and Repeat were calmly sitting on the porch; had there been an intruder, the big hybrids would be anything but calm. The early morning was bright with stars.

Waiting for the coffee to brew, Barry sat down on the back steps. While he slept, his mind had been busy. Someone had gone to a great deal of trouble and expense to bring in John Ravenna. Who? Organized crime? Maybe. But for some reason he could not readily explain, Barry doubted that. While he had absolutely no basis for his suspicions and ultimate conclusion, Barry believed this planned assassination to be totally political.

Barry hated politics. He had lived under just about all forms of government, and had found that in the end, very few of them were worth a damn. Power corrupted and politicians would inevitably lie, disregard their constituents, and vote a straight party line, or simply ignore the wishes of the majority of taxpayers. The only thing Barry despised more than politics in general and politicians in particular was the Internal Revenue Service. It was totally out of control, and all the politicians would do about it was blow hot air.

The simplest and best form of government Barry had ever lived under had been during his time with the American Indians. You did not lie, you did not

steal, you did not cheat, you did not assault a member
of the tribe, and you did not commit murder against
a member of the tribe. Do any of those things, and
the punishment came down swift, hard and harsh, and
in some cases, very final.

Barry poured a mug of coffee and returned to the
back porch. All right, he mused, so who has what to
gain by the death of Congressman Madison? The party
that was not in control of the House and Senate, of
course. With the twenty-first century just around the
corner, Barry had been forced, for the sake of survival,
to keep up with as much technology as possible, and
to read up on current politics, as distasteful as the latter was.

He knew that Cliff Madison was an avowed conservative, and many liberals hated him for it. Especially a
U.S. senator named Madalaine Bowman—nicknamed
Tax and Spend. She had other nicknames, but they
were not printable. Senator Bowman was capable of
doing anything. She despised the military, despised
conservatives, and loved all liberal causes. She had
publicly announced that if she had the power to do
so, she would outlaw all forms of guns . . . except
those in the hands of the police and certain other selected individuals (all of them members of her political
party, of course).

Barry also knew that President Hutton, while a
Democrat, was a very conservative one, and Madalaine
Bowman hated him.

Barry had read, much of it between the lines, that
as much as Madalaine hated the president, she hated
Cliff Madison a hundred times more intensely. But that
was no reason to think she would go so far as to hire
an assassin to kill either one. Was it?

Yeah, it was.

Barry would tell Don Salter of his suspicions, and

how the sheriff handled it from that point was up to
him. But from where Barry sat, the needle of suspicion
pointed straight back to Washington.

And, Barry thought with a sigh, he was finished here
in this lovely and quiet part of North Arkansas. "If I
had any sense, I'd pull out right now," he muttered.

But he knew he wouldn't do that. He'd take the risk
and stick around, see how this thing turned out. He
knew he had to stay because Stormy might well be in
danger.

Barry sat on the back porch, sipped his steaming
coffee and watched as the dark eastern sky gradually
began to take on a silver hue. And as the horizon began to shift from dark to light, a germ of suspicion
began to worm its way into his mind. He had lived far
too long to accept anything at face value, and something about this planned assassination just did not add
up. The Speaker of the House was an important man
in politics, but killing him would really not alter very
much in the day-to-day operation of the House of Representatives. Another member of the majority party
would just step in and take over. So other than personal motives, what would be the point?

Barry finished his coffee while mulling over that
question in his mind.

Diversion.

Sure. It was so obvious it was elusive.

But if this planned assassination was a smoke screen,
then who was the real target?

The president of the United States, of course.

Now things were beginning to fit.

It was common knowledge that VP Adam Thomas
and President Hutton did not get along. VP Thomas
was a good and close friend of Senator Madalaine Bowman, as was Congressman Calvin Lowe, who would be

next in line for the Speaker's position. And then the VP's slot.

"Well, now," Barry muttered. "Isn't that something?"

But it was all conjecture. No proof.

Barry stood up, a smile curving his lips. No proof—yet!

Thirteen

Nine A.M. Stormy and Ki were at Will's Grocery & Bait Shop waiting for John Ravenna to make an appearance. They were chatting with Mr. Will and thoroughly enjoying the man's anecdotes and background on the area. He had told them stories about how rowdy Chief Monroe had been in his youth, and how Sheriff Salter had been no angel while growing up.

"I think men who were about half-rogue while growin' up make the best cops," Will said. "They know firsthand the pitfalls of standin' too close to lawlessness and what it can lead to."

"Don't men like that tend to overreact in any situation that turns violent?" Stormy asked.

Will shook his head. "No. At least that's been my experience. You take men who grew up dependin' on their wits and their fists to survive, they can see trouble buildin' and head it off." Mr. Will shifted his gaze to the outside. "Company's comin'."

"My God," Stormy whispered. "That's Robert Roche!"

Even Mr. Will was impressed. "*The* Robert Roche? The richest man in the world?"

"One of the richest. In the top five, at least. Maybe higher."

"He was in here yesterday, buyin' bait and such. I should have recognized him. I must be gettin' senile."

Ki smiled and put a hand on his arm. "You've always seen pictures of him in a business suit and shirt and tie. The way he's dressed now, he looks like a farmer." She glanced at Stormy. "You want me to start shooting him now?"

"Now wait just a minute, ladies!" Mr. Will blurted, alarm in his voice.

Stormy laughed. "With a camera, Mr. Will. Relax."

"Oh," the store owner said, relief evident.

Stormy shook her head. "No. Hold off. Let's try to get on his good side. After all, he is our boss, in a way."

Robert Roche recognized Stormy immediately and was all smiles and cordiality. "Ladies!" he said, taking the hand of each. "How good to see you. I knew you were in the area, covering the Speaker's visit. I've been making inquiries as to where you were staying."

"Oh?" Stormy said.

"Yes. I'm planning a little informal get-together for the Speaker. I wanted to invite you both, and gentlemen friends of yours, too." He smiled at Stormy. "I knew you were here, of course. I won't take no for an answer. You see, I know your little secret, Ms. Knight."

"What little secret, Mr. Roche?"

Robert leaned close. He smelled of very expensive cologne. "The mystery man in your life, Stormy. Your secret love. You really didn't think you could keep something like that quiet for very long, now, did you? Besides, I've already included your names on the guest list. It will have to be given to the FBI for them to look at. But then, none of us has anything to hide, now, do we?"

Ki looked at her friend in amazement. As long as

they had known each other, this was the first time she had ever seen Stormy rattled.

"Ah, why, ah, no. Of course not," Stormy finally managed to mutter.

"Of course you don't. That's settled then." The billionaire smiled, but his eyes were as hard as flint. "I'm so looking forward to meeting your gentleman friend," Robert said. "I know how to get in touch with you; I'll have my aide give you a jingle, ladies. Until then." He turned away, bought his bait and supplies, and left without another word.

"So you're seein' Barry Cantrell, eh?" Mr. Will said, a twinkle in his eyes.

Stormy sighed. Were there any secrets in this part of the world? "Yes, sir. I am."

"Barry is a real nice young feller. I like him. Liked him from the git-go." Again, the man cut his eyes to the front of the store. "But here comes one I don't much cotton to, ladies. This here is John Ravenna pullin' in the drive. And I'd sooner stick my hand into a gunnysack full of rattlesnakes than mess with him. He's a bad one, ladies. I don't know why he's here. But he's up to no good. I'll bet on that."

Mr. Will introduced Ravenna, and while John was ever the gentleman, both women fought back the urge to recoil from him. The eyes of the man were fish-cold, the voice just too unctuous.

"I do enjoy your reports on the telly, Miss Knight," John complimented Stormy. "I watch them whenever possible."

In Ireland? Stormy thought. You must have one hell of a satellite system, buster. "Thank you. 'Telly' gives you away, Mr. Ravenna. England, perhaps?"

"Ireland, actually. But I do spend a great deal of time in London. Business, you know?"

Killing business, the words jumped into Stormy's

head. "I have an idea, Mr. Ravenna. I'd like to do what we call a human interest story. An Irishman's views on America."

Stormy watched Ravenna's eyes change from ugly to awful. But the smile never left his lips. "An interview, Miss Knight? I'll certainly give that some thought. Yes. I really will."

John Ravenna bought a pack of cigarettes and left the store without another word. But his back was stiff with anger.

"I ain't the most brilliant feller in the world, Miss Knight," Mr. Will remarked, "but I do know this: you just made a bad enemy there."

"Yes," Stormy said softly. "I believe I did."

"Feds were damn firm in what they want from us," Chief Monroe said to Sheriff Salter.

"Yes. And?"

"They can go suck eggs, far as I'm concerned. You heard me tell them that Jim Beal's bunch is not involved in this thing and I won't give them a list of people I think are part of his AFB. You know damn well they've got a snitch in that group, and we both know it's Wesley Parren. I don't know about you, but I don't blame Wesley for rollin' over for the feds. Hell, the IRS had him bent over a barrel with his pants down around his ankles and were fixin' to stick it to him. Poor guy had no choice in the matter. Goddamn government."

Don said nothing. He did not want to start the chief off on the government, even though he pretty much agreed with him.

When Russ saw that Don was not going to take any bait, he asked, "How about this John Ravenna?"

"I gave the feds his name, and they said they'd check

him out. But they didn't seem too excited about it; said they'd get back to me."

"Don't hold your breath until they do. If the people out of the Little Rock office were handling this, they'd work with us. But these are back east feds. And to tell you the truth, I don't think they really trust us, Don."

Don said nothing. He sat and stared off into the distance with a faraway look in his eyes.

"What's wrong with you, Don?" the chief asked, after a moment of silence. "You've been actin' odd since yesterday afternoon."

"Just have a lot on my mind, I guess, Russ." Yeah. Like a man who turns into a wolf right before my eyes, and then tells me he's seven hundred years old. You could say I have a lot on my mind. If I'm not losing it, that is.

"People tell me that Ravenna fellow's a nice guy. A little on the odd side, but nice."

"That's what I hear," Don replied. And he's a *thousand* damn years old.

Maybe I am losing my mind.

"You got people on him, don't you, Don?"

"Following every move he makes." Provided he doesn't pull a Barry Cantrell and change into a god-damned wolf and go loping off into the timber.

"Good. You'll keep me informed?"

"You know I will. Russ? We still have a few red wolves in this area, don't we?"

"Damn few. I haven't heard of a sighting in a long time. Why?"

"How about gray wolves?"

"Wiped out nearly a hundred years ago, so I'm told. I've never seen a timber wolf in the wild. Why all the sudden interest in wolves?"

"Oh, just curious. I wonder if they're as vicious as people claim they are?"

"Not from what I see on the TV." He chuckled. "You're thinking about those big hybrids of Cantrell's, aren't you?"

"Yes. Well, sort of. They're more than half-wolf; anyone with eyes can see that. Yet I've seen dogs that were a lot more vicious than Pete and Repeat."

Russ laughed. "Did Cantrell name those hybrids, you reckon?"

"Yes. Both of them."

"Well, the man's sure got a sense of humor. I have to say that."

After seven hundred years on this earth, he'd better have a good sense of humor, Don thought.

Don's walkie-talkie cracked out his name. He took it out of the leather carrying case attached to his belt and keyed the mike button. "Go ahead."

"Mr. Ed Simmons, the Speaker's chief aide, and family just picked up the keys to their lake house, Sheriff. Thought you'd like to know."

"That's ten-four. Thanks." He turned to Russ. "You heard?"

"I heard. That means Congressman Madison is only a couple of days behind him. I better get all my reserves ready to go."

"Yeah. Me, too. Those that can take time off from work, that is."

"I'm gettin' a real bad feelin' about this thing, Don."

You are? I've got two men in this area who can't die, and to make matters worse, one is under contract to kill the Speaker of the House. And you've got a bad feeling, Chief? Don nodded his head. "Yeah. I do, too, Russ. A real bad feeling."

* * *

"So are we going to Robert Roche's little 'get-toether'?" Stormy asked Barry.

"It would look awfully odd if we didn't. Sure, we'll go."

"That place is going to be swarming with federal agents," Ki reminded him. "As soon as Roche turns that guest list over to the feds, your life is going to get very interesting."

Barry smiled. "My life has been interesting since about 1315, Ki. But you're right. I've never really faced modern technology before. Not to this extent. I have a hunch Roche has already turned that list in to the feds. He probably did it before he talked to you. One doesn't get to be worth billions of dollars without having the ability to stay one step ahead of everybody else, all the time. I'm thinking that Robert Roche planned all this very carefully."

"It's time to go public, Barry," Stormy urged. "Time to stop running."

He shook his head. "Not just yet. Oh, if I thought my doing that would throw a kink into this planned assassination, I would do it without hesitation. But my going public would only cause more confusion in this area, at a time when it's least needed. Within twenty-four hours after the announcement, there would be a thousand or more reporters in here, from around the world. Plus about ten thousand rubberneckers wandering all over the place and clogging up the highways—with more coming in by the minute. Just think about it for a moment. My God, there would be a traffic jam stretching out for miles in all directions. And we certainly don't need that now."

"You think the feds are going over that guest list now, Barry?" Stormy asked.

"If Roche has turned it in, and I strongly suspect he

has, the feds are scrutinizing that guest list as we speak."

"Everybody on this list checks out clean," Special Agent Van Brocklen said. "Except for this Barry Cantrell."

"Have you run him?" Special Agent Miller asked.

"As far as I could. I'm checking on his social security number now."

"Good luck. That might take a week. What else do you have on him?"

"He just moved into the area a few months back and doesn't have a job."

"So?"

"So why the hell would he be invited to a party at Robert Roche's house?"

"That is a very good question. What did he used to do for a living?"

"I don't know. Like I said, I'm waiting on social security to give me a background."

"Let's don't wait on them. Go see the local sheriff. The people out of our Little Rock office say he's a real straight-arrow type."

"On my way."

"Inspector Van Brocklen?" an agent called, hanging up the phone.

Van Brocklen turned. "Yes?"

"Congressman Madison decided to leave early. He and his wife will be landing in Memphis tomorrow morning at ten o'clock. They'll be here about the middle of the afternoon."

"Well, that's just friggin' wonderful!" Van Brocklen said. "Why doesn't he make our jobs just a little bit more difficult?"

Special Agent Miller smiled. "Ours is but to serve, Van."

"Yeah, right," Van Brocklen said sourly. "You bet."

Fourteen

Stormy received the call from New York about Congressman Madison's decision to start his vacation early and was advised that Coyote's affiliate in Memphis would cover his landing. She and Ki left to do a pre-arranged interview with the mayor and the city council.

Barry glanced at the clock on the mantel. Just past noon. He felt in his guts that matters were about to pop wide open in this area, and decided he'd better get ready for it.

He got out his .375 Winchester and carefully cleaned and oiled the lever-action rifle. He propped the rifle in a corner of the bedroom and decided to take the hybrids out for a walk in the woods. At the back door, Barry paused, and reflected for a moment, his expression hardening. Then he returned to the bedroom and picked up the rifle, slipping a few extra rounds into his jeans pocket. The feeling he'd suddenly developed of impending danger was building strong within him. Every fiber of his being was screaming *get out get out.*

But he knew he wouldn't do that. He'd already made up his mind he was not running. Not this time. At least not yet.

Barry took the hybrids for a short walk, then put

them back into the house and locked the doors. He returned to the woods and began making a slow circle of his property. His highly honed senses rarely failed him, and he was certain they were accurate now: somebody, or some*thing*, was on his property . . . and he, it, or they did not belong here.

He squatted down behind a huge old tree and remained rock-still. His eyes caught a quick flash of movement, a burst of blue denim that was gone as quickly as it came. New blue denim, Barry thought.

Barry did not move a muscle. He waited. If the person was a hunter, he was poaching, for no season was open. And Barry hated poachers.

Moments later, he spotted the flash of blue again. It was much closer to his location. Barry slowly laid the rifle on the ground and tensed his leg muscles, ready to jump. The person came closer until he was only a few yards from Barry's position. Barry emerged from concealment in a burst of motion. He slammed into the man, knocking the intruder sprawling on the ground. He jerked the man to his feet and stopped his right fist just a split second before he made contact.

Only it wasn't a man.

It was a woman. Her cap had fallen off, spilling a shock of auburn hair. Barry stared at her in amazement for a few seconds. She tried to knee him in the groin, but he blocked the move. He gave her a hard shove, and she landed on her butt, on the ground. She cussed him and reached for the pistol holstered at her side. Barry none too gently kicked the autoloader from her hand. The gun went sailing off into the brush.

"Oww!" she hollered, her eyes flashing anger. "That hurt, you son of a bitch!"

"It isn't nice to point guns at people, lady. Who are

you and what the hell are you doing skulking about on my property?"

"I wasn't skulking!"

"Yes, you were. And you aren't a very good skulker either. Now get up and behave yourself."

The very attractive lady slowly rose from the ground and brushed herself off. "I'm Susan Green, United States Secret Service. You're in big trouble, mister."

"That's crap!" Barry popped right back. "You were the one trespassing on posted property. Let me see some identification."

The woman took a leather case from her back pocket and did the famous federal badge flip. Before the two leather halves could meet, Barry jerked the case from her hand and looked at it.

"Well, it looks genuine," Barry conceded, handing the leather folder to her. "What the hell are you doing here, lady?"

"That is none of your business."

"Really? Well, I understand. I guess you were inspecting these old nuclear missile silos on my place."

That shook the woman, widening her eyes. She looked all around her. "What nuclear missile silos?" Then she saw the grin playing around Barry's mouth, and that put a disgusted look on her face.

"Gotcha, didn't I?"

"Very funny, Mr. Cantrell. Cute."

"You know my name."

"And that's about all I know."

"Does that make me a criminal, Ms. Green?"

"I didn't say that."

"Well, obviously it makes me some sort of suspect about something or you wouldn't have been snooping around my property."

The woman said nothing in reply. Barry stared at her for a moment. She was dressed all in denim: blue jeans and cowgirl shirt with pearl snaps in place of buttons. Auburn hair cut fairly short. Hazel eyes. He guessed her in her late twenties. Very pretty. Very well endowed.

She met his gaze for a moment, then suddenly flushed in embarrassment.

"I'm sorry if I made you uncomfortable, Ms. Green. Forgive me. But you are a very pretty lady."

"Thank you, Mr. Cantrell."

"Call me Barry, please. Look . . . let's go up to the house where it's cool. I'll get you a soft drink or water or coffee and we'll talk. I'll answer any question you might have. How about it?"

Susan opened her mouth to speak just as Barry twisted around at the sound of a faint click from the woods around them. Susan turned just as a rifle slammed, the bullet passing between the man and woman. If Susan had not turned with Barry, she would have caught the bullet in her chest. Barry threw himself against the woman and rode her down to the ground.

"Next time, you federal cunt!" the voice ripped out of the deep timber. "Remember Waco and Ruby Ridge!"

The woods fell silent. Barry scrambled over to where Susan's pistol had hit the ground, scooped it up, and tossed it to her. They both knelt on the ground, listening intently. But whoever had fired the shot was gone as silently as they had come.

"You'll want to call this in," Barry said, still kneeling. "I have a phone in my house."

"I would hope so," the Secret Service woman said drily. "Most people do."

Barry grinned and helped her to her feet. Susan's face was flushed, but other than that, she showed no signs of being very shaken. "You've been shot at before."

"Just one other time. A gunfight isn't very pleasant."

Neither is a battle with spears, lances, swords, or bows and arrows, Barry thought.

"Where is your car?" Barry asked her.

"Parked on a gravel road over that ridge," Susan said, pointing. "Why?"

"I'll make a bet you've got four flat tires, among other damage."

"No bet, Mr. Cantrell." She took a small transceiver from a belt pouch, inserted a tiny plug into her ear, and called in. She spoke only for a few seconds, then listened. "They'll meet us at your house," she said. "Now, I'll take you up on that offer of something cold to drink."

"You're not going to pursue the attacker, Ms. Green?"

She shook her head. "There are people throwing up a cordon around this area now." And she would say no more.

A few minutes after they arrived at the house, two cars pulled up and three men got out of each one. Barry left Susan inside with Pete and Repeat and opened the sidewalk gate, waving the men inside. They did not offer to shake hands and neither did Barry. They didn't smile, either.

"You boys take life entirely too seriously," Barry told the six agents. "Lighten up, you'll live longer."

"Thank you for the health tip, Mr. Cantrell," one said, walking toward the house.

"You're welcome."

"Is Agent Green all right?" another asked.

"She's fine. She's inside, playing with my dogs. And speaking of my dogs, don't make any sudden moves until they get a chance to sniff you and see that you're not here to harm me or them."

"Those big bastards move toward me and they're dead dogs," an agent wearing a very surly expression popped off.

Barry had sized that one up as an iron pumper; his neck was about the same size as his head. Which, under a thick mop of hair probably came to a point, Barry concluded.

"And should that happen," Barry told him, stopping the walk toward the house and facing the government agent, "I can guarantee you that you will be dead approximately two seconds later."

"Are you threatening me?" the agent almost shouted the question.

"As a matter of fact, yes," Barry replied in much softer tones.

The mouthy agent opened his trap to retort, and an older man said, "Close your mouth, Ray. You're out of line."

"I don't have to take that kind of crap from—"

"Shut up, Jones!"

"Yes, sir," Ray said.

"What a fun afternoon this is going to be," Barry said, stepping up on the porch and opening the door. "My tax dollars at work are coming in, Susan. Pete and Repeat, stay."

Barry had cut his eyes to the older man, and saw a small smile play at the corners of his mouth and a twinkle spring into his eyes at Barry's words.

The hybrids sniffed the men, then, at Barry's command, went out into the fenced backyard. But Barry could tell that both hybrids had taken an instant dislike to Agent Jones.

He could certainly understand why the dogs reached

that decision. So far, there wasn't very much about Agent Jones to like.

The older man took Susan off to one side and spoke in low tones for a moment; then they rejoined the group, taking seats.

"Sorry for any inconvenience we've caused you, Mr. Cantrell," the older man said. "Let me assure you that you have not been singled out. As a matter of precaution, we're checking out a number of people in this area." He stuck out a hand. "I'm Chet Robbins, Secret Service."

Barry took the hand; then Chet began introducing the others. One name jumped out at him: Special Agent Don Branon. Branon had been one of the agents in Idaho who had come in after the rogue agents, and the man was studying Barry with a very careful and critical eye, his brow furrowed in concentration.

"Found anything interesting about me, Agent Robbins?" Barry asked.

"We can't find out much about you at all, Mr. Cantrell," the senior Secret Service man said. "That's really why we're here."

"Maybe there isn't very much *to* find out, Agent Robbins. I live a very quiet life. My grandfather left me with a small inheritance, and I get by on that." He gave them the name of the San Francisco law firm that handled his estate. "Would you like for me to call them and clear the way for you to check me out?"

"Oh, that won't be necessary," Chet said evenly. "But it's kind of you to offer."

"Anything to help." Barry met the eyes of all the agents sitting in his living room. He could not understand why they all seemed so unconcerned about the shooting.

As if reading his mind, Chet said, "This area has

been sealed off, Mr. Cantrell. Not that it will do us much good. I'm sure the person who shot at either you or Agent Green—and that has not yet been determined—is long gone. The thing that bothers us is this: how did they know Susan would be here, and how did they know Susan was a federal agent?"

"I'm sure I don't know the answer to either question."

Chet stared at Barry for a moment. "Perhaps," he finally said.

Barry shrugged his shoulders. He didn't really give a good goddamn whether the federal agent believed him or not. He'd been questioned by agents of kings, queens, princes and princesses, potentates, Indian chiefs, premiers, prime ministers, presidents, and every type of royalty in between. None of them had been able to intimidate him.

"The sheriff tells us you moved here from Idaho, Mr. Cantrell," Special Agent Branon said. "What part of the state?"

Barry smiled. "The part where all the action took place last year. It got just a little bit noisy around there for me."

"How come your name never came up from any of the teams who went in there?" Branon questioned. "Everybody who lived in that area was questioned."

Barry smiled. "Friend, you people didn't talk to one tenth of the folks who live in there. People move into the wilderness to avoid human contact."

To Barry's surprise, Branon nodded his head in agreement. "Yeah, you're probably right about that. That op was a screwup from the word 'Go.' "

Chet put a hand to the plug in his ear and then lifted his handy-talkie and keyed the talk button. "All right. That's about what we expected. I'll be around there in a few." He turned to the room full of agents.

"The shooter slipped out before our people could get into place. No surprise there. But we do have some good boot prints we're casting now, as well as some tire tracks. We could get lucky there, but I wouldn't count on it. We'll call a garage to tow your car in, Susan. It's got four flat tires."

Susan Green said several very ugly words, and the other agents laughed.

"I didn't hear any vehicle leave," Barry said.

"Neither did I," Susan added.

Chet shook his head. "The tire tracks probably don't belong to the shooter. But he could have been there earlier checking out the area. A team is coming in now to try to find the slug."

"Good luck," an agent said softly.

Chet cut his eyes to Barry. "May I use your phone to make a credit card call, Mr. Cantrell?"

"Of course. There is a jack in the kitchen if you'd like more privacy."

"Someone pulling up outside," Branon said, glancing out the window.

"Stormy," Barry said.

"Stormy?" Chet questioned.

"Stormy Knight. The reporter."

"No kidding?" Agent Jones said. "What's she doing here?"

"She's staying here while covering the Speaker's visit. The lady with her is her camera-person. Ki Nichols."

New respect for Barry sprang into the eyes of the male agents in the room while amusement danced in Susan's eyes. "My, my," Susan said. "I thought I detected the scent of perfume in this house. I didn't think it belonged to you, Mr. Cantrell."

Barry said nothing in reply.

Stormy pushed open the front door and stepped inside, questions in her eyes as she looked at Barry.

Before Barry could speak, Agent Robbins said, "Don't be alarmed, Ms. Knight. We're federal agents. Somebody took a shot at Agent Green and Mr. Cantrell. Nobody was hurt."

Stormy kissed Barry, much to the envy of the men, and said, "Big news in town, Barry."

"What news?"

"The president is coming into Little Rock for a fundraiser, then taking a helicopter up here to visit for a few hours with the U.S. representative from this district. Steve Williams. They're old friends."

"What?" Agent Robbins almost shouted the one-word question.

"It was on the radio," Ki said. "The president and first lady will officially begin their vacation in this area."

"Shit!" Agent Robbins said, and quickly moved to the phone. He didn't bother with privacy. When the call went through, he said, "Will somebody kindly tell me what in the hell is going on? I have to get the news secondhand about The Man coming into this area." He listened for a moment. "I see. That really makes my day, people. Can somebody up there impress upon the President that this trip is very unwise? We've got a volatile situation building here, and I don't think it's a good idea for the president to be here. As a matter of fact, it's a lousy idea." He listened for another moment. "I see. The First Lady and Mrs. Williams were sorority sisters in college. That's wonderful. Can't this reunion take place in Little Rock?" Again, he listened. "Yes, sir. I understand, sir. Perfectly, sir. And a good day to you, too, sir." He stood looking at the buzzing phone for a moment before slowly replacing it in the cradle. He sighed heavily, then turned to face the group.

Before he could speak, Susan asked, "The President and First Lady are really coming here?"

"Yes," Chet said. "They really are."

"Well, goddamn!" she said.

That seemed to sum up the feelings of all the federal agents in the room.

Fifteen

On the day that Congressman Madison was due to arrive, Barry awakened before dawn with a morbid feeling of dread. Not even Stormy lying warm against him, breathing evenly in very deep sleep, could wrest the feeling away. Their lovemaking had been long and satisfying, and afterward Stormy had wasted no time in successfully reaching the arms of Morpheus. Barry had slept his usual few hours and was wide awake long before dawn.

He slipped from her side and, from countless years of habit, dressed as silently as a spider spinning a web. He let the dogs out in the backyard and quietly made a pot of coffee, filled a mug, and sat on the back porch.

Get out of here, Barry, the silent urging popped into his brain. Head for Canada and get yourself lost up there. If you stay here, you're going to get involved in this deepening mess.

But as he had pondered this very thought a few days past, he knew he was not going to leave. And he was certain that deep in her heart, Stormy realized he would not run away.

Barry was working on his second cup of coffee, the hybrids lying peacefully by his side on the back porch, when he heard Stormy moving around in the house. A moment later, she stepped out onto the darkened porch and sat down beside him, a cup of coffee in her hand.

"How long have you been up, Barry?"

"About half an hour or so. Just sitting out here thinking."

"I don't have to ask what you were thinking. You really believe there is going to be some sort of coup within our government, don't you?"

"It's the only thing that makes any sense, Stormy. You said yourself that you didn't believe Senator Holden's death was suicide. From what I've read and heard about Senator Bowman, I think the woman is very dangerous. I suspect there are power plays that go on every day in Washington—most of them relatively harmless. But not this one. This power play is going for broke, as folks used to say. This nation is ripe for revolution. Seeds of discontent are sprouting everywhere. I've seen and heard the same scenes and words in dozens of countries over the years. President Hutton walked into a powder keg when he took office. And I believe the fuse is now lit."

Stormy sipped her coffee in silence for a moment. Then she sighed. "I don't doubt your words, Barry. It's just difficult for me to accept them. But after what I saw in Idaho last year, I know that armed rebellion is certainly possible."

"There are millions of Americans who are fed up, Stormy. They're weary of taxes that just keep going up and up and never seem to stop. Government programs that the majority of people don't want and would like to see abolished. Nothing is sacred anymore. The government listens to our phone conversations, reads our mail, monitors electronic bulletin boards, and snoops into our bank accounts."

"Seems to me I've heard this conversation before," Stormy said with a smile. "But it always seems newer and fresher each time you say it."

Barry chuckled. "Thank you. But I think it's because I'm not mouthing theories or hypothetical situations, Stormy. I've seen revolutions, close up and personal. I've been involved in them and bloodied by them. I've watched them build from the grass roots, as the saying goes here in this country, and that's what this nation is heading toward. And revolution is no longer crawling in that direction; it's running all out."

"That's scary."

"It's pathetic, that's what it is. And so avoidable." He shook his head and cut his eyes to her in the dimness of predawn. "The networks have been awfully quiet about the death of Senator Holden, Stormy. Not even Coyote has had much to say about it. Are your people hitting a stone wall?"

"If the senator's death was murder, Barry, it was done by a very skilled assassin. All the law enforcement agencies involved in the investigation say it was suicide."

Barry grunted. "John Ravenna swears he did not kill Senator Holden, and I believe him. John was contracted to kill Congressman Madison. No one else. At least not yet. I've told Sheriff Salter about John. I don't know what else to do . . . speaking from a legal standpoint."

"But you're going to stop John, aren't you?"

"I'm going to try. Immortals don't fight each other. Call it an unwritten agreement among us. We don't fight each other because to do so would be pointless. We would mark each other, quite savagely, but in a few days, we would be healed, and the confrontation would have accomplished nothing. I don't know how I'm going to stop Ravenna; only that I must try."

Barry was conscious of Stormy's unwavering gaze. She said, "I get the feeling you're holding back from me."

"Not intentionally, I assure you. I just . . . well, have no proof of my suspicions."

"Bounce it off me. Let's talk about it."

"I think the president is the main target. Congressman Madison, while certainly a target, is also a diversion. But President Hutton's sudden decision to visit here just makes things easier for the coup planners."

Stormy's hands were shaking as she lifted her cup and finished her coffee. "You think someone is going to try to kill the president of the United States."

"Yes. With Hutton out of the way, VP Thomas—a man who is in Senator Madalaine Bowman's pocket—would be sworn in as president. With Congressman Madison dead, Congressman Lowe—also a quiet ally of Bowman, and a very weak person—would become Speaker, then vice president. Next in line for the Speaker's slot in the House is Congressman Valli. A closet liberal; easily manipulated. There are three years to go on Hutton's term. Three years during which the liberals could get their train back on track, divide this nation even further, and quite possibly bring it into full armed revolt by irate citizens."

Stormy stared down into her empty coffee cup and for a moment was silent. "What would happen to this country if there was some sort of revolution, Barry?"

"It would be awful. The next revolution—if there is one—will not be great battles between thousands of troops. It will be done by sneak attacks. The bombing of federal buildings and sniper warfare. Anyone who is employed by the federal government will be fair game. The insanity of Northern Ireland brought to the shores of America. I've seen it, Stormy. I know what I'm talking about. The free travel that Americans have always enjoyed will be a thing of the past. Papers will be required to move from state to state. In a small way, that's already started at our major airports. It can do nothing except worsen."

The sky was beginning to tint silver in the east. Stormy stared out at the fading night for a moment and said, "What are we going to do, Barry? The Speaker will be here in a few hours."

"I'm going to make one last attempt to try to talk John Ravenna out of this. If that fails, and I'm sure it will, you've got to go to the FBI and lay it all out for them."

"Mentioning your name?"

"Just tell them you got a tip about John Ravenna. They'll act on it."

"You hope."

"Yes. I hope."

Barry pulled into the driveway just as Ravenna was leaving his rented lake house, carrying a rod, reel, and tackle box.

"Well, cousin!" the assassin called brightly. "How good to see you. I hear the fish are really biting today. Care to join me?"

"I came out to talk, John."

"Oh. Well. I suppose I could give you a few minutes. My, but you do have a terribly serious expression on your face, cousin."

"I'm here to ask for a favor."

"You? Ask me for a favor?" He set his fishing gear on the ground. "I can't believe it. If memory serves me correctly, the last time you asked me for a favor was two hundred years ago, in France. I was in the employ of Burgundy, and you were fighting with those miserable street rabble. Did I grant you the favor, cousin?"

"No."

"Ah! Pity. What was the favor?"

"A life."

Ravenna waved that off. "Oh. I thought perhaps it might have been something important. What favor do you request of me on this glorious day?"

"A life."

"Really? Let me guess. Your windbag politician, right?"

"That's correct."

"Then I must disappoint you again. The answer is no."

"You leave me no choice, John. I've got to expose us both."

Ravenna laughed, but the laughter held no mirth. It was dark-tinged with evil. "My cover is perfect, cousin. I'm a well-respected citizen in my little Irish village. Actually, I'm known as quite the generous person. I give money to all the right causes. I've saved many a poor widder woman from being tossed out into the street. The folks there love me. Interpol has already checked me out, a few years ago. They apologized for any inconvenience they might have caused me. You can't touch me, cousin. So go ahead, make a fool out of yourself."

"Is that your last word on the matter?"

"It is. I don't care to discuss it any further. As a matter of fact, you're becoming quite the bore."

"Then you go right straight to hell, Ravenna!"

"Sometimes, cousin," John said, a wistful note to his voice, "I wish I could."

* * *

"I have no choice in the matter," Sheriff Don Salter said to Chief Monroe. "Not now. You heard my deputy say that it appears Ravenna and Cantrell quarreled about something. He couldn't hear the conversation, naturally; but his binoculars are good, and he said the men became quite heated. My guess is that Barry went to see him to try to talk him out of this assassination plan. He obviously failed."

The chief of police was still shaken by what the sheriff had just moments before told him about immortals and wolves. He wondered if Don was on the verge of a nervous breakdown. He shook his head. "Don, ah, I know you think what you saw out at Cantrell's place was real, but, ah, really, Don . . . there is no such thing as a shape-shifter. That's Indian folklore. Legend. This Cantrell person is some sort of magician. He's got you bamboozled, Don."

"I know it's hard for you to believe, Russ. Hell, I fainted! Passed slap out when he did it. It's no trick, Russ. And he is not alone in the ability to do that. I told you, Ravenna is also a shape-shifter and he's here to kill Congressman Madison."

Chief Monroe rose from the chair and paced the room nervously. These stories brought back vivid memories of when his half-Choctaw grandmother used to tell him stories about shape-shifters. Used to scare the crap of the young boy. He never wanted to believe the old woman's stories, but a part of him always did. He turned and slowly nodded his head. "You know I'm part Choctaw, don't you, Don?"

"Yes."

"My grandmother used to tell stories about shape-changers. She said she saw one back around the turn of the century, when her father took her to visit relatives over in Oklahoma." The chief paused to light his pipe.

Don waited. He had learned never to push Russ Monroe. The chief would get to it, eventually.

When Russ got his pipe going, he returned to his chair and asked, "I remember reading last year, I think it was, a story about a man who could not die?"

"That's Barry Cantrell."

"I was afraid you were going to say that." The older man sighed. "You want to go to the feds with this story?"

"Do we have a choice?"

"Not really, I suppose. But the whole story?"

"I think we can get away with just the assassination plot. We can say we got a phone tip from a man who refused to give his name."

"All right." The chief rose to his boots. "Let's do it before I lose my nerve."

"Now, let's go over this one more time, Ms. Knight," Inspector Van Brocklen said. "You say you received a phone tip from a man claiming to have knowledge about a plot to kill Congressman Madison?"

"That is correct. The call was received at my camerapersons motel room."

"Not your room?"

"You people know perfectly well I am not staying at the motel. Stop playing games, Inspector. If you don't find this serious, then to hell with it."

"Just calm down, Ms. Knight. We take death threats very seriously. The caller mentioned John Ravenna by name?"

"For the fourth time, yes."

The door to the adjoining motel room opened. "Inspector? Agent Chet Robbins on the phone. I think you'd better hear this."

Van Brocklen picked up the phone. "Go, Chet." He

listened for a moment, his expression hardening. "That is interesting. I have Ms. Stormy Knight with me now, telling me that she received an identical call, also anonymous. Let's coordinate this, Chet. Right. I'll see you in a few minutes." He turned to Stormy. "Thank you, Ms. Knight. You've been very helpful."

Outside the motel room, Ki said, "You think he bought it?"

Stormy nodded. "Yes. I think that phone call cinched it. That must have been Sheriff Salter. Let's stick around and see who shows up."

"We're being watched," Ki said. "A man and a woman. And they're not making any effort to hide that fact."

"As far as I know, Ki, there is no law against two people standing in a motel parking lot."

"Yet."

They watched as several cars pulled into the parking lot, among them the units of Sheriff Salter and Chief Monroe. The men disappeared into that section of the motel occupied by federal agents and closed the door.

"You want to drive on out to Mr. Will's store and wait for the feds there?" Ki suggested.

"No. I think they'll send a couple of people out there to keep an eye on Ravenna and wait until they get something back from Washington; the State Department, maybe. I don't want to do anything that would tip the agents' hand."

The sound of a horn honking up the street caused them to turn their heads. A man and woman walked out of the motel restaurant and paused by Stormy and Ki. "Well," the woman said, "I guess the Speaker of the House has arrived."

BOOK TWO

We must remember not to judge any public servant by any one act, and especially should we beware of attacking the men who are merely the occasions and not the causes of disaster.

—Theodore Roosevelt

Sixteen

Congressman Cliff Madison stopped at the mayor's office for some glad-handing and was immediately surrounded by reporters. Ki and Stormy were there, filming, but Stormy asked no questions. That would come later, for she had already requested and received a block of the Speaker's time later on. That is, Stormy thought glumly, providing the Speaker's time has not run out.

Since the Coyote Network had taken a decidedly conservative stance in news reporting, conservative politicians always found time for any reporter from Coyote.

Stormy had been covering politicians for years, and she noticed immediately that security was very tight. There were agents on rooftops with rifles, and a helicopter slowly circled the area. Looking around, she saw Barry sitting on the tailgate of his truck, and leaving Ki to film, she walked over to him.

"Big doings," Barry said with a smile.

"Security is tight."

"John isn't here. I just left him on the lake. He's fishing, and looks as though he plans to stay out for quite some time."

"You went out there twice today?"

"Yes. The sheriff has two men watching him at all times, and I'll bet that after Don talked to the feds,

John will be blanketed with agents. Not that it will do any good."

"Well, there he goes," Stormy said, pointing. "Off to his cabin on the lake."

They stood and watched the caravan of vehicles pull away from the courthouse square and head out of town. Moments later, the town had settled down to its normal routine.

Ki strolled over and leaned against the bed of the truck. "As much security around the Speaker as around the president," she remarked.

"I imagine the president ordered it," Barry said. "According to what I read in the papers, they're old friends. But with the president making this surprise trip, the coup planners have had to do some sudden changing of plans."

"What do you mean?" Stormy asked.

"I told you I thought the president was the main target in this plot. I don't know what the plan was, of course, but let's say it was to hit him at his home in Ohio. Now all that's had to be revised. According to the papers, he's flying to Little Rock directly from Washington, then leaving from this area for his vacation out west. Hitting him here would be the logical choice, considering all that has happened; two birds with one stone, so to speak."

"You think the feds have put all that together?" Ki asked.

"I would certainly hope so."

"And if they haven't?" Stormy asked.

Barry shrugged his shoulders. "It's going to get real interesting around here."

"Perhaps we should tell the Secret Service and the FBI about those suspicions." Ki suggested.

Barry smiled. "And when you do, they'll be very interested in how you reached that conclusion."

"Yeah," the woman said slowly. "I see what you mean."

"I just hope the president does not take a helicopter from Little Rock up here," Barry said softly.

"Why not?" Stormy asked. "That's the way he usually travels on short hops."

"A helicopter is easy to bring down. It would only take one nut with a shoulder-fired SAM to bring down the chopper."

"I did a report a couple of years ago on how easy it is to get one of those things," Stormy said. "Jesus Christ, Barry. Do you think . . . ?"

Barry held up a hand. "It's a possibility, that's all. As far as I know, it's never been tried. But there is always a first time for everything."

"Ravenna could get one of those SAMs, couldn't he?" Ki asked.

"As easily as snapping his fingers," Barry said. "He's got contacts all over the world."

"And has had a thousand years to develop them," Stormy said drily.

"You want to hear more bad news?" Barry asked.

"Why not?" the women said.

"Some of those contacts are immortals."

The feds got a search warrant and served it on Victor Radford. When ten agents in two cars and a van pulled out of the motel parking lot, Stormy and Ki followed them straight to Victor's compound. Ki jumped out filming.

"Just stay back, ladies," one agent shouted.

"Oh, hell, no!" Vic hollered. "Come on in, ladies. This is my property. You're welcome. Please come in. I want you to see your government at work."

"Goddammit!" one FBI man muttered.

Inspector Van Brocklen held up a warning hand. "Stay back, ladies. We're in the process of serving a federal warrant. String that tape!" he shouted to another agent, then turned to the Coyote Network crew. "Stay back of the tape, ladies. Please."

Stormy nodded, and she and Ki remained behind the warning tape.

Stormy had no idea what was being said by the federal agents on the other side of the tape, but whatever it was, Vic Radford wasn't taking it well. She and Ki could hear him shouting.

A dozen or so of Vic's followers drove up in cars and trucks, and the federal agents had to warn them repeatedly to stay behind the tape.

"Why aren't you filming this?" one of the men shouted to the Coyote Network crew.

"Yeah!" another shouted. "What's the matter, are we the wrong color?"

Ki started to lift her camera. "Forget it," Stormy said.

Several of the men started making chicken-clucking sounds.

"On second thought," Stormy whispered.

"Right," Ki said, and clicked on her camera as Stormy picked up the mike and headed toward the knot of red-faced, angry men gathered by the road.

The hen-house sounds stopped abruptly as the women approached, and the men began casting wary glances at each other.

Stormy walked up to one pus-gutted man with a mouthful of teeth that looked as though they would be more at home on a well-used garden rake. "Do you know why federal agents are serving a federal warrant on this man, sir?" she asked.

"Hell, yes, I do!" the man blustered. " 'Cause we won't kowtow to them damn communist politicians in

Washington, that's why. 'Cause we believe in the right to keep and bear arms. And 'cause we believe in the purity of the races."

Stormy knew how easy it would be to make this man look like the fool he obviously was, but Coyote reporters didn't play that game, except with politicians. Before she could frame another question, a shout came from the men gathered by the tape. "Hey, they got Vic in handcuffs!"

Ki swung the camera. A violently struggling Vic Radford was red-faced and cussing the agents. Each agent had a firm grip on Vic, left and right arm.

"Hang in there, Vic!" one of the men by the road shouted.

"We'll get you out, Vic!" another yelled.

The men started chanting, *"Sieg heil, Sieg heil!"*

Stormy and Inspector Van Brocklen exchanged brief silent glances seconds before Vic Radford was placed in the van, and two agents drove away with the still cussing and shouting prisoner.

"See where they take him!" a man shouted, pointing at two men sitting in a pickup truck. "Go!"

The pickup sped after the van.

The other agents quickly stepped behind the tape and walked back toward the house, refusing to acknowledge any questions shouted at them by Radford's followers.

After a moment, Van Brocklen walked out of the house and motioned for Stormy and Ki to approach. An agent lifted the tape, and the Coyote crew walked up the hard-packed gravel drive.

"I have a statement for you," the inspector said. "When you are ready."

"Go," Ki said, swinging the camera to her shoulder.

Van Brocklen said, "Acting under orders from the attorney general of the United States, agents of the

Federal Bureau of Investigation, Secret Service, and Federal Marshal's Service attempted to serve a search warrant upon the person and premises of Victor Radford. Mr. Radford became verbally abusive and physically violent and began fighting. He struck two agents with his fists and was immediately taken into custody. He will be charged with resisting arrest and battery upon a federal officer."

"What were you searching for, Inspector Van Brocklen?" Stormy asked.

"Illegal weapons."

"Did you find any illegal weapons?"

"We have found several weapons we believe have been converted from semiautomatic to fully automatic."

"But you don't know that for a fact?"

Van Brocklen's look was not friendly. "Not until we fire them, Ms. Knight."

"Would you grant us permission to be present when the test firing is performed?"

"I don't have that authority."

"Where do we get that permission?"

"I'll have to get back to you on that."

"There ain't no goddamn automatic weapons in that house!" a man yelled from the road. "I know every weapon in that house. This ain't nothin' but a damn setup by the government. That's all it is."

Inspector Van Brocklen stepped out of the house, carrying what many referred to as an assault rifle. He walked halfway down the drive, stopped, pointed the muzzle to the sky and pulled the trigger. A second and a half later, he had blown a thirty-round magazine into the air.

"Holy shit!" one bystander said. "I never knew Vic had nothin' like that."

"Them feds must have toted that gun in yonder," another said defensively.

"No, they didn't," Stormy corrected. "We watched and filmed their every move."

"Thank you, Ms. Knight," Van Brocklen said. "Please don't lose that film."

"We won't," Ki assured him.

The women looked at each other. "What happens now?" Stormy asked.

"We break him out," Alex Tarver told his group of skinheads. "Then we can start planning the revolution."

"What revolution?" George Willis asked. George was not the swiftest person, mentally speaking.

"The revolution we've been talkin' about for months," Jason Asken told him.

"Oh!" George said.

"When do we do it?" Lorrie Morrow asked.

"Tonight," Alex said. "The feds won't be expectin' anything this soon."

"People are gonna get hurt, maybe kilt," Phil Allen pointed out.

"Does that bother anybody?" Alex asked, looking around him at the faces of his group.

The young men and women all shrugged their indifference.

"Fine. We go tonight."

"I ain't gonna stand for this," Tom Devers said, popping open another beer. "I just ain't a-gonna stand for it."

Noble Osgood stared at him for a moment. "What have you got in mind, Tom?"

"Bustin' Vic out of jail."

"And then what?" David Jackson asked.

"Vic'll think of something. Maybe even start the revolution."

Hal Chilton looked at each of the men gathered in the woods west of town. "That ain't for us to say, boys."

Paul Crenshaw nodded his head. "But Vic's been talkin' about it. He's been in contact with other groups around the nation."

"We bust Vic out of the bucket, we won't have no choice in the matter. We'll have to start it," another ventured.

"I got an idea," Tillman Morris said. "Let's coordinate this with the skinheads. Alex's a reasonable guy and he's got some sense. 'Sides, he might be thinkin' of doing the same thing. We don't want to get all balled up here."

"I can't stand them goofy-actin' bunch of nuts in Alex's group," John Hammit said. "I think they're all about two bricks shy of a load."

"They're unpredictable, for a fact," Bert Landers said. "And I don't think they's a one of them that has yet to reach age twenty-one."

"So we use them for cannon fodder," Tom Devers replied with a dirty grin.

"What do you mean?" Sam Evans asked. Sam was not real quick when it came to thinking, or anything else for that matter, except for beating his wife, which he did on a regular basis. Whether she deserved it or not, was Sam's favorite saying.

"I'll explain it to you later, Sam," Tom told him.

"Oh. Okay."

"When do you want to do this?" Tillman asked.

"I'll go see Alex right now. But the sooner the better, I say."

"Hell, it might be tonight," Noble said with a smile. "I'll go home and get my guns."

"Hell, yes!" the rest of the group shouted, followed by, *"Sieg heil! Sieg heil!"*

Seventeen

"We don't want to give these people any excuse to start trouble, " the attorney general told Inspector Van Brocklen. "Not while the Speaker is in the area and the president is due in a few days. The situation is volatile enough as it is. Bail has been set. If he can make it, release him."

"Yes, sir."

It was late in the day when Vic walked out of the local jail, still mad as a hornet. He waited for a few moments, looking around; but none of his people were there to meet him, and that made him still angrier. He hitched a ride to his home, and none of his people were there, either. Furious, Vic began making calls to members of his group. He could not make contact with anyone.

"Well, where in the hell is everyone?" he shouted to a blown-up poster of his idol, Adolf Hitler.

In the woods outside of town, a group of men met, planning Vic's breakout from jail.

Disgusted, Vic fixed a tall, stiff drink and sat down in his favorite recliner. He drank his whiskey and water and fixed another, just as strong as the first. It wasn't long before Vic had a buzz on. After his third very strong drink, Vic grew sleepy and leaned back in the chair. He was soon asleep, dreaming of a nation filled with the master race; all inferiors were slaves, doing their bidding.

Barry watched John Ravenna fish for a time, then returned to his house. He knew John was aware of his presence and also of the several carloads of feds getting into place at various locations around the lake. He was convinced that John would pull some stunt this day, but he didn't know what. Barry puttered around his house the rest of the day. It was after five when Stormy returned; and Barry fixed them drinks and they sat in the den, watching the Coyote Evening News.

During a commercial break, Barry asked, "And you heard that Vic was about to be released?"

She nodded her head. "He should be out by now. He swears he did not know that rifle was fully automatic. Of course, no one believes him."

"They probably figured that holding him would only cause more trouble, and they don't want that, with Congressman Madison in the area and the president coming in." Barry sipped his drink and grimaced at the commercial on the screen, featuring dancing underwear. "Progress is certainly a wonderful thing," he muttered.

"Did you say something?" Stormy asked.

"Ah . . . no. Is Ki coming over for dinner?"

"No. She's beat. Said she was going to take a long, hot bath, have an early dinner, and hit the sack."

"My goodness," Barry said with a smile. "Whatever will we do to pass the time?"

"I'm sure we can think of something."

"No doubt."

The ringing of the phone cut into the growing mood

like a hot knife through butter. With a sigh, Barry rose from his chair and picked up the receiver. "Hi, Don. Oh? Well, I told you that would happen. You sure about this? Okay. I'll be ready."

He hung up and turned to Stormy. "Ravenna has slipped his watchers, just as I said he would."

"And the sheriff wants you to find him?"

"You got it."

She smiled. "I'll be waiting."

"Definitely a point to keep in mind."

Barry looked up at the sky as he stood on the front porch. About an hour and a half of good daylight left. Ravenna's sudden shaking of the feds didn't alarm him; this was still only a game to John. He was playing with them.

It was deadly play, to be sure, if the agents got too close to him. But still just a game to John.

Before leaving the house, Barry had spoken silently to the hybrids. They would guard Stormy with their lives. He drove into town and linked up with Don at the sheriff's office, climbing into Don's unit.

"Ravenna's playing with you, Don," he said, closing the door. "He knows you're onto him, and this is his way of showing you his contempt."

The sheriff looked skeptical.

"Believe me, Don. I've seen him do this many, many times over the years."

"Macabre sense of humor," the sheriff grunted.

"Oh, more than you know, Don. Much more than you know."

The sheriff pulled away from the lighted parking area and into the road.

"Did you tell the feds anything about me, Don?"

"Good God, no! But I did tell Chief Monroe."

"And what was his reaction?"

"Unbelieving, at first. But now I think he's about half-convinced. Says he is." He cut his eyes to Barry. "Where do you want to start?"

"Where was he last seen?"

"In his backyard. One second he was visible then he was gone. Agents entered the home, but he was not there. He just vanished."

"Shape-shifted."

"You said he doesn't, ah, shape-shift into a wolf. What does he change into?"

"Something very unpleasant. But something very dangerous. Very strong, very quick."

"Sheriff?" the voice jumped out of the speaker.

Don picked up and keyed the mike. "Go."

"Bl0 reports, ah, well, he's on Haney Road just south of 375. You'd better get over there. I don't want to get on the air with this."

Don hesitated, then said, "That's ten-four. Rolling."

"What is it?" Barry asked.

"Something dispatch doesn't want the scanner freaks to hear. And that usually means it's grim."

It was a body, lying just off the blacktop near a clump of woods, and it was worse than grim. The face was gone, the throat had been torn out, and the stomach had been ripped open, leaving the intestines scattered about. One young deputy had already lost his supper at the sight.

"Go over to your unit and sit down, Jimmy," Don told the young man, as he pulled on a pair of rubber gloves. "And puking at something like this is no disgrace. We've all done it."

The other deputies glanced at Barry, wondering about his presence, but said nothing. Who the sheriff hauled around in his unit was his business.

"What the hell kind of animal did this?" Don asked,

kneeling down by the mangled body. "It looks like the neck was broken." He gently touched the head. It wobbled loosely.

"It was done within the hour," a deputy said. "Rigor mortis has not yet set in."

"A pack of wild dogs?" another deputy ventured.

"No," Don said, shaking his head. He pointed to the ground. "Just one set of tracks. But if it's a dog, it's got to be the biggest damn dog I've ever seen." He glanced up at Barry. Barry's face was expressionless.

"There was no ID on the body, Sheriff," the first deputy on the scene said. "And I couldn't find any wallet in the first search."

"Does anybody have any idea who this might be?" Don asked, standing up.

"Hard to tell without a face, Sheriff. But what the hell happened to the face? It looks like it was just ripped off."

"Maybe it was eaten?" another deputy opined.

"Oh, shit!" The young deputy who had lost his supper had returned to stand with the others. He hurriedly exited the scene. Again.

Don looked up at his chief deputy, who had been the second officer on the scene and so far had said nothing. "What do you think, Steve?"

The older man shook his head. "I've never seen anything like it. I don't know what to think." He pointed to the ground. "Those tracks belong to the dog family, for sure. Only different. Look how they're sunk into the ground. This animal must weigh close to two hundred pounds. There are no dogs around here that size. I've never even *seen* a dog that large."

"All right," Don said. "Steve, use the cell phone in your unit and call Inspector Van Brocklen at the motel. Ask him as a favor to come out here ASAP."

"Right."

Don cut his eyes to Barry. "You want to stick around?"

"Might as well."

"You don't seem too upset by this."

"I've seen worse."

"Jesus, where?" a deputy asked.

Where indeed? Barry thought. How about hundreds of men and women impaled on stakes by Vlad the Impaler? How about human beings drawn and quartered until their limbs were torn from them? Men and women dragged to death. Name it, young man, and I've damn sure seen it over the long and bloody years as the world made its slow march toward more civilized behavior.

"Van Brocklen's on his way," Steve called.

Don nodded. Deputies began taking pictures of the mangled body, and Don and Barry leaned against the sheriff's unit, waiting for the Bureau to show. They didn't have a long wait.

The inspector took one look at Barry and said, "What's he doing here?"

"He was riding with me when I got the call. He's all right."

Van Brocklen grunted and walked over to the body. "Good Lord! What happened to this poor bastard?"

"It looks like some sort of animal attack," Don said.

"What kind of animal, a man-eating tiger?"

"We were hoping you could tell us."

Van Brocklen shook his head. "Have you established the identity of the victim?"

"No. And there was nothing in the pockets. There have been no carnivals or circuses through here; no reports of missing animals."

"Anyone reported missing?"

"No."

An ambulance moaned up, and the county coroner

stepped out. He took one look at the body and said, "Jesus Christ!"

"I have to ask this, Dr. Varner," Don said. "Do you recognize the man?"

"No. What the hell happened to him?"

"Some sort of animal attack, we believe."

The deputies had taken both casts and pictures of the tracks around the body.

"Just one animal?" the doctor asked.

"Only one set of tracks around the body."

"Are you people through here?"

"Yes. You can have the body."

Dr. Varner was kneeling beside the mangled corpse. "An animal with very strong jaws and large teeth did this," he said. "This arm has been crushed, the bone shattered. No domestic animal did this. This was not done by a dog."

"A wolf, perhaps?" Van Brocklen asked. He looked at Barry. "Or a hybrid wolf."

The coroner shook his head. "No. I doubt that very much." Using tweezers, he was carefully picking strands of very coarse hair off the body and putting them in a plastic bag. He closed the bag securely and held it out to Don. "Can you dispatch a deputy to the university with these? See Professor Garrison. He'll identify the hair."

"Right now," Don said, taking the evidence bag and handing it to a deputy. "Go."

Inspector Van Brocklen pulled the sheriff off to one side and spoke in low tones for a moment. Then the inspector walked to his vehicle and drove off. Sheriff Salter returned to the knot of men around the body.

"Still no sign of Ravenna," Don said to Barry. "The man just vanished."

"Not really," Barry told him. "Are we through here?"

"Oh, yes. My deputies will secure the area and begin an evidence search. Why?"

"Let's take a ride."

"Why? You know something I don't?"

Barry smiled.

"Forget I asked that," Don said wearily. "Of course you do. Come on."

Rolling away from the death scene, Don said, "What's on your mind, Barry?"

"Ravenna killed that man back there, Don. I don't know why; perhaps the man startled him while he was his Other. But that was Ravenna's work. No doubt about it. I've seen his work many times before."

The sheriff looked doubtful. "The coroner said it wasn't a wolf that killed him."

"He's right. Ravenna does not shape-shift into a wolf. He can only become a hyena."

Don almost ran off the road at that. He quickly corrected his path and cut his eyes to Barry. "A hyena? You mean one of those big ugly African things? A scavenger?"

"Yes. Very big, and very dangerous. Capable of crushing a large bone with one snap of his jaws."

"This Professor Garrison will be able to identify the hair, won't he?"

"Very quickly."

The sheriff sighed. "We've got to sit on this. News of this gets out, every redneck in three counties will be out in the woods blasting away at anything that moves." He was silent for a mile. "Barry? When this is over, will you do me a favor?"

"What?"

"Would you consider moving?"

Eighteen

The two men rode in silence for a time, wandering the back roads of the county. After a few miles, just as dusk was settling over the land, Don said, "He could be anywhere."

Barry glanced out at the gathering gloom. "Probably back at his rental house, sitting in the dark. Don, has Vic made bail yet?"

Don shook his head, stepped on the brake, cut down a gravel road, and said, "Not to my knowledge. This is a shortcut to the lake. We'll be there in fifteen minutes or so. I want to talk to this bastard."

"And what will you say?"

"I don't know. I'll think of something. If he gets too lippy, I'll have the boys throw a net over him and lock him down. Then he can shape-shift all he likes, but he won't be able to get past steel doors and bars."

Barry smiled. "That would certainly be a sight to see."

"Sounds as though you'd like to see it."

"Oh, I would. John and I are not exactly what you might call friends."

Don pulled into the driveway just in time to see John Ravenna walk out of the woods behind the lake house and pause by the side of the house as the sheriff pulled in. He walked over to the unit.

"Gentlemen," Ravenna said with a mocking smile. "Ah! Good evening, Sheriff Salter. Out for a little drive in the twilight, are we? I've been walking in the woods for the past hour or so. It's such a lovely part of America. How may I be of assistance to you?"

"We, ah, saw you coming out of the woods," Don said. "Didn't recognize you at first, Mr. Ravenna. Thought you might be a prowler and wanted to check it out."

"Heavens, me!" Ravenna replied with that same mocking smile. "A prowler. Think of that. I'd probably have a heart attack if confronted by some criminal element. Violence is something I try to avoid. But I do thank you for your concern."

"Have a nice evening, sir," Don told him.

"Thank you, I shall."

Don backed out of the drive and headed back to town. Just around the bend, he slowed and pulled in beside a van with two men in the front.

"Federal agents?" Barry asked.

"Yes." Don lowered his window and spoke to the driver. "He's back in his house now. Said he's been out walking in the woods."

"He's slippery as sheep shit," the driver said, giving Barry a visual once-over. "There is more going on here than meets the eye. I just wish I knew what it was."

"Yes. Well," Don said, suddenly uncomfortable. "You boys take it easy. See you around."

A few hundred yards down the road back to town, Don's radio began squawking. "Sheriff!" dispatch hollered, panic in the man's voice. "The damn jail just blew up!"

* * *

When the heavy charge of dynamite blew, it threw one jailer through an office window, depositing him in a trailer load of watermelons that a deputy had brought in just that day, the vehicle having expired plates, no brake lights, and defective brakes, among other charges.

The deputy was not badly hurt, except for about a dozen minor glass cuts, but when the watermelons exploded under his impact, he was covered with a red stain. The deputy felt sure he was mortally injured and began shrieking to high heaven.

Another deputy was blown under a desk, and since he was more than a bit overweight, he got stuck in the leg hole and panicked. He began hollering for someone to get him out.

A third deputy had just brought in one of the town's regular drunks, with the help of a city policeman. All three of them were rolled down the tiled hall from the concussion and found themselves in a tangle of arms and legs and total confusion.

The jail quickly filled with black-jumpsuited men, wearing ski masks and carrying a variety of weapons. They began searching the cells. But their leader was nowhere to be found, for Vic was sound asleep in his recliner, miles away, smiling in his sleep, dreaming of a pure Aryan nation.

"Yahoooo!" one of the ski-masked skinheads shouted, pointing his AR-15 at the ceiling and pulling the trigger just as fast as he could, sending plaster and concrete and dust flying everywhere. The rapid fire sent everybody into a panic.

Two FBI agents and one Secret Service agent were having supper at a small cafe just across the street from the jail when the blast occurred. The heavy charge of dynamite had been placed at the back door of the jail. Just inside the door, the men's room was on the left, the ladies' room to the right. Commodes and urinals and sinks and bricks and pipes and paper towel dispensers went flying through the air. One commode landed in the middle of the street and exploded into a thousand pieces. The concussion blew out the windows on all the storefronts on two sides of the courthouse square; falling debris dented cars and trucks and smashed vehicle windows.

The federal agents were knocked off their stools and dumped on the floor, addled but unhurt.

Inspector Van Brocklen had just driven into the center of town and was stopped at a red light when the back wall and part of one side of the jail blew apart. Part of a urinal landed on the hood of his car, knocking a huge dent in the metal and popping out the windshield. Van Brocklen exited the passenger side faster than he had moved in a long time, and crouched on the street, pistol in hand, looking wildly all around him. He couldn't see much, for the dust from the explosion and the gloom of near dark cut his vision down to nearly nothing.

"What the hell happened, Inspector?" one of his men called from the cafe.

"Part of the courthouse blew up," Van Brocklen called. "Or maybe the jail. I can't tell until the dust settles."

"Might be a diversion, sir."

"Maybe. Call in. See if the Speaker is all right."

"I can't call in, sir."

"Why the hell not?"

"Because there's a toilet in the front seat of my car. Radio's gone."

Van Brocklen cautiously opened the passenger side door to his car and grabbed the mike and called in.

While Van Brocklen waited for a reply, Vic's men and the skinhead group, seeing that Vic was not in the jail, decided to split. They ran out a side door and disappeared into the dark alleys on the undamaged side of the square.

Slowly the dust began to settle in the still and humid air.

"Help!" the deputy trapped deep in the trailer load of watermelons hollered. "Help! I'm mortally wounded."

Sheriff Don Salter put on the brakes and slid to a halt on the damaged side of the courthouse. "Holy shit!" he whispered, gazing at the huge hole in the building.

The deputy who had called it into the sheriff was trapped in his unit. A huge chunk of concrete had landed on the roof of his vehicle, jamming all four doors. He had managed to kick out the glass on the driver's side and was struggling to climb out of his car without cutting himself.

Crowds were beginning to gather on the fringes of the courthouse square, to look and point and wonder.

"Keep those civilians back," Van Brocklen yelled, as more and more federal agents began to gather. "We don't know what we've got here."

Leroy Jim Bob "Bubba" Bordelon, chief klucker of the local KKK, had driven into town with two of his people. They were stopped at roadblocks set up by Chief Monroe's men and had to walk the rest of the way to the square. There, they bought popsicles at a drug store and stood licking and looking at all the excitement.

"Gawddamn," one of Bubba's men said.

"Yeah," the other one said. "Gawddamn."

The deputy, the city police officer, and the drunk they had been escorting to the bucket staggered to the front of the courthouse.

"Hold your fire!" Sheriff Salter, Chief Monroe, and

Inspector Van Brocklen all yelled simultaneously, as the three men appeared in the doorway.

Several deputies rushed up to escort them to safety—more or less, since no one really knew what the hell was happening.

"Oh, Lord, help me!" the deputy in the trailer load of watermelons hollered. "I'm bleedin' to death."

"Who the hell is that?" Chief Monroe asked, after carefully working his way over to Don.

"Sounds like Ricky," the sheriff said.

"Where the hell is he?"

"I think he's in that there load of watermelons," a citizen ventured.

"He must have got blowed through that courthouse window," another allowed.

"All right," Don said. "I'm going to get him. Cover me."

"You want some company?" Barry asked.

The sheriff thought about that for a moment. "Yeah. I do. Consider yourself deputized, Barry."

"Wonderful," Barry said drily.

The two men ran to the trailer and crawled up the side, peering over into the mashed mess.

"Jesus," Don said. "He's cut all to pieces."

"I don't think so," Barry replied. "I think that's stain from the watermelons."

"Give us your hand, Ricky," Don urged.

"I'm dyin'," Ricky said.

"No, you're not. Give me your hand."

Don and Barry hauled the deputy out of the trailer and stretched him out on the grass. They quickly checked him over and discovered he was far from dying; just cut up a bit.

"Stay here," Don told him. "EMTs will be with you as soon as we get this mess straightened out." He keyed his walkie-talkie. "We're going inside. Hold your fire. Pass the word to the feds."

"Ten-four, Sheriff."

Barry and Don cautiously entered the building through the blown-out hole where the back door and most of the back wall used to be.

"Get this fuckin' desk off me!" the words drifted to the two men as they stood in the rubble-littered hallway. "I'm trapped in here. Help!"

"That's Frank," Don said. "Come on."

Barry started laughing at the sight of Frank stuck beneath the desk, and his laughter was infectious. Don soon was chuckling as the two men tugged and pulled and finally managed to get Fat Frank free of the heavy steel desk.

"Don't say nothin' about this Sheriff," Frank pleaded. "Please?"

"Your secret is safe with us, Frank. Just try to lose a few pounds, will you?"

Frank went staggering off toward the gaping wall, muttering to himself.

The few prisoners in the lockup were all right, just scared. Other than that, the jail was empty.

"Come on in," Don radioed. "It's clear."

"Christ, what a mess!" Van Brocklen said, standing in the hall.

Federal agents, deputies, city cops, and a few local and county officials began filling the long corridor, all of them staring in disbelief.

None of the jailers could shed any light on who the people were who blew up the jail, since none had actually seen any of them.

Van Brocklen whispered to one of his agents, "See if John Ravenna is at home."

"Maybe they weren't after anyone," a deputy said. "Maybe this is in retaliation for arresting Vic Radford."

"That's a thought," Van Brocklen said. He pointed to several agents. "Get on that. Go over that list of members we got from Radford today. Start knocking on doors."

"Tonight?"

"Tonight. Move!"

Van Brocklen turned to the sheriff. "I saw your name on the guest list for that shindig out at Robert Roche's. I need to get with you on security."

"Tomorrow morning at nine in my office?"

"Sounds good." The FBI inspector slowly looked all around him at the damage and shook his head. "Jesus, what else is going to happen?"

"Nothing, I hope," Don said, taking off his hat and wiping his face with a handkerchief.

Don't bet on that, Barry thought, standing off to one side. He looked at his wristwatch. Forty-eight hours until the party at Roche's house. And that, he was sure, was when all hell was going to break loose.

Now just how do I know that? Barry silently questioned.

Because that would be John's style, came the reply. Ravenna likes to do things with a flourish.

"Let's get some help in here and clean this mess up," Don said. He looked up at a sudden burst of harsh light. Ki and Stormy were standing just outside the ruined wall, filming.

"The press is here," Van Brocklen said, then gave Barry a very dirty look.

"What'd I do?" Barry asked the Bureau man.

"I don't know," Van Brocklen said, keeping a steady gaze on Barry. "Yet."

Nineteen

The next two days were very frustrating for law enforcement. The Bureau rounded up every name on the membership list of Vic's neo-Nazi group but were unable to link any of them with the bombing of the jail. They all alibied for each other, and no one broke the code of silence. Vic was ruled out that very same night. He had downed several very stiff drinks on an empty stomach and was still drunk when the agents finally managed to rouse him from a deep sleep. Vic Radford thought the destruction of the jail was highly amusing.

"It's just too bad," he added, looking at the federal agents with open hate in his eyes, "you people weren't standing next to the blast."

Leroy Jim Bob "Bubba" Bordelon and his white-sheeted night riders were also questioned, but they all had unshakable alibis.

Every friend, colleague, and advisor to the president did his best to talk the president into changing his plans to travel from Little Rock to North Arkansas, but to no avail. The trip was on and that was that. The president was not going to change his mind.

More federal agents were sent into the area.

The FBI, Secret Service, and Federal Marshal's Service now had two entire wings of a local motel and one wing of another. One local wag commented, "There's enough antennas around them places to talk to Mars."

Undercover agents were quartered all over town. The motorcycle boys and girls were sleeping in tents out at a campground on the lake.

Work on repairing the jail had begun at dawn the morning after the bombing. Those few prisoners who had been in lockup had been transferred to the old city jail. Adding to all the federal agents, the governor had sent about a dozen Arkansas state troopers into the area to help out.

Stormy and Ki were shopping for something to wear to Roche's party that night, and Barry decided to stop in at Nellie's Cafe for a cup of coffee and a piece of pie.

He had just sat down when Sheriff Salter, Inspector Van Brocklen, and Secret Service Agent Chet Robbins joined him.

"Morning, gentlemen," Barry said. "The apple pie looks awfully good."

"I leveled with them, Barry," Don spoke in a whisper.

"Did you, now?"

"I just didn't have any choice in the matter."

"I don't blame you. Relax."

The waitress walked over and took their order, then left. The table where they were seated was in a far corner of the cafe, and at midmorning, Barry, Don, and the two feds were the only customers.

"So you are the mystery man from the Idaho shootout?" Van Brocklen asked.*

*Hunted—Pinnacle

"That's me."

"You didn't have to run, Barry," the Secret Service man said. "There are no charges against you. Inspector Wallace and Special Agent Murphy saw to that."

"Thank them for me."

"But there is a little matter of six rogue agents who seemingly dropped off the face of the earth," Van Brocklen said. "Max Vernon and the five men with him. I don't suppose you'd know anything about that."

"I imagine they fought the wilderness and lost," Barry said with a straight face. "You can't fight the wilderness. You have to work with it."

"I'll be sure and put that in my report," Van Brocklen said drily.

"How long have you known John Ravenna?" Chet asked.

"About six hundred and fifty years. I met him in Italy. He'd been hired to kill the pope. I stopped that assassination, and John has hated me ever since."

Van Brocklen suddenly had a very pained look on his face, Chet Robbins wore an expression of utter disbelief, and Don Salter ducked his head to hide a smile.

"We've run into each other every two or three decades since then. This has been the longest time between meetings."

"How long since you've seen him?" Chet asked. He quickly added, "Not that I believe any of this."

"World War II. In France. He was working for the Nazis. I was in the American Army, going by the name of William Shipman. I was dropped into France and was working with the French Resistance. You can check that. It's all true."

Conversation stopped while the waitress brought their coffee and pie. When she had left, Van Brocklen asked, "Assuming any of this is true, Barry, are you two the only immortals?"

"Oh, no. There are at least several hundred of us

around the world. I suspect there are several thousand. None of us know for sure."

After a full minute of silence had ticked by, Secret Service asked Bureau, "Do you believe any of this?"

Van Brocklen shook his head. "I don't know, Chet. I don't know what the hell to believe anymore."

Robbins chewed on a bite of pie for a moment, sipped his coffee, looked at Barry. "Let's put this hocus-pocus business aside for a moment. Do you think this John Ravenna is here to whack Congressman Madison?"

Barry hesitated, then said, "Yes. But now another target has been added."

"Who?"

"The president of the United States."

After a session with Walt Reynolds, head of the president's Secret Service security detail, the president agreed to take a small jet from Little Rock to his friend's home town in North Arkansas. The runway there was plenty long to accommodate a Lear. With that decision made, everybody concerned started breathing a little bit easier, since there was no way in hell anyone was going to dissuade the president and first lady from visiting their friends.

The squadron of fully armed air force Eagles, which always accompanied the president's plane, flying in a diamond formation, would land at Tinker AFB in Tulsa. When the president decided to leave, the fighters would be notified, and by the time the president's plane lifted off, they would be waiting, up in the wild blue yonder. Security surrounding the president was much tighter than the average citizen knew.

But in this case, it wouldn't be tight enough.

* * *

"Max, I've decided to back a flat tax," President Hutton startled his chief of staff. "Or if someone can show me that a user tax would be fairer, then I'll back that legislation. But the IRS, as presently structured, has to go."

Max sat down in front of the president's desk in the Oval Office. "What percentage rate, Dick?"

"Ten percent."

The chief of staff shook his head. "You've seen the figures, Dick. That isn't enough by at least five percent."

"It will be if we do away with several departments. And I plan to back that, too. I'm going to discuss it with Congressman Williams. As a matter of fact, advise the Secret Service that I've decided to spend my entire vacation in North Arkansas. Max, you fly down today and rent me a house on the lake."

Max sat for a moment, stunned. "Dick, this is going to send the Secret Service into a tailspin. They spent weeks setting up your vacation spot. They—"

The president waved that aside. "The service is accustomed to sudden changes in plans. As a matter of fact, Max, you and Honey go on down there together and get yourselves settled in." Honey was Max's wife's nickname. "You can meet me in Little Rock for the fund-raiser and we'll fly back together. Arrange for a meeting with Congressman Madison. This damned partisan politics has got to stop. We've got to move this country along and for once do what is best for the majority of the people instead of kowtowing to special interest groups and . . . ," he paused and smiled, "others," he added.

Max leaned back in his chair and smiled at his longtime friend. "You're going to break with party philosophy, Dick."

"Can't be helped. Our party has got to face reality.

This nation cannot continue to try to be all things to all people all the time. We've almost bankrupted ourselves attempting to do that. It has to stop."

"The Coyote Network is going to love this."

Dick frowned. "It'll be the first damn thing I've done that they love. Get to it, Max."

Max rose from the chair. "On my way." He looked at his friend for a few seconds. "This just might get you reelected, Dick."

The president shook his head. "Whether it does or not suddenly doesn't matter much to me, Max. And that is the truth. For once I'm going to toss party politics right out the window and do what is right. And that feels good."

"I'll call you from Arkansas."

"I'll be right here."

"Three bus loads of folks just rolled in from Little Rock and Memphis," Chief Monroe told Sheriff Salter.

"Don't tell me, Russ. Let me guess. Willie Washington's bunch."

"Mohammed Abudu X."

"Yeah. Right. Where the hell are they all staying?"

"They're all camped out and in and around Mohammed's house. I drove out there. Looks like squatter city. You know his daddy left him that three hundred acres west of town."

"Russ, that land butts up against Bubba Bordelon's place!"

"Yeah, I know that, too."

"Bubba is not going to like that."

The chief spread his hands in a gesture of helplessness. "I can't do anything about it, Don, and neither can you. What really bothers me is what will happen when they all gather to march. My informants tell me they're going to gather in the town square and then march out to where the Speaker is staying. And it's going to be coordinated while Congressman Williams and wife are there. And the president of the United States."

"I don't even like to think about it, Russ."

"Way I see it, we got one hope: they'll all get to quarrelin' among themselves, callin' each other names, and all get to fightin' before they reach the lake, and we can move in and arrest ever' damn one of them and put them in jail."

"What jail, Russ? My jail's got a big hole in the wall. I've still got to get plumbers and electricians in."

The chief shook his head. "I got that figured out, too. We'll use the high school football stadium."

Don nodded his head slowly. "That'll work. Yeah. *If* they start fighting."

"Oh, they'll do that, Don. Think about it. We're gonna have the Klan marchin' along with the Back to Africa movement marchin' side by side with the Hitler worshippers and the skinheads and God only knows who else." The older man had a wistful expression on his face. "I wish we could get them armed so's they could maybe all kill each other."

"Russ!"

"Just a thought, Don. Just a thought." He smiled. "You all set for the big party tonight?"

"As set as I'll ever be. You're not going?"

"No. I've got every man I can find on duty tonight. Town council's gonna hit the roof when I hand them the bill for all this. But it can't be helped."

Don looked at his watch. "I guess I'd better get going. Wish me luck."

"Wish us all luck," the chief replied somberly.

* * *

"Let them fancy-pants people have their party," Vic

told his followers. "We don't do nothin' until the march."

"Hell, Vic," Tom Devers said. "What can we do? The feds got us covered like a blanket."

"Yeah," Sam Evans said. "We're bein' watched right now!"

"Piss on 'em," Vic said. "What I want to know is who put that damn machine gun in my arsenal? Somebody pulled a switch, and I want to know who done it."

"You mean you really didn't know it was there?" Noble Osgood asked.

"Hell, no, I didn't know! We got twenty Colt AR-15s in the gun room; they all look alike 'ceptin' for the selector switch. Hell, I don't inspect each one ever' damn day. It's been two/three months since we been out shootin'. Somebody switched one deliberate, tryin' to get us in trouble." Vic's expression turned deadly serious. He eyeballed each member of his Aryan Nations group. "Boys, we got us a traitor in our midst."

That caused everyone's lower orifice to pucker up in shock. A traitor? That was unthinkable.

"I don't believe it, Vic," David Jackson said. "We all been knowin' each other for years. More'un likely some damn fed slipped in here whilst you was away and planted that gun."

The others agreed with that.

"Maybe you're right, Dave," Vic said, after a moment's thought. "Yeah. I guess you are, at that. All right, boys, let's talk about this march. We've got a lot of planning to do."

"Brothers and sisters of the sun," Mohammed Abudu X said to the group of a hundred or so gathered in the old family barn, which was over fifty years old and not in real good shape. "The day of decision is nearly upon us. We must plan carefully . . ."

"Don't take no shit from no honky!" someone in the crowd hollered.

"Well, that, too," Abudu agreed.

"Damn right," said a woman who was dressed more or less as Nefertiti might have appeared after a hearty romp in the sack with Akhenaton. "Screw a bunch of ofays."

The elder Washington, who had driven up from Little Rock with his wife to see what their youngest and, in his opinion, their dumbest son was up to now, shook his head and walked back to the house he had left years before. Mr. Washington, who had recently retired after forty years with the railroad and farming in his spare time, told his wife, "Pack up, Ophelia. We're gettin' the hell gone."

"We just got here!"

"Well, we're leavin' again. That foolish boy of ours is gonna get his gimlet ass kicked plumb up between his shoulder blades, and I don't want to be around to have to bail him out of jail . . . again. I've never seen such a bunch of screwballs all gathered together in one place in my life. I feel like I'm on a Hollywood set of the remake of Cleopatra."

His wife ducked her head to hide a quick smile. But when she looked up, her expression was sober. "There's going to be trouble here, isn't there, Clarence?"

"Yeah. And I don't want to be anywhere near when it blows." He shook his head. "I should have never given this land to William. I had it leased out and we were making a nice profit. But no. William wanted it. I thought he was going to farm it. Instead he turns it into a home for wanna-be King Farouks. Let's go, Ophelia."

The front door to the old farmhouse opened, and

a young man stood there, dressed in brightly colored robes. "I arrived late," he said. "Can you tell me where I can find Abudu X?"

The elder Washington frowned, then slowly nodded his gray head. "Yeah, I can, boy. You go back to the highway, turn east, and start walkin'. It's about sixteen thousand miles."

"I beg your pardon, sir?"

"It's called the continent of Africa, boy. And this ain't it!"

Twenty

Stormy and Barry had changed out of their party clothes and into jeans and were sitting on Barry's porch. Stormy reached over and took his hand.

"You're disappointed that Ravenna didn't pull something at the party tonight, aren't you?"

"Not disappointed. But I was sure he'd do something. I wish I could get into his mind."

"That would be like taking a stroll through hell," Stormy said. She shuddered, then cut her eyes to him in the darkness. The night was surprisingly cool, with very low humidity. "Barry? Do you believe in the Hereafter?"

"Oh, yes."

"Heaven and hell?"

"Yes. But not as the preachers describe those places."

She waited; finally stirred impatiently. "Well?"

"I believe there are levels of rewards and levels of punishment. I also believe that when the day of judgement comes, there are going to be a lot of very disappointed people. I heard a preacher say one time that heaven is going to be a very sparsely populated place."

"And you, Barry?"

"Me, what?"

"Heaven or hell?"

Barry smiled in the darkness. "None of us knows that, Stormy. For a mortal, I would think that a person would want to spend eternity with close family members, all the pets he or she has owned and loved over the years, good friends."

"And for an immortal?" Stormy asked softly.

"Peace, I think. Rest." He chuckled. "Could you get along with all the women I've known in the past, Stormy?"

"Ummm," she said. "I think we'd better drop this subject."

Pete and Repeat suddenly sprang to their feet, ears laid back, fangs glistening white in the night, growling low.

"Get in the house, Stormy," Barry said.

"Oh, no need for that." John Ravenna's voice came out of the gloom. "I'm not here to cause trouble. Just to talk. May I open the gate and take a seat on the porch, cousin?"

"Come on, John. But let me put the dogs up before you do. Once you're seated they'll settle down. I don't think they like you very much."

"So much for a dog's ability to judge character. Oh, all right. Put those hounds away. I can wait." He laughed softly. "I've had years of practice."

The dogs in the house, and told to calm down, Barry stepped back onto the darkened porch. "Come on up, John. Can I get you something to drink?"

"A large glass of water would be nice. I ran all the way over here."

"You ran ten miles?" Stormy blurted.

"As his Other," Barry told her.

"I'll get the water," Stormy said, standing up.

John walked up the steps and took a seat. "You always choose the quaintest places to reside, cousin. I live in a castle."

"You would. Do you commiserate nightly with the ghosts?"

John chuckled. "Would it surprise you if I said yes?"

"Not at all. Did you have anything to do with the bombing of the jail, John?"

"Heavens, no! That was done by some local boobs. Vic Radford's neo-Nazis. They didn't know their leader had already been released. What a pack of nitwits."

"That's one thing we can agree on."

"Surprised that I didn't turn up at Roche's party this evening, cousin?"

"Actually, yes. You must have been tired after killing that local the other day."

Barry felt Ravenna's eyes on him. "What local, Vlad?"

"Oh, come on, John. The man was ripped to shreds. I've seen your work before."

Ravenna was silent for a time. "I haven't killed anyone in this area, Vlad. I have been leading those silly federal agents on several wild goose hunts, for my own entertainment, but I have killed no one."

"Then . . . ?"

Stormy opened the front door and stepped out onto the porch, a large glass of ice water in her hand.

"Cousin," Ravenna said slowly, "I think we have another cousin in the area." John stood up and took the glass of water. "Thank you, dear. You're very kind." He drank deeply, wiped his mouth with a handkerchief from his pocket, and said, "I gather you know all about me, Ms. Knight?"

"I know only what Barry has told me."

"Ah! Well, I suppose that is quite enough. Please, sit down. Let's be comfortable. We have much to discuss."

The phone rang, and Barry left the porch to answer it. He was back in a moment and took his chair. "That was Sheriff Salter. The body that was found was not a local. It's been identified as an escaped prisoner from an Arkansas penal institution. The hair samples came from a large panther . . ." Barry smiled. "The scientists agree that the hair samples came from a species that has been extinct for thousands of years. They are on their way here to investigate. The first team will arrive in the morning, others to follow from various university anthropology departments."

"Shit!" Ravenna swore softly.

Barry again smiled. "What's the matter, John?"

"Don't try to be funny, Vlad. You know very well what's the matter. Jacques Cornet."

Barry chuckled. "Ah, yes. Dear Jacques. I haven't seen him since 1917. He doesn't like you very much, does he, John?"

"Am I missing something here?" Stormy asked, looking from Ravenna to Barry. "Who is Jacques Cornet?"

Both men were silent for a moment. Barry glanced at Stormy and said, "Jacques is an immortal. You probably gathered that much. Jacques has been on the side of the law for centuries . . ."

John Ravenna muttered an obscenity under his breath.

"He's also been after John. Back in the thirteenth century, John picked the wrong side in a fight: he chose the English over King Philip Augustus. Augustus won, and John had to flee to England. Then, during the Hundred Years' War, John again chose the English side and ultimately lost. A few years later, John was hired to kill Charles VII. He failed, and Jacques has been after him ever since."

"Charles VII," Stormy muttered. "That was . . ."

"He was crowned July 17, 1429."

Stormy leaned forward, her expression incredulous. She stared at Ravenna. "Jacques Cornet has been chasing you for over five hundred years!"

"More or less. He's persistent, if nothing else," John grumbled. "Vlad, this man that Jacques killed . . . he was in prison for doing what?"

"Murder, among other things."

"Is that all? Well, still, Jacques would have no way of knowing that. Jacques may have been in his Other and overheard some mumblings from this miscreant. Knowing how he feels about law and order, he killed him."

Barry was not at all convinced of that. Jacques had never been entirely stable. Really, the only difference between John Ravenna and Jacques Cornet was that Ravenna would kill anyone for money and Jacques had roamed the world for centuries, killing anyone he perceived to be a criminal . . . whenever the mood struck him.

"Don't you agree, cousin?" Ravenna pressed.

"I don't know. I do know this area is certainly getting crowded."

"Yes, it is. Why don't you leave and reduce the population?"

"Oh, I think I'll stick around for a while longer. John, what did you want to talk about? You didn't run all the way out here just for exercise."

John finished his water and set the empty glass down carefully on a low wicker table. "Your adopted country is falling apart, Vlad."

"I certainly won't disagree with that."

"It won't be long—perhaps only a few years—before men like me will be in great demand."

"Maybe."

"Oh, come on, Vlad. You know I'm speaking the truth. This nation has had it. It's fragmenting, breaking up, coming apart at the seams. Armed groups representing this, that, and the other thing are forming in every state. Hundreds of thousands of people are stockpiling food and guns and ammunition. Race relations are worse than they've been since the civil rights movement of the 1960s. Morals and values have reached an all-time low. There is nothing but rot and drivel on television. For the most part, Hollywood is cranking out mindless slop. People are killing each other over a pair of tennis shoes or a jacket. Drive-by shootings are commonplace; drug abuse is up. Have you noticed any of which I speak, Vlad?" The last was said with a great deal of sarcasm.

Barry ignored the derision and said, "Get to the point, John."

"Pick a side, cousin. The war is coming."

Barry did not reply, but he agreed with the assassin. The United States of America was facing open revolt if the politicians did not get off the backs of its citizens, and do so damn quickly. Actually, everything that Ravenna had said was true. It was only a matter of time before a few armed citizens got angry enough to start shooting. And as with all revolutions, it only took a spark to start it.

Ravenna rose to his feet. He looked down at Barry. "Think about it, cousin. And think about Crazy Jacques while you're at it. With him in the area, we both have something to worry about."

"If it is Jacques."

"Cousin, you are the eternal optimist. You know it's Jacques. The man is insane and you're fully aware of that. You're also well aware that while he hates me, he isn't exactly filled with love for you."

Sitting in his chair in the darkness of the porch, Barry slowly nodded in agreement. Jacques' dislike for Barry went back more than two centuries, back to the

American colonies' fight for independence. Jacques had wanted to hang a young British soldier who had been captured by Washington's troops, a boy, really, about sixteen years old. Barry had spoken on the boy's behalf and the lad had been spared the noose. Then, during the Indian wars on the American frontier, Barry had again gone against Jacques' wishes, successfully arguing to spare the life of a young Cheyenne boy. Jacques had disliked Barry ever since.

"And you are suggesting what, John?" Barry asked.

"That in dealing with Jacques, we work together. It's to our mutual benefit."

Barry had to admit that was certainly true. The thought of Jacques Cornet padding around as his Other, killing whenever the mood struck him, was disconcerting. "I'll think about it," he told John.

"Well, that's something," John said. "If this trend continues, think of the progress we might make during the next thousand years." The last was said with no small amount of sarcasm.

Barry looked up. But Ravenna was gone, having shape-changed into his Other and blended silently into the night.

"Mr. Washington stopped by to see me before he and Ophelia pulled out for home," Chief Monroe told Sheriff Salter and federal agents Van Brocklen and Robbins as they sat at a table in Nellie's Cafe. "Told me he and his wife raised seven kids. Six successes and one idiot. Said if we have to put Willie in jail, don't call him to go his bail."

"You knew this man well?" Van Brocklen asked.

"All his life. One of the finest men I ever knew, and you won't hear me say that about many black folks.

Even Jim Beal would sell Mr. Washington supplies . . . on the QT, of course."

"Why are there no minorities in this area?" Robbins asked.

"Klan ran them out. That was, oh, hell, ninety years ago, I guess. Maybe longer. Those that didn't leave were hanged. Just east of town, 'bout three miles, to the south of the highway, there is a large hill with a stand of timber. That used to be known as Ku Klux Hill. That's where the hangin's took place. Over the years people have forgotten about that. All of the people who took part in the hangin's are dead. Includin' my father."

"Your father was a member of the Klan?" Van Brocklen asked.

"Yes. So was I until I was about thirty years old," the chief admitted. "But when this local bunch got all involved in the American Nazi movement and all sorts of weird-assed other philosophies, I got out. I ran for chief of police the next year and won, and I've been chief of police ever since. The Klan walks very light around me."

"There is still an active chapter here?" Van Brocklen asked, surprise in his voice.

Chief Monroe smiled. "You betcha there is. But they, like so many other antigovernment resistance groups, went hard underground. *Posse comitatus* is very strong around here. But they went deep underground after Gordon Kahl was killed. The posse is stronger than ever."

"How come you never told us any of this?" Van Brocklen asked.

"None of you boys ever asked me."

"Why were the blacks run out of this area?" Robbins asked. "Or hanged," he added.

"According to my daddy, it all started with a robbery and a killing. That much is documented. A young colored fellow got himself all juiced up on Sweet Lucy one evenin' and decided to rob a store. Durin' the robbery, the owner of the store, a white man, was killed. As the colored fellow was runnin' out the store, the constable showed up, and the two of them exchanged shots. The constable was killed. The young colored fellow ran down into colored town and hid in his mother's house." Chief Monroe shook his head. "From this point on, it gets a little vague. I don't think there is anyone alive today who really knows the truth. I sure as hell don't. I do know that my father was involved in it. He told me so. My daddy was an older man when I was born. He's been dead fifty years. He was born about 1880." The chief finished his glass of iced tea and waved to the waitress for a refill.

When the waitress had come and gone, Chief Monroe said, "Well, it didn't take long for the Klan to get cranked up that night. I have a suspicion they'd been waiting for something like this to happen. They rode their horses down to where the young colored fellow was holed up and demanded his mother turn him over. She refused and they shot her. Right there on her front porch. Killed her. That much is, again, documented. What happened next may or may not be what really occurred. The masked riders pulled the colored fellow out of the house and hanged him. Right then and there. There was a riot. I don't know who started it, and there is no one living who does, but colored town was burned to the ground. Every building destroyed. There were a lot of colored folks killed. Men and women, and I suspect, some kids, too. Those that didn't leave that night were hunted down and hanged, right out there on Ku

Klux Hill. The next day, folks went out there and cut down the bodies and burned them. By the time word got to the governor about what happened and he sent people in here—you have to understand there were no telephones back then, and it probably took weeks or months for the governor to learn of it—there was not a trace left of colored town. What was left of the charred buildin's had all been removed and the ground worked clean, usin' mule teams and road scrapers. My daddy said there wasn't a board or a nail left. The governor's people looked around, talked to some people, and went back home, and that was the end of it. The Washington family lived way out in the country and wasn't involved in it in any way. Course, like me, Willie's father wasn't born when it happened. We've never talked about it."

"I wonder why the relatives of some of the survivors haven't come forward with this story?" Van Brocklen mused aloud. "Survivors of other similar incidents have come forward."

Chief Monroe shrugged his shoulders. "Stories fade with time. None of the original survivors who could remember it would be alive. Their kids would be at least fifteen or twenty years older than me, and more than likely dead. Hell, the survivors scattered to the wind after that night and were probably afraid to talk about it."

One of Don's deputies walked into the cafe, looked around, and spotted the sheriff. He quickly walked over to the table. "Sheriff, Chief, gentlemen."

"You want to sit down and have something to drink, Mark?" Don asked.

"No, sir." He squatted down and whispered, "Another body was found about an hour ago, Sheriff. Scattered all over the place. It's in worse shape than that escaped convict's body. Although I can't imagine how that could possibly be."

Don cursed under his breath for a few seconds. "Where?"

"On the north end of Bubba Bordelon's farm. Bubba's hired man found it. He's pretty shook up. Had to call for the EMTs to come out."

"The coroner been notified?"

"Not yet."

Don nodded and reached for his hat, then looked at the feds. "You boys coming along?"

"We'll follow you, Sheriff."

"I'll be going to the house for a few minutes first." Don glanced at the deputy. "Get in touch with Mr. Hardesty and his hounds. We're going tracking and tree this damn animal. Tell Hardesty we're going to stay out until we find this . . . whatever the hell it is. Tell Steve to take over until I get back. Tell Jess and Davy to get their rifles and pack some food and water for each man—enough for a twenty-four-hour period. Hiking boots and extra socks. Go!"

Bureau and Secret Service stood up; Bureau said, "We'll head back to the motel and change clothes. Meet you . . . where, Don?"

"City limits sign. North end of town by the supermarket."

"We'll be there."

In his car, Don used his car phone to call Barry and bring him up to date. "I want you with us, Barry. I think you know what's going on here."

"Yes, I do. But who would believe me?"

"Well, we're about to find out. No press on this, Barry."

"Stormy and Ki are gone. Meeting with the Speaker later on today. I'll leave a note telling them I'm helping you on a case."

"I'll see you in a few minutes."

"Ten-four, as you professionals say," Barry replied.

Don hung up before the urge to tell Barry what he could do with his sarcasm became too great.

Twenty-one

"This is Phil Unger," Don said, kneeling down by the body. "Or what's left of him. See the tattoo on his left arm?"

"Where is his other arm?" Inspector Van Brocklen asked.

"We haven't found that yet," a deputy said. "But we did find his guts. They're over yonder, about fifty yards, under that tree." He pointed.

"This is a damn shame and a disgrace!" Bubba Bordelon hollered, waving his arms. "I'm gettin' the boys together."

"You do and I'll put you all in jail, Bubba," Don told him. "I don't want you nitwits wandering around shooting at everything that moves."

"*Nitwits!*" Bubba squalled. "Who you callin' a nitwit, you nigger-lovin' son of a bitch!"

Don stood up quickly and faced the Klan leader. "Bubba, you better put a zipper on that mouth of yours and close it up tight."

"This is my property, Salter! All bought and paid for and legal. You can't tell me what to do on my own property. Phil was my friend, and by God I'm gonna avenge him."

"Go back to your house, Bubba," Don told him. "Stay out of the way."

Bubba stalked off, muttering threats and obscenities.

"Is he dangerous?" Agent Robbins asked. "We have only a very sketchy outline on Bordelon."

"So far, he and his bunch are all mouth," Don told the Secret Service man. "But I've always believed he has the potential to turn violent. He's worth keeping an eye on." Don looked up at Barry. "What about this, Barry?" He pointed to the mangled body.

"Don't touch anything!" The shout came from the middle of the pasture. "Get away from there before you destroy the tracks."

All heads turned. A half dozen men and women were trooping across the pasture, doing their best to keep from stepping in the cow patties that littered the field.

"What the hell . . . ?" Inspector Van Brocklen muttered.

"I think your archaeologists and animal behavioralists and what have you have arrived," Barry said.

"Wonderful," Don said. "They have such great timing."

A man about five and a half feet tall and about five and a half feet wide huffed to the group of lawmen. "I'm Dr. Waller," he announced, wiping his face with a large purple bandanna. "From the university. These distinguished ladies and gentlemen with me are the leading experts in our field. They've flown in from various institutions of higher learning all over the United States. From left to right, Doctors Thomas Dekerlegand, Harris Ramsey, Irene Biegelsack, Gladys Dortch, Inez Hopper."

"A pleasure, I'm sure," Don said with a long sigh. "I think," he said under his breath, frowning at Barry's ill-concealed smirk.

"My word!" Dr. Irene Biegelsack blurted, getting her first good look at the body of Phil Unger. "Would you look at that!"

All the Ph.D. types suddenly wanted to crowd closer to the body. Sheriff's deputies held them back.

"Let us finish our work first, ladies and gentlemen," Don told the group, all of them very ample in size. "Then you may make your examination."

"I can tell you from the size and depth of those bites, this was not done by any ordinary panther," Dr. Ramsey said. "And look at those paw tracks. This animal weighs two hundred and fifty pounds, at least."

"Could we possibly have a mutant here?" Dr. Dortch questioned.

"Oh, quite," Dr. Hopper said.

"Marvelous!" Dr. Waller cried.

"Wonderful!" Dr. Biegelsack clapped her hands.

"Oh, shit!" Sheriff Salter muttered.

After the pictures were taken and the deputies concluded their immediate examination, Don left two deputies with the body and walked to the center of the pasture to meet with Mr. Hardesty and his tracking dogs. Just before he left the crime scene, he overheard the Ph.D. types' conversation:

"Definitely caught somewhere in the evolutionary chain."

"Oh, definitely."

"Not a saber-tooth, but not yet evolved to the present panther form."

"Quite right."

"I'm thrilled at this find."

"I'm absolutely ecstatic."

"What world do these people live in?" Don asked Agent Robbins.

"The very tight little world of academia," the Secret Service man replied.

"What the hell language are they speaking?" a deputy asked.

Before anyone could reply, they all looked up at the rattle of several trucks pulling up to the fence line.

"What the hell . . . ?" Don said.

"Rental trucks," Inspector Van Brocklen said, as about a dozen young men and women began pouring out of the vehicles and dropping the tailgates.

"Those are our assistants," Dr. Waller said. "They're bringing in our supplies for an extended stay. Also the capture equipment."

"Capture!" Don blurted.

Dr. Waller looked very offended. "Certainly. What were your plans?"

"To kill the goddamn thing!"

"Barbarian!" Dr. Biegelsack shrieked.

"Unthinkable!" Dr. Dekerlegand wailed.

"Call the president!" Dr. Hopper yelled. "The animal must be taken alive."

"What president?" Don asked.

"The president of the United States, of course, you ninny!" Dr. Hopper said indignantly. "We were classmates. He'll put a stop to your primitive urgings."

Barry had backed away from the main group, standing off to one side with a smile on his face.

Van Brocklen looked heavenward. "Just think," he muttered. "All I ever wanted to do was be a cop in Philadelphia like my daddy."

"Call Jacques Cousteau!" Dr. Ramsey yelled.

"Call Marlin Perkins!" Dr. Dortch hollered.

Don shook his head in disbelief and walked off to meet with Hardesty and his dogs.

"Who the hell's all them people?" Hardesty asked.

"Scientists."

"You don't say. What are they scientistin' 'round here?"

"Animal behavior, more or less."

"Hell, we got both kinds in this part of the state."

"What do you mean?"

"Two-legged and four-legged. Have they seen Vic Radford yet?"

Don chuckled. "Your dogs rested and ready to go?"

"They're ready. What are we after, Sheriff?"

"A panther."

"No kidding! Have you kept people away from the tracks?"

"As much as we could. Come on. And ignore whatever the scientists have to say."

"Hell, I wouldn't know what they was talkin' about no ways."

Don waved at Barry and the two deputies, Jess and Davy, who would go with him, and the men gathered around the sheriff and the dog handler. The deputies both carried 30-.06 rifles in addition to their side arms. Each had two canteens of water attached to a military-style web waist belt, and each carried a small packet of food. Don strapped on his own gear just as agents Robbins and Van Brocklen joined the group.

Don glanced over at Barry. The man carried neither water nor food and was weaponless. "You're traveling light, Barry. Where is the food and water I gave you?"

"I won't need it."

"Why?" Robbins asked.

"We won't be out here that long."

"You seem damn sure of that, Cantrell," Van Brocklen challenged.

"Just a hunch," Barry replied evenly.

"Your dogs got the scent, Mr. Hardesty?" Don asked.

"They got it."

"Is everybody ready?"

"Sheriff, all them kids with nets and such is right behind us," Hardesty pointed out. "All they got's them tranquilizer guns. And from lookin' at these here tracks, I got to say this is a big son of a bitch we're after, and a mean one. This cat's tasted human blood. He'll prob'ly attack without no warnin'."

He's been doing that for hundreds of years, Barry thought. But he won't attack us unless he's cornered. That is, unless Jacques has gone completely around the bend.

"They were warned to stay back," Don said. "I'm on record as advising them to stand clear. I won't nursemaid them. Turn your dogs loose, Mr. Hardesty."

"You don't say?" Congressman Madison said, after the aide had interrupted the meeting with Stormy and whispered in his ear. "Lots of excitement around here."

Ki had cut the camera at Stormy's signal.

"What's going on, sir?" Stormy asked. "If I might ask."

"Some sort of wild animal attack outside of town. A man has been killed. The sheriff has called for tracking dogs and is out there now. It should be wrapped up quickly."

Don't bet on that, read the silent glances that passed between Stormy and Ki.

Twenty-two

The hounds took off with a bay of excited voices and soon were out of sight. Hardesty, although far from being a young man, loped effortlessly behind them. The other, followed in a fast walk.

"When the baying changes," Don told the federal men, not knowing if they had ever been a part of anything like this, "we'll know the hounds have something."

"We've done this before," Van Brocklen told him.

"Just checking."

"But it's been a while for me," Robbins admitted.

Conversation stopped as the men concentrated on maintaining a fast walk through rough terrain. After only a few minutes, the baying of the hounds changed.

"Listen!" Van Brocklen said.

"I heard it," Don replied. "That's MacFarlane Road just up ahead."

It took fifteen minutes for the men to cover the distance, and by that time, the baying had stopped altogether.

The lawmen emerged out of the brush on a wide gravel road. Hardesty stood by the road, his dogs back on leashes.

"What the hell . . . ?" Don asked him.

"They lost the scent," Hardesty told him. "Right over there on that turnaround." He pointed across the gravel. "I worked the dogs in a wide circle, but they came back to that spot. Judging from the tire tracks, your big cat got in a car and drove off."

"Somebody trained a cat to do this?" Davy asked.

"Not no cat like this," Hardesty said. "I been trackin' in ever' state that has panthers and pumas. I ain't never seen no cat the size of this one. This son of a bitch will weigh a good two hundred twenty-five, two hundred fifty pounds. You sure we ain't after a jaguar that got a-loose?"

"Not according to the scientists," Don said, getting up from a squat and reaching for his walkie-talkie. He keyed the mike. "This is the sheriff. I'm at MacFarlane Road, just to the north of that burned-out old farmhouse. I want a team up here to take some plaster of tire tracks ASAP. We'll secure the area."

The scientists' assistants, students on their summer break, came panting up with their nets and tranquilizer guns and sized up the scene immediately. One of them lifted a handy-talkie and said, "The cat got away," while the other young people cheered.

"I swear to God," Hardesty said, slowly shaking his head. "Young people nowadays ain't got sense enough to pour piss out of a boot." He looked at Don. "You done with me, Sheriff?"

"If you're sure the scent is gone and not retrievable."

"I'm sure."

"Send your bill to my office."

"I'll shore do that, Sheriff. I'll just follow this road a bit and then cut crost-country to my truck. See you fellers."

Deputies Davy and Jess were busy keeping the scientists' assistants out of the turnaround while Barry stood aside with the two feds and the sheriff.

"All right, Barry," Don spoke in low tones. "What's going on here?"

Barry shrugged his shoulders. "You're not going to believe me."

"Try us."

"You're chasing a shape-shifter . . ."

"Oh, shit!" Inspector Van Brocklen muttered. "More hocus-pocus."

Agent Robbins said nothing, just stood and stared at Barry, a puzzled look on his face.

"Go on," Don urged.

"His name is Jacques Cornet. He hates criminals. He's been killing them for centuries. He's . . . well, not entirely sane. He also hates John Ravenna and isn't real fond of me."

"Ah . . ." Agent Robbins was the first to speak, after he cleared his throat. "How old is this, ah, person?"

"Oh, about the same age as John, I suppose."

"And that would make him . . . ?"

"About a thousand years old."

Both federal agents sighed heavily with very pained expressions on their faces. "I had to ask," Robbins muttered.

Van Brocklen lifted his walkie-talkie at a burst of sound. "Go."

"That info you wanted on that, ah, certain subject, Inspector? The military records back to the Indian wars?"

"Yes."

"It came back. Just like the man said."

"Okay. We came up dry on the cat hunt. I'll be in shortly." He turned to face Barry. "Sergeant Billy Wilson?"

"I was, at one point in my life, yes."

"Sergeant William Shipman?"

"During the Second World War, yes."

"Ranger Sergeant Dan Gibson?"

"During the Vietnam War, yes."

"Son of a bitch!" Van Brocklen swore softly. "This is f'ing incredible." Then his eyes narrowed. "If any of it's true, that is."

"It's true. I've leveled with you all the way. I'll do whatever I can to stop these planned assassinations."

"And then . . . ?" Agent Robbins asked.

"I want to be free to go my own way. I want the government to stop hunting me. I'm tired of being human prey."

"I don't know if I can guarantee that," Van Brocklen said.

"But you can try."

"Yes. I can try."

Barry smiled and nodded. "That's good enough for me. I used to have a friend back during the First World War who was from Missouri. One of his favorite sayings was 'try his best' was all a mule could do."

"Whatever happened to your friend?" Robbins asked.

"He became president of the United States. His name was Harry Truman."

Barry returned to the motel with the federal agents to give depositions about himself, John Ravenna and Jacques Cornet, and to call Stormy and Ki for their corroboration of what they knew of his story. Sheriff Salter went with them, after trying to dissuade the scientists and their assistants from staying on the property adjoining Bubba's farm, but to no avail—not even after Bubba told them if he caught any of them on his property he'd take a shotgun to them.

"Cretinous oaf!" Dr. Biegelsack told the Klan leader.

"Fuck you!" Bubba retorted.

"It is my opinion that people who must sprinkle their conversations with the vilest of profanity possess very limited intelligence," Dr. Dekerlegand told the man.

"Thank you," Bubba replied.

"Imbecile!" Dekerlegand muttered.

By the time the feds got back to their motel, they had another surprise waiting for them.

"The president has decided to come into Little Rock early," a Secret Service agent informed Chet Robbins. "This afternoon."

"What? What the hell for?" Chet hollered the question. "The fund-raising dinner is several days off."

"The candidate got sick and the fund-raiser was called off."

"What's the matter with him?"

"Chicken pox."

"Oh, shit!" Robbins and Van Brocklen said as one voice.

"I suppose," Van Brocklen said to the agent, "that now you are going to tell me the president is coming up here earlier than scheduled?"

"He'll be here tomorrow afternoon. The first lady is coming in the next day. She and a college friend are going to do some sight-seeing in Little Rock for a day."

"What the hell is there to see in Little Rock?" Van Brocklen questioned. "A statue of Orval Faubus?"

Chet Robbins turned to Barry. "We'll take your deposition tomorrow, Barry. We're going to be jumping through hoops here for the next twenty-four hours."

"You know where to find me."

Barry met Stormy and Ki in the driveway of the motel, and the three of them returned to Barry's house. Seated in the coolness of the living room, Barry told them about the president's early arrival.

"Seems to me that the president is ignoring his security by coming up here at all," Ki remarked.

"Nothing has happened that directly affects him," Stormy said.

"Yet," Barry corrected.

"Jim has turned into an old woman," Beal's second in command, Nate Williams, told a gathering of the AFB. "Now is the time to start the second revolution. But all he can do is shake his head and say no."

Seventy-five out of the AFB's two hundred and fifty members had gathered at Nate's summons. Seventy-five men and women who felt that the time had come to strike, to stand up and show their discontent with the U.S. government.

"How far are you talkin' about us takin' this, Nate?" Clyde Mayfield asked.

"Marching," Nate responded. No one noticed the ugly gleam in the man's eyes. "That's all. Just marching in the protest parade that's planned."

Several of the others in the natural amphitheater in the timber exchanged furtive glances and faint smiles at that reply.

"I don't see nothin' wrong with doin' that," Barbara Ashland said.

"Me, neither," her husband, Dick, agreed.

The rest of those present began falling into agreement, nodding their heads or vocalizing their assent.

Nate held up a hand for silence. "One more little matter we've got to agree on, people. I have word that Mohammed Abudu X and his people will be armed and looking for trouble . . ."

"That don't come as no surprise to me," Lenny Ford said.

"Me, neither," his brother, Leo, said.

"And they'll also have supporters scattered along the march route, on both sides of the streets and roads, and they'll be really armed, ready to hand over rifles to Abudu and his people," Nate continued. "So, people, I just can't see us being set up for target practice."

"Black folks will stand out pretty plain in this part of the country," Nolan Wade said. "We can have people close by ready to jump them should they reach for guns."

"They won't be black people," Nate said. "They'll be turncoat whites. People we've called friends and neighbors for years. Government sympathizers."

"How do you know all this, Nate?" Hugh Morgan asked.

"From Jim's own plants in the Justice Department," Nate lied. "I seen the note Jim received, just before he destroyed it. He's holdin' back from us. And that ought to tell you all something about Beal."

"I never did trust that son of a bitch," Conrad Hastings said.

"Me, neither," Leon Moore said.

Others in the room began nodding in agreement. Tish Thompson said, "I told you all last year Jim was turnin' soft, didn't I?"

"That's right, Tish," her friend, Helen Wheeler, said. "You sure did."

"I 'member that, now," Roy Blanchard said. "We should have paid attention to you then."

"So what are we gonna do, Nate?" Stephen Smith asked.

"Several things. First of all, play it real close to the vest," Nate replied, his eyes burning with a hot fever.

"Jim must never know that we've met. Secondly, when you get home, pick out your favorite pistol and clean it up good—preferably a semiauto. When we gather to march, wear loose clothing and have the pistol hidden under your clothing. Have plenty of spare ammo, for when the nigras start their violence—and we all know that's what they're going to do—we've got to be ready to defend our loved ones and country."

"Damn right!" George Rogers said, considerable heat behind his words.

Mimi Fowler said, "I got me a feelin' that there's more to this than you're tellin' us, Nate. What are you holdin' back?"

Nate took a deep breath. Now for the big lie. This one would either tear his breakaway group apart or weld them solidly together as one like-minded unit. "Jim Beal has been meetin' secretly with Wesley Parren. I been followin' them to their meetin' place out in Nolan's Woods. I don't have to tell none of you what that means. And the third party meetin' with them is that new man in town, Barry Cantrell."

"I knew it!" Lester Crowson almost yelled the words. "I told y'all when that son of a bitch come to town he was a government plant. Now, didn't I tell you he was?"

After the babble of angry voices had died down, Nate said, "Yes, you did, Les. You did for a fact. And I want to take this opportunity right now to apologize to you for not heedin' your words. I was wrong and you were right."

"Takes a big man to admit something like that, Nate," Jeanne Masters said.

"Damn sure does," Albert Simpson said.

"Aw," Les said, grinning and ducking his head. "It wasn't nothin'."

"I believe the time has come for us to stand up and be counted," Wilfred Wilkes said, rising to his feet.

Wilfred was the pastor of the Hand of the Lord Non-Denominational Church of the Hills. Most of those present attended his services. Wilfred was also the chaplain of the AFB. Prior to his getting the "Call" and feeling the hand of the Lord touch his skinny shoulders, Wilfred had run a honky-tonk in the Bootheel of Missouri, with several trailers in the back of the joint where any one of a dozen ladies could be rented for twenty-five dollars a lick, so to speak. Wilfred had married one of the girls after receiving the nod from Above. Sophie was not exactly the quintessential pastor's wife, possessing a mouth that once caused four drunken sailors to stand speechless in awe at her ability to sling profanity to the winds.

"What are we goin' to do about all these government cocksuckers in town?" Sophie questioned.

"Now, dear," Wilfred said soothingly.

"Fuck off, baby," Sophie told him. "Read your Bible and let me handle this."

"If they get in the way," Nate said, "they're gonna get hurt. We all know whose side they're on anyway, so what difference does it make?"

"Damn right!" Paul Mullins said, standing up. Several more men stood up with him.

"To the revolution!" Howard Dill shouted.

"To true freedom!" Mary Lou Nichols yelled, dragging her husband, Philip, to his somewhat reluctant feet.

Soon everyone in the clearing was chanting "Revolution!"

Nate stood on a rise of earth and smiled. Now, by God, he thought, he'd show the government a thing or two. And he'd do it in just about forty-eight hours.

Twenty-three

Jim Beal sat for a long time behind his computer in his office. He had received the coded messages from both his deep plants in Washington. The messages alarmed him. The president and first lady were coming here, ahead of schedule, and after a day or so of meetings with Congressman Williams and Congressman Madison, the president was to hold a press conference, during which he would announce some drastic new cuts and a total shift away from liberal democratic dogma.

So why did that fill Jim with such alarm?

He grimaced at the thought. No mystery there. He knew the answer only too well: lately, for whatever reason, there were people within his own AFB who had been secretly (so they thought) advocating open violence against the government. Jim knew who most of them were, and certainly that Nate Williams was the leader of the breakaway bunch. What he didn't know, for sure, was what they were planning. Nate was Congressman Williams' cousin. The two men hadn't spoken in years.

But Jim had seen Nate Williams slowly change over the past few years. And Jim knew where to put the blame for that: the government. There was no one else to blame.

It had all started when a lady bought a souvenir from Nate's wife—or rather, the lady who used to be Nate's wife—at her arts shop in town—or rather, where her arts shop used to be. Liz had a knack for making things out of what nature provided, real pretty things. Several times a week she could be seen wandering the fields and woods, picking up bird feathers, which she would use to make knickknacks and doodads to sell to the tourists. Only problem was, Liz didn't know a parakeet feather from a blue-footed booby. She just picked up pretty feathers and made pretty things with them.

No one knew for sure who turned Liz in to the federal wildlife and fisheries people, or why, but Jim suspected it was a local. Liz was charged, among other things, with possession of feathers from endangered species. Dozens of people came forward, testifying that Liz didn't hunt birds, she just wandered the countryside picking up fallen feathers off the ground. But in the end it didn't do any good. Nate and Liz exhausted their savings fighting the charges, but despite their efforts, Liz had to pay a huge fine and was placed on probation for several years. Then the IRS came down on Nate and wiped them out. Their marriage ended in divorce, and Nate and Liz were ruined financially, including losing their home.

Liz now clerked at a local supermarket, and Nate did handyman jobs wherever he could find them.

And both of them hated the government.

Jim stood up and paced the floor, making up his mind. Damned if he was going to the feds with this. The goddamned feds brought it on themselves, so they could pay the price. As far as Nate was concerned, anyone who worked for the government was the enemy, and while Jim didn't entirely agree with that, he could sure understand why Nate felt that way.

While Jim was mulling over the current state of affairs in his locale, the president of the United States and the first lady were stepping off the plane in Little Rock. Bands played, crowds cheered, and President Hutton and the first lady smiled and waved. Then they were hustled into the president's limo, which had just a few hours before been flown into the area, and were driven off.

Sitting in a comfortable chair in the living room of his rented house by the lake, John Ravenna smiled. It was almost time to earn his pay. And he was certainly looking forward to that.

Mohammed Abudu X and his followers were busy in the barn painting placards and affixing the heavy cardboard to long poles. The slogans read: NO JUSTICE NO PEACE; WEALTH REDISTRIBUTION NOW; AMERICA IS RACIST; SPEAKER MADISON IS A JERK; MORE MONEY FOR WELFARE, LESS FOR THE MILITARY.

No one paid any attention to the half dozen or so men and women who slipped away from the barn and went to a van. There, they removed a side paneling and took out weapons, each person inspecting the guns carefully: pistols, sawed-off pistol-grip shotguns, MAC-10s, and Uzis.

If the march went off according to plans, the day of the parade was going to be very interesting.

Vic Radford had given it much thought before finally reaching a decision; he'd even taken a chance and visited Alex Tarver. Only after the two whackos had discussed the situation at length, the conversation often interspersed with glowing praises of Hitler and the master race, had he reached a decision: the two groups would march together and they would be heavily armed, with friends along the way holding extra weapons and ammo. If the nigras started something—and they were both sure of that happening—it would be foolish not to be prepared for it.

Vic then drove to each member's house and personally told them the plan. No damn way was he going to use a phone, not with the feds covering him like white on rice. His plan was received with enthusiasm; all his people would be ready.

Then Vic thought of Bubba Bordelon. He decided he'd best go talk to Bubba, too. The more people he had on his side, the better off they'd be.

Vic's oldest son, Carl, was home for a visit, just released from jail for inciting to riot during a protest march in Los Angeles, and Carl was ready to do anything his father suggested.

"I'm gonna whup that Willie Washington's ass again, Pa," Carl said.

"Wait 'til the march, son," Vic cautioned him. "You got to be patient."

"Right, Pa."

"Ah, son, I got to ask you a question: them people you got with you, can they be trusted?"

Carl had showed up with a dozen of the most disreputable-looking men and women Vic had ever seen.

"Sure they can, Pa. I was in prison with all the men, and the women is okay, too. The men is part of the Brotherhood."

"The Brotherhood?"

"They don't like niggers."

"Oh. Well . . . they must be all right, then. But they sure are a rough-lookin' bunch, boy."

"Each one of them shanked a coon in the joint," his son replied proudly.

Vic wasn't real sure what that meant, but his son was so proud of it he decided he'd not push the conversation. He'd figure it out later.

"Goddamn right I want to march alongside you, Vic," Bubba was quick to agree to Vic's plan. "I wouldn't miss it for the world."

"Good, Bubba, good. Have your people armed. I'm pretty sure there's gonna be trouble."

"We'll be ready," Bubba said grimly.

"Are we going to march?" Nate Williams asked Jim Beal.

"No, we are not." Jim's reply was quick. "I'm ordering all our people to stay away from the march route."

"Then I reckon it's time for me to take those who agree with me and split from the brigade, Jim. I just can't get through to you that it's time to act."

"You can do what you want to, Nate, but you can't use the Arkansas Freedom Brigade's name."

"We'll come up with our own name. I don't want nothin' to do with you and those pantywaists who follow you."

"I hate to see you do this, Nate. I know what the government put you and Liz through, and you got a right to be pissed off. But now is not the time to do anything stupid. This area is blanketed with feds. You know that."

"I ain't scared of no goddamn fed!"

"I didn't say you were. I just want you to think about whatever it is you're planning. Don't go off half-cocked and do something you'll regret for the rest of your life."

"Life? Life, Jim? What life? The fuckin' feds have ruined me and Liz. We lost everything. Just like Wesley. But Wesley rolled over for them. I wouldn't. And never will. Me and Liz talked it over the other night. We're trying to get back together. We both agreed that if we have to be the ones who die first in this revolution, then so be it. I can't tell you how much I hate this goddamn government. Now, I guess you're going to run and tell the feds everything I just said?"

Jim shook his head. "No, Nate. You know me better than that. Regardless of how you feel now, we were friends for years. I just hope you'll change your mind."

"I won't. Far as I'm concerned, it's now or never. Just stand clear of this march, Jim. For your own good."

"I don't plan on being anywhere near the march route, Nate. And you can count on that."

Nate Williams left Jim's office without another word being spoken.

"Shit!" Jim breathed, slowly shaking his head. "All hell is gonna break loose around here."

"You won't be seeing much of us for the next couple of days," Stormy told Barry over dinner. "We'll be covering the president and first lady and Congressman Madison." She smiled. "But mostly what we'll be doing is waiting."

"I want to be with you when you cover the march," Barry said. "I've got a real bad feeling about that."

"Have you heard when it's going to be?"

"Day after tomorrow. It's going to start about noon. That's the rumor. Nothing firm."

"That's the same thing we heard," Ki said. "But what

can happen, Barry? There are federal agents, local cops, deputies, and state police all over the place."

"A bullet doesn't have a brain, Ki. It doesn't care who it hits. Have either of you noticed that this area is filling up with some hard-looking men and women?"

They both shook their heads.

"I've been driving around, looking the place over. Must be fifty or so new skinheads staying out at Tarver's place, living in tents. About the same number of men and women have pulled into town and are staying with various members of Jim Beal's AFB. But what is odd is that none are staying with Jim or any of his close associates. I think there's been a major split in the ranks. If that's true, then look out, anything is apt to happen. About a hundred men and women are camped out on Bubba Bordelon's farm. Maybe fifty or so staying at Radford's place. To me, that's a dead giveaway that something is about to pop. Or explode might be a better word to use."

"Have you talked with Sheriff Salter about it?" Stormy asked.

"I haven't been able to get through to him. But he's a good lawman; I'm sure he's noticed."

"How about out at the Washington farm?" Ki asked. "Have you been out there?"

"I drove past. It looks as though some new people have arrived." He cut his eyes to Stormy. "Have you been able to interview Mohammed yet?"

"He refuses to grant me an interview. He says the Coyote Network is racist."

"And the guards on the farm are armed with shotguns," Ki added.

Barry arched an eyebrow, but said nothing.

"Have you talked with John since he came out here?" Stormy asked.

"No. And I have no idea where Jacques might be

hiding. But I can tell you both very firmly that I am not going out looking for him. I'll fight John Ravenna if it comes to that . . . although I hope it doesn't. But if Jacques shifts into his Other, I wouldn't have a prayer of coming out unscathed. I've seen what he becomes, and it's truly awesome. There isn't an animal in all of North America that could fight him and win, and that includes any type of bear you might want to name. Jacques' Other is the size of the largest jaguar that ever lived, and five times as vicious. His teeth and claws are prehistoric. His strength is phenomenal, and for his size, his speed is unbelievable. If any of those scientists or their assistants ever get a picture of him, it will rock the scientific community back on their heels."

"So will you, Barry," Ki said.

Barry nodded in agreement. "I have just about resigned myself to that fate, ladies. Regardless of how hard the Bureau tries to work out a deal for me, I don't think the government will agree to it. But I am not looking forward to going public."

"I'm sure the government will be more than happy to work something out that will meet with your satisfaction," Stormy said.

Barry fixed her with a very jaundiced look. "Then you have infinitely more faith in big governments than I do, dear."

Twenty-four

The day before the march dragged by slowly and uneventfully. None of the participants made an appearance anywhere near town. Liz Williams did not report for work, and she did not call in with any sort of explanation for her absence. Every foot of the small county airport was checked out by the Secret Service, the FBI, federal marshals, BATF personnel, state troopers, and county deputies. Every foot of the route that would be taken by the president was walked over and checked out as carefully as time permitted. Locations were picked out for Secret Service sharpshooters to be placed. Residents along the way were checked out all the way back to the moment of conception and interviewed. To the dismay of the feds, many of the residents who lived along the route thought that while President Hutton was a damn sight better than that incompetent prick he replaced, Hutton was still an asshole.

"What this country needs is for Ben Raines to step out of the pages of those books and take over," one resident said. "He'd straighten this damn country out in a hurry."*

*The *Ashes* Series—Zebra Books

"Who?" Chet Robbins asked.

Inspector Van Brocklen said nothing. He just stared off into space and silently cursed. He knew exactly what the citizen was referring to. A couple of years back, the Bureau had been asked to check out the author of the *Ashes* series. They had done so, thoroughly. Much to the disappointment of a number of radical extremist liberals in Washington, elected and appointed, the Bureau could find nothing about the man his political enemies could use to shut him up.

Not that the Bureau would have had anything to do with any attempt to silence a writer, Van Brocklen quickly amended his thoughts. That would have been up to the political party in power at the time. And just how they would have gone about that—if it had occurred—was something Van Brocklen did not care to dwell upon.

It was long after dark when the exhausted teams met back at the motel. They had done all they could do in the short time allotted them. Now it was all in the hands of God, or fate, or luck, or whatever one believed in.

"Hey, gloomy," Stormy said to Barry. "You are really down this evening."

"You're right. I don't recall being this depressed in several hundred years." He tried a smile that almost made it.

Ki had gone back to the motel for some sleep; the next day was going to be a brutal one. Her words. She had no way of knowing at the time just how accurate that statement would prove to be.

"Barry, there are several hundred federal agents in this area. And probably a hundred or more undercover. There are Arkansas State Troopers all over the place, in addition to everybody Chief Monroe and Sheriff Salter could hang a badge on."

"Yes," Barry conceded. "And we've also got John Ravenna here. The feds just won't take me seriously about him. We've got Crazy Jacques Cornet, who has already killed two people—that we know of. Plus we've got about five hundred kooks—that we know of—who hate each other, all getting ready to march. And you can bet they will all be armed. I wish I could just go to sleep for two or three days."

"Well"—Stormy reached over and took his hand— "I can't help you with that deep a sleep, but I might be able to help you sleep for this night."

Barry gently squeezed her hand and smiled. "Oh? What do you have in mind?"

She stood up and tugged him to his feet. "Come on. I'll show you."

"My, my," Barry said. "I just love surprises."

All over the county, those who were to take part in the march were meeting, finalizing plans. With the exception of Abudu X's group, all were checking their weapons one last time. Abudu did not know it, but even many of those who were not a part of the outside agitators had made up their minds to enter the march armed. Some had friends along the way, ready to hand them weapons should the need arise, and all felt it certainly would, here in what they all referred to as redneck country.

Since there was not a motel room to be had in town, the scientists and their young assistants were camping out near the lake. They were restless as they lay in their sleeping bags and blankets, eager to get an early start the next day and track this big cat and capture it. The scientists were sure the cat was some sort of throwback to prehistoric times . . . which it was, sort of. What a find this would be! What a paper they could write!

Secret Service agent Chet Robbins sat in his motel

room having a much needed and welcome bourbon and water. Inspector Van Brocklen sat across the room, having a scotch and water. Both felt in their guts that tomorrow was going to be a real son of a bitch.

"I've asked for more people," Van Brocklen broke the silence.

"So have I," Chet said.

"Think we'll get them?"

"No."

"Neither do I."

"Shit!" said Chet.

"Me, too," said Van Brocklen.

Sheriff Don Salter sat in Nellie's Cafe with Chief Russ Monroe. Each was having a cup of coffee that neither one of them really wanted, or needed. Both looked up as Congressman Steve Williams walked into the cafe, spotted the lawmen, and walked over to the table and took a seat. He came right to the point.

"My nutty cousin, Nate, is going to pull something tomorrow, gentlemen. I feel it in my guts."

"I can't arrest someone on the basis of your gastronomical problems," Don said shortly. He didn't like Steve Williams, had never voted for him, and never would. It all went back to high school days. Steve had been a damn sissy liberal puke back then and, in Don's eyes, still was. If it hadn't been for Steve's daddy's money, Steve would never have been elected to Congress . . . not in this district. But Steve's daddy was one of the richest men in the state, and people were scared to death of him. The man had a nasty habit of coming back on people who crossed him . . . therefore, no one crossed him, or his puky son. No one, that was, except Sheriff Don Salter and Chief Russ Monroe. When Don was running hard for sheriff, pitted against the elder Williams' hand-picked man, the older man had tried pulling some shady political deals against Don. But this time, the people didn't buy any of it. Don went out to see the elder Williams at his hunting camp and placed a cocked and loaded .357 magnum against the man's neck. The muzzle was very cold, and the older man began shaking like a leaf in a stiff breeze. He knew he was closer to death at that moment than he had ever been.

"If you don't back away from me, you old son of a bitch," Don told him, in a very menacing voice, "I promise you, I will blow your goddamn head off and shit down your neck."

Williams replied, in a very shaky voice, "You just might be the right man for sheriff after all, Don."

"Believe it," Don told him.

The next day, Don's opponent dropped out of the race.

Country politics could get just as nasty as big city politics, and much earthier.

"Don, Chief Monroe," Steve said, "I know that neither of you like me. But this is serious."

"Right on both counts. And we're aware of the seriousness of the situation, boy," Chief Monroe said, knowing how Congressman Williams hated to be called "boy."

"So what are you going to do about it?"

"Let the feds handle it," Don told him.

"That's it?"

"That's it, boy," Chief Monroe added.

"Don't call me boy," the congressman said automatically; he'd had years of practice doing so with Chief Monroe.

"Right, boy," Chief Monroe said.

"Well, I think you're both being very cavalier about this whole matter!"

Chief Monroe sighed, and Sheriff Salter rolled his eyes. "Steve, what would you have us do?" the sheriff asked. "Go out and arrest five or six hundred people? On what charge? All we've got on them now is preparing to march without a permit, and until they do march, they've broken no laws. Vic is out of jail legally; he paid the bond set by a judge. We know who blew up the jail, but we can't prove it. None of the groups we're looking at has broken any laws . . . yet."

Steve stood up. "Well, I'm going to the FBI and the Secret Service with this. Maybe they'll do something about it."

"I'm sure they'll be glad to see you," Chief Monroe said.

Steve left the cafe, his back stiff with anger.

"Better the feds than us," Don said.

"You got that right."

"You ready for tomorrow?"

"No."

"Well, it's coming."

"I can't see no way of stopping it." The chief pushed his coffee cup away and stood up. "I'm goin' home and get some sleep."

"See you for breakfast right here 'bout six?"

"You got it."

Slowly the lights began going out all over town. It was peaceful. For a few more hours.

Barry slipped from Stormy's side long before dawn began coloring the eastern sky to sit on the front porch and drink coffee. The hybrids had done their morning business and had gone back into the house, to sleep on the bedroom floor.

Barry walked soundlessly back into the house, refilled his coffee cup, and returned to the front porch.

He looked up at the cloudless sky. It was going to be a beautiful day. At least in some respects. The weather forecaster had said clear and very hot with a chance of late afternoon thunderstorms. Thunder-bumpers, he'd called them.

There was going to be some thunder, all right, Barry mused, but it wasn't going to be caused only by some weather system.

Too many factions with various axes to grind were getting together. Anything was apt to happen this day, and probably would.

Despite his gloomy feelings, Barry had to smile. For a fellow who professes to want only peace, he told himself, you sure can get yourself into some real predicaments, Vlad.

Barry stared out into the gloom of predawn. Then with a sigh he rose to his feet. Might as well get ready to face the day. Whatever else it might turn out to be, it was damn sure going to be interesting.

Twenty-five

Ki picked up Stormy at seven o'clock, and Barry left the house minutes later, after being sure Pete and Repeat had plenty of water. He ordered them to stay inside and knew they would obey. At the last minute, Barry tucked his lever-action Winchester .375 behind the seat of his pickup and added several boxes of ammunition and a full bandoleer, although he really wasn't sure why he was doing it.

Sheriff Salter straightened that out as soon as Barry ran into him, moments later, outside Nellie's Cafe.

"You're still a sworn-in deputy sheriff, Barry," Don told him. "With full arrest powers. You see something going down, you stop it. I'll back you one hundred and ten percent."

"Wonderful," Barry said sarcastically.

Agents Robbins and Van Brocklen were in the cafe. They both looked as though they had not gotten enough sleep.

Barry ordered coffee and biscuits and gravy, for he had skipped breakfast at the house.

"Does anything ever affect your appetite, Cantrell?" Van Brocklen asked. "Or whatever your name is."

"Vlad Dumitru Radu. The answer to your question is no. Why should it?"

"Radu?" Robbins spoke in low tones. "What nationality is that?"

"Rumanian."

Van Brocklen looked at him. "How'd you get to America?" He held up a hand; shook his head. "Never mind. I don't want to know."

An agent came in and whispered in Robbins' ear, then left. The Secret Service man sighed heavily. "Lots of strangers in town, and more gathering by the minute."

Van Brocklen finished his coffee in a gulp and stood up. "Time to get back to work. See you fellows."

FBI and Secret Service left the cafe.

Don waited until Barry had finished his breakfast before asking, "You ready to go to work?"

"What do you want me to do?"

"Circulate. Report back to me if you see or hear anything suspicious."

"Don, a full twenty-five percent of the people in this town look suspicious."

"You know what I mean!"

"All right, all right."

"Are you armed?"

"No." He shook his head. "Rather, I'm not carrying a pistol on me. I stuck a rifle in the truck."

"That cannon I saw?"

"Yes."

Shaking his head and muttering about a rifle capable of bringing down a polar bear, the sheriff left the cafe, Barry right behind him. Barry began slowly walking around the courthouse square. He had not gone half a block when a man fell in step with him. Barry recognized him from the party, one of Robert Roche's security men.

"Mr. Roche wants to see you, Cantrell. His car is parked in a garage just around the corner." He pointed. "That way. He said to tell you no tricks of any kind. He just wants to talk. He's waiting outside the car."

"If anything hinky goes down, I'll tear your arms off first and stick them up a part of your anatomy that will be very uncomfortable."

"I don't want to tangle with you, Cantrell. All Mr. Roche wants is a few minutes of your time. That's all. Regardless of what you might think, he is a man of his word."

"Sure he is. All right. Lead the way."

"We'll dispense with handshaking, Mr. Cantrell," Roche said, as Barry approached. "I have this, ah, call it an eccentricity about people touching me."

"Fine."

"Do you have time to listen to a business proposition?"

"A short one. I've been pressed into service by the sheriff."

"How admirable of you to accept such a responsible position during these trying times. Mr. Cantrell, I'm a blunt man. Name your price."

Barry stared at the man for a few seconds. He knew exactly what Roche meant, but the abruptness of it took him by surprise. "Robert," he started slowly, choosing his words carefully. "I and the others like me are a fluke of nature. We possess no magic gene to give eternal life to anyone else . . . it isn't transferable by blood transfusion or surgery. We come from all walks of life. And there are immortals being born even now, perhaps one or two every fifty or hundred years or so. We don't die, Robert. At least I don't think we do. I met a wanderer in Egypt once who had walked with a holy man called Jesus. I met another who remembered the flood. I met a beautiful woman who was once in Cleopatra's court, another who marched side by side with the Phoenicians . . . when they explored what is now called North America. They're still alive, Robert. They have all married dozens of times and had children. Ninety-nine point nine percent of those offspring lived normal lives, aged, and died. We all believe that a tiny percentage of offspring who are born immortal got that way because somewhere far back in their past they were related to an immortal . . ."

"Then there is a possibility that I might have an immortal in my past?" Robert interrupted impatiently.

"Anything is possible. But I would guess the odds at about ten million to one." Barry paused to stare at the billionaire, sensing that the man's mind was working furiously, coming to some strange conclusions.

Robert slowly nodded his head. "Then I need a female immortal if I am to achieve immortality," he spoke softly.

Barry shrugged his shoulders. "I can't say that for certain."

"Tell me where I can find one." Robert's voice had turned harsh and demanding.

"Sorry. I won't do that."

"Oh, I think you will," the billionaire said, a mocking smile playing on his lips.

Barry knew then he'd been suckered. He spun around, but too late. He felt the lash of a needle burying deep in his hip, the crack of a tranquilizer gun. His world began to fade. His legs felt rubbery, unable to hold his weight.

"Oh, you'll tell me," Robert Roche's voice came through the gathering mist in Barry's brain. "Sooner or later, you'll tell me. That's the only way you'll ever gain your freedom."

"So much for your being a man of your word," Barry managed to mumble the words.

"There is that adage about all's fair in love and war, Barry," Roche said mockingly.

"I seem to recall something like that." And that was the last thing Barry would recall for hours.

Twenty-six

"Drive Cantrell's truck out to his house and park it there," Roche instructed. "You follow the truck," he told another man.

One of Roche's security men stripped Barry of his shirt and put it on. Moments later, Barry's pickup was driven from a side street parking area and out of town. Barry was tossed onto the rear seat of Roche's car and covered with a blanket.

"We'll take him to the lake house and wait until the march starts," Roche said. He grinned nastily. "We know there will be a great deal of trouble, don't we?" He quickly sobered. Roche's moments of levity did not last long. "Then we'll drive to Little Rock and fly out."

"Hadn't we better handcuff him, boss?" one of the goons asked.

"Don't be ridiculous! The drug we injected him with is used to tranquilize elephants. He'll be out for hours."

For several hours, yes, but not nearly as long as Roche thought. He had no way of knowing just how advanced Barry's recuperative powers were.

* * *

"Any of you people seen Barry Cantrell?" Don asked several of his deputies, who were just reporting for their usual eight-to-four shift.

"I seen his truck headin' out of town," one replied. " 'Bout ten minutes ago." The deputy frowned.

"What's the matter?" Don prompted.

"Well . . . you know how friendly Barry always is? He didn't return my wave. And I could swear he was lookin' right at me."

"Maybe he had his mind on Stormy," another deputy suggested with a smile.

"Was he heading out toward his house?" Don asked.

"Yes, sir, he was. And there was a car right behind him, stayin' close."

Don nodded. "You guys go on to work, and stay loose. I got a hunch this day is going to be busy."

The sheriff drove out to Barry's house. The pickup was parked in the drive, but outside the fenced-in area; Barry never parked there. Pete and Repeat were on the porch, refusing to come off, and while Don was friendly with the dogs, and believed he could enter the grounds without being harmed, he was wary of the big hybrids, even though they were not behaving in an unfriendly manner.

Using the cell phone in his unit, Don dialed Barry's number. He got the answering machine. He tried three times, and three times the answering machine clicked on. Barry was not at home.

Don walked over to Barry's truck and looked inside. The same shirt that he had seen Barry wearing just about half an hour or so before was lying on the seat.

"What the hell . . . ?" Don muttered. He looked behind the seat. Barry's .375 Winchester was in place. Don walked back to his unit and got behind the wheel. "What's going on here?" he said aloud. He drove around town, then out into the county for the next hour. Barry had vanished.

Don pulled over to the narrow shoulder when he spotted a large group of people trooping across a field. He sighed when he recognized Dr. Waller and his group of scientists and assistants.

"We're on the trail!" Dr. Irene Biegelsack hollered at him.

"Wonderful," Don replied.

"We found a fresh track in a marshy area just a few hundred yards back!" Dr. Dekerlegand yelled.

"Stay with it," Don said.

"Oh, we shall!" Dr. Inez Hopper shouted, puffing along like a miniature locomotive. "But I'm sure I'll see you at President Hutton's reception tomorrow evening."

"Right." Don sat in his unit and watched the parade until they disappeared into a clump of woods.

"I'm due for a long vacation," he muttered. "I've earned it, I deserve it, I need it."

Don drove over to Vic Radford's place, parked in the drive just off the road, being careful not to enter Vic's property, and stared in disbelief. There were at least a hundred people milling around, the hardest-looking bunch of men and women Don had ever seen.

"My God," Don breathed, and backed out and drove away.

He continued on to Bubba Bordelon's farm. Same thing. Kluckers from all over the state had pulled in; there were so many Confederate battle flags waving in the slight breeze Don couldn't count them. "Good Lord!" he muttered, and reached for his mike, keying it.

"Hazel," he said to the woman working the radio at headquarters. "Has that National Guard unit arrived yet?"

"Yes, sir. Just about an hour ago. They sure cut it fine, didn't they?"

"How many of them?"

"About a company, I think. A hundred or so. They're meeting with the federal people now."

"Good. We're sure going to need them."

"Where are you now, Don?"

"Out at Bubba's place, looking at a sea of Confederate flags and white sheets."

"Sheriff?"

"Yes, Hazel."

"My great-granddaddy fought for the Confederacy."

"Well, hell, Hazel!" Don blurted. "So did mine. What's that got to do with anything?"

"Nothin', I guess. Where are you off to now?"

"Over to Jim Beal's warehouse."

"He isn't there, Sheriff. I just saw him havin' breakfast in town."

"You see Nate Williams?"

"No, sir."

"Then I'll go over there and check him out."

"That crazy Alex Tarver's in town with about fifty or more of those bald-headed idiots that run with him. They're stompin' around wearin' army clothes and combat boots and carryin' Nazi flags."

"Wonderful. That's all we need. I'll be in the office in about an hour."

"Ten-four."

The breakaway AFB people were gathered at Nate's. They were dressed in army battle dress and carrying American flags. Don got out of his car and walked up to the man. "Nate. I'm warning you now: if you march, I'll arrest you. You don't have a permit."

"Neither do the nigras, Sheriff. You goin' to arrest them, too?"

"You damn right I am!"

"I'll believe that when I see it," Clyde Mayfield said.

"Yeah, me, too," his wife popped off.

Don sighed. "Don't say you weren't warned."

Somebody in the crowd gave Don a very wet raspberry.

"This is going to be a very interesting day," Don muttered, as he got in his car and headed back to town.

Barry was tossed in the back of a panel truck parked behind the lake house and locked in, but not before a security man tied his hands and feet with rope. The security man had heard all about Barry Cantrell, and wasn't about to take any chances. But he needn't have worried, not for several more hours, at least.

The march was due to start about noon, but like all events of that nature, it would be late in kicking off—just about the time Barry would start coming around.

Stormy called Barry about ten o'clock that morning, but got the answering machine. Then she remembered that Barry had promised he would help Sheriff Salter. She thought no more about it. She and Ki returned to work filming the gathering crowds that were milling about the courthouse square, interviewing a few of the people . . . those who would consent talk to her, that is. Some of the people were waving American flags; others held Confederate flags.

Sheriff Salter walked up. Before he could ask if the women had seen Barry, Ki asked, "Is Congressman Madison really going to speak to this . . . ah, gathering?"

"Far as I know his appearance is still on."

"Jesus!"

"Yeah. I agree. Stormy, have you seen Barry?"

She cut her suddenly narrowed eyes to the man. "Not since early this morning."

"He checked in and then vanished. His truck is parked out at the house. His house. But he's nowhere around. Something's going on, and I don't like it."

"Maybe he's riding with another deputy?" Ki suggested.

Don shook his head. "No. I checked."

"Robert Roche," Stormy said. "Barry told you about him, didn't he?"

"A little. You want to ride out there with me and nose around? We've got a couple of hours before this mess kicks off."

"Let's go."

On the way to Don's unit, they ran into Robbins and Van Brocklen. "What's up?" the Bureau man asked, casting a look at Stormy.

"Barry's disappeared," Don said, then told the feds all he knew, including Stormy's suspicions about Robert Roche. "We're heading out that way now to check it out."

"The Speaker's due in town in just about an hour," Robbins said. "We've got to stay close. Keep us informed about Cantrell, will you? I just don't trust him." He glanced at Stormy. "Sorry, Ms. Knight. I've got a suspicious nature."

"You're off base on this one," she told him.

"Maybe."

Stormy spun around and got into Don's unit. Don looked at the feds. "I think you're wrong, too."

"I hope I am, too, Don," the Secret Service man admitted. "I sort of like Cantrell."

"And I can't stand Robert Roche," Van Brocklen

added. "We've tangled with him before. And I would appreciate if you didn't repeat that."

Don smiled. "I won't. I'll call in just as soon as I know something. One way or the other."

After Don had pulled out, Chet turned to Van Brocklen. "What the hell are we going to do with all these National Guard troops, Van? These people are a public affairs unit, or something like that, not military police or anything remotely connected with combat."

"We can all pray fervently they don't shoot some innocent citizen by accident."

A horrified look passed the Secret Service's face. "You mean they have live ammunition?"

"Governor's orders."

"My God, Van! These people aren't soldiers. They're civil servants and CPAs and bureaucrats."

"I know. And I wish I didn't."

A Bureau man walked up. "The Speaker's on his way into town."

Robbins looked at his watch. "He's early."

Van Brocklen slowly shook his head and sighed almost painfully. "Here we go, gang."

By eleven o'clock, all the various groups that had threatened to march were in town, and no stranger bunch had ever gathered in the North Arkansas town. Vic and his neo-Nazis were there. Bubba Bordelon and his Kluckers were there, resplendent in their robes and Confederate flags. Nate Williams and his breakaway AFB people were milling around, dressed in camouflage battle dress and black berets. Alex Tarver and his skinheads were in attendance, with their tattoos and cut-off jackets and heavy boots and chains, stomping around, scowling at everybody and frightening little children.

Alex stomped up to one little boy, about six years old, made a face at the child and said, "Boo!"

The little boy reared back and kicked the shit out of him, landing one small cowboy boot on Alex's shin.

"You little son of a bitch!" Alex hollered, hopping around on one boot.

The boy's mother smacked him on the side of the head with a very large purse. Alex hit the sidewalk in a sprawl.

"Freak!" the woman yelled at him.

"Old bag!" Alex shouted at her.

The woman's husband pulled her away and glared down at Alex. "I ought to kick your scummy butt, boy."

"Yeah!" Alex hopped to his feet. "Come on, hot shot. Try it." He balled his hands into fists and started jumping around.

"Break it up!" Chief Monroe said, walking up. He pointed a finger at Alex. "You—move!"

"I didn't start this, Chief! That little bastard yonder kicked me."

"Move, or I'll lock you up, Tarver."

Muttering dire threats, but keeping them well under his breath, Alex and his group moved on.

"And the day is just getting started," the chief said.

Monroe turned at the sounds of laughter. While he had been dealing with Alex Tarver, several large buses had pulled up onto a side street and parked. Abudu X and his bunch had arrived, and it was quite a sight. It looked to Chief Monroe as if a large group of extras had arrived for the filming of a modern Tarzan movie. He had never seen so many colorful flowing robes and funny-looking little hats in all his life. Quite a crowd had gathered around, some of them just standing and staring, some of them doing their best to contain their laughter, others making no effort to hide their amusement.

Chief Monroe stood and shook his head at the sight. Trouble was right around the corner unless Willie kept a firm hand on his followers. This was not Africa; this was solid conservative North Arkansas, and people just weren't accustomed to seeing such bizarre sights.

Agent Robbins walked up, a worried look on his face.

"Now what?" Chief Monroe asked.

"More trouble on the way. They'll be here just about noon."

"Who?"

"A bunch of gay activists."

"Gay? You mean queer?"

Robbins looked pained. "The term 'queer' is not politically correct, Chief."

"Who gives a shit?" Russ came right back. "How many of those . . . homosexual persons . . . are on the way?"

Robbins had to duck his head to hide his smile. Personally, he agreed with Chief Monroe; politically he had to curb his tongue if he wanted to keep his job. "About a hundred or so."

"A hundred fags!" Chief Monroe shouted. "Here! In this town! Hell, we got two here on a permanent basis, and that's five too many."

Much to Agent Robbins' chagrin, a crowd was gathering. "Three bus loads of them. They don't like Congressman Madison's position on homosexuality and plan to demonstrate."

"Oh, my God!" a woman yelled. "They'll spread the ebola everywhere."

Agent Robbins sighed heavily. He was doing a lot of sighing lately.

Chief Monroe lifted his walkie-talkie. "Don? You got your ears on?"

"Go ahead, Russ," Don replied.

"We got three bus loads of fruits and fairies comin' in."

There followed about ten seconds of silence. Then, "Ten-nine?"

"About a hundred fags on the way."

"That's what I thought you said. I was hoping I misunderstood you."

"You didn't."

"We'll just have to make the best of it."

"I'm gonna call the highway patrol and have them block the road and turn those damn people around. You ten-four that?"

"You can't do that, Russ. They haven't broken any laws."

"Don, if those people march and protest, there will be a goddamn riot and you know it. People 'round here ain't gonna put up with that crap!"

"I'll be back in about thirty minutes, Russ. We'll handle it."

"The county is your call, Don, the town is mine. Monroe out."

Don was just pulling into the drive at Robert Roche's lake house. He sat for a moment, conscious of Stormy's eyes on him. He expelled a long breath and said, "Good Lord, what next?"

Twenty-seven

"Dr. Hopper!" a young student called excitedly. "We've found the creature's lair."

"Wonderful!" Dr. Hopper cried. "I'll radio the others. We've agreed this find is something we will all share."

Soon the scientists and their young assistants were gathered around a hole set into a knoll, the entrance hidden behind a thick stand of bush.

"Careful now," Dr. Irene Biegelsack cautioned. "We really don't know what we're dealing with here."

"It's a panther," Dr. Waller said.

"No, it's a leopard," Dr. Dekerlegand contradicted.

"I believe it's some sort of mountain lion that is, or was at one time, indigenous to North America," Dr. Dortch said.

They were all both wrong and right, to some degree, as they were about to find out. Very abruptly.

Inside the small cave, Jacques Cornet, as his Other, lay on his belly on the cool ground and listened to the humans talk. He sensed these people were not criminals, and certainly not dangerous—except for the tranquilizer guns they carried. Jacques was very familiar with those.

He did not want to harm these silly people, just scare

them away. And he had a good idea just how to do that. His prehistoric teeth bared back in an animal smile. As his Other, Jacques weighed nearly three hundred pounds, stood three and a half feet tall, and was just over seven feet long.

"Get the nets ready," Irene said. "I'll go in and see what we've got."

Which was going to be a good trick, for Irene's ass was just about as wide as the cave entrance.

Irene removed her pith helmet and laid it to one side. She wriggled her bulk halfway into the darkness and suddenly came nose to snout with a prehistoric sabre-tooth beast of as yet undetermined species. As his Other, Jacques' fur was as black as midnight, and his teeth very long and very white.

Jacques was in reality a throwback to the jaguar family, and jaguars screamed about as often as they roared. And Jacques screamed. Irene banged her head on the cave entrance, unhinged her ass, and left the lair with her hair standing straight up on end. She knocked over her colleagues like bowling pins and sent the young assistants scurrying in all directions, nets and tranquilizer guns forgotten. Jacques bounded out of the cave to stand for just a couple of seconds in front of the brush and scream at the frightened group. Then he was gone, leaving the area with amazing strength and speed.

"After the beast!" Dr. Thomas Dekerlegand hollered, crawling to his hands and knees.

"Come on, people!" Irene bellowed, finally managing to stand up. "This is the greatest find of the century!"

And off they went, stumbling across the fields and over the hills and through the timber of North Arkansas. The route they were following would take them straight to the highway which led to the lake—the same road the marchers planned to use. Jacques knew this. Jacques may have been slightly around the bend, but he still had a sense of humor . . . albeit a rather strange one.

In the panel truck, Barry's fingers began to twitch. But he was still a couple of hours away from full consciousness.

The gates of the driveway leading to Robert Roche's rental house were closed, and no amount of horn honking would bring any response. Don shook his head. "They're not going to come out, and I can't go in there without a warrant."

Ki had stayed back in town to do some filming. Stormy said, "Go back down the road and let me out at Will's store. I'm certain that Roche has Barry."

"How will you get back to town?"

"When you get back, look up Ki and tell her to drive out to the store. I'll be waiting."

Don was dubious about the idea, but he couldn't hold the woman against her will. He nodded. "All right. But I don't think it's a good idea."

Stormy grinned at the sheriff. "I'm pretty good at taking care of myself, Don."

Don let her off at Will's store and headed back to town.

Jacques Cornet had put some distance between himself and his pursuers, then shifted into his human form. He wanted to time their arrival at the road just right. Overland, they were still a good three hours from the road, through some rough country. Jacques smiled as he walked, thinking this was going to be more fun than Marie and the food riots in France.

Congressman Cliff Madison took one look at the mob of people and flags and placards and manner of dress around the courthouse square and paled. "Good God!" he said.

"This was not a good idea, Mr. Speaker," a federal marshal told him. "This crowd is very volatile. Too many factions involved here. It's not safe."

But by then it was too late to back out. The mayor and members of the town council had rushed up and were all talking at once, shaking his hand and patting him on the back. Just about that time, the buses carrying the gay rights activists pulled up at the edge of the square.

"Hey!" hollered Jason Asken, one of the skinheads. "The faggots is here!"

"I would suggest, Mr. Roche," one of the billionaire's aides said, "that we leave now."

"We'll leave as planned," Robert said, without rancor in his voice. He was feeling too good for anger. He was closer to eternal life than ever before. Absolutely nothing could spoil his mood. He held up a county map. "Taking the route I have outlined. Not before."

"Yes, sir. As you say, sir."

"Always, as I say, Richard."

"Yes, sir."

In the panel truck, Barry stirred in his unconsciousness and moaned faintly. His eyelids fluttered, and he clenched his hands into fists. Then drifted back into darkness.

* * *

"We'll park the car at that empty house just up from Roche's place and go in the back way," Stormy told Ki. She spoke openly in front of Will, for she liked and trusted the older man.

"You ladies better think some on this," Will warned. "That Roche is a mean man; he's got ruthless written all over him. And some of Vic Radford's nuts have been prowlin' around here this mornin'. They're not so much mean as they are plumb crazy."

"We'll be careful," Stormy assured him. "And Ki is armed, if that makes you feel better."

"Will you use that weapon?" Will asked.

"I'll use it."

Will stared at her for a moment, then nodded. "Yeah. I believe you will."

The two women left the store and drove off. Will sat for a time behind the counter, then slowly shook his head. "I got me a bad feelin' 'bout all this. There ain't no good gonna come of it. No matter how it turns out, somebody is gonna get hurt." He thought for a time longer, then stood up and got his shotgun, loading it up full with double-ought buckshot. "I think I'll just take me a ride," he said.

Will hung the CLOSED sign on the front door and locked up. Behind the wheel of his pickup, he checked to make sure his .38 was in the glove box and loaded up. He knew a mostly forgotten old dirt road that he could circle around on that would take him right up to the rear of Roche's rental house. He'd just keep him a good eye on those two ladies.

President Hutton had quietly flown into the small county airport and had been hustled out to Congressman Williams' home without incident. Since Hutton and Congressman Madison were about to bury the hatchet—for a change not in each other—and try to work together for the good of the country, the press had been asked to leave the president alone with his thoughts. They had agreed and for the most part had done so. Now it was just about time for him to drive out, or rather, take a ride out to the airport to pick up his wife.

One of his aides entered the room. "The first lady will be a couple of hours late arriving, sir. She decided at the last minute to visit a children's hospital."

"Thank you. Then we'll leave for the airport about . . . ?"

"Two-thirty, sir."

"I believe I'll take a nap."

"Very good, sir. I'll wake you in plenty of time."

In plenty of time for the president to look death right in the eye.

A thousand miles away, Senator Madalaine Bowman looked at the men and women seated around her in the den of a lodge in the Virginia mountains. She was quite pleased with herself and with the way matters were beginning to shape up in Arkansas. She glanced at her watch and then lifted her eyes to the small group.

"We have only a few moments before the others arrive. Later, when we hear the news, we must all be shocked, stunned, sickened, and horrified at what has happened. In approximately three hours, events will have taken place in Arkansas that will shape the destiny of our party, our philosophy, and the nation well into the next millennium and, hopefully, beyond. What makes it all so perfect is that none of us can be even remotely linked to the tragedy that is about to befall Congressman Madison and President Hutton." She smiled and spread her hands wide. "What could be more innocent than a party planning committee meeting over the weekend?"

The others in the room chuckled their approval at how well the senator had planned.

Jim Beal just couldn't stand it any longer. He locked his warehouse office and told his store manager he was gone for the rest of the day. Jim got into his truck and drove to the courthouse square. Maybe he couldn't stop the march or the violence he knew was going to come with it, but by God he could be a part of putting an end to it.

He found Sheriff Salter. "What can I do to help today, Don?"

The sheriff stared at him for a moment. "Are you serious, Jim?"

"As serious as a crutch. You know that Nate took about seventy of my people and left the AFB?"

"Yes. They're here in force and going to march. Are they armed, Jim?"

"I could be wrong, Don, but I just don't think they would be that stupid. But you can bet they'll have people along the way ready to hand them weapons if the need arises."

Van Brocklen walked up and gave the AFB leader a hard look. Don caught it and said, "He's all right, Van. He's offering to help us."

The FBI man knew that Jim had forbidden his AFB people to march, knew his brigade had split up over that decision—among other things. And knew that most people in the community felt Jim was a decent man—despite, or because of, his views on race—and agreed with about ninety-nine percent of the local militia's beliefs. Van Brocklen shrugged his shoulders. "That's your call, Don."

Don didn't hesitate; he'd known Jim Beal all his life. "Ride with me, Jim. Let's see if we can't defuse some of these walking time bombs."

"You'll never do it, Don," Jim was quick to reply. "Nate Williams, Alex Tarver, Bubba Bordelon, Vic Radford . . . they've all been waiting for a moment like this. This is their chance to blow the lid off and bring themselves national attention."

"And you, too, Mr. Beal?" Van Brocklen couldn't resist asking.

"No," the AFB leader said softly. "That isn't true. What's left of my militia feels just like the majority of militias around the country: we don't want a lot of publicity, because the type of coverage we get from the press is always biased. Look, Mr. Van Brocklen, don't you think I know who Wesley Parren works for? I've known it since the day he rolled over for you feds and started informing on us. You people must have a thousand or more guys like Wesley around the nation, spying on men and women who call them friend. But it works both ways, and you're fully aware of that, too. Let me tell you something, Federal Agent, you think your stats are right about two hundred million guns in the hands of private citizens in America. Try half a *billion* guns and you'd still be short. Most of us in the militia or survival movements don't want a damn war. Hell, that's the last thing we want. It's just that we've got enough foresight to see that one is coming." He shook his head in disgust. "Jesus, Van Brocklen, this is not the time to be discussing political ideologies. We're going to have a war on our hands right here in this little North Arkansas town if we can't clamp the lid down tight, and do it today. Now what's it going to be, Mr. Federal Agent?"

Van Brocklen stepped closer to Jim Beal, conscious that Agent Robbins had walked up and had been listening. But there was no back up in Jim Beal. The two men stood nose to nose and eyeball to eyeball on the side street. "Let me tell you something, Mr. Militia Leader." The Bureau man's voice was low. "Do you think the majority of us in the Bureau, the Secret Service, BATF, Federal Marshal's Service, DEA, or what have you, like to take orders from pantywaist egg-sucking liberals? Do you think we actually *enjoyed* watching the events at Waco or Ruby Ridge . . . ?"

"Yeah, I do, you federal prick!" Jim popped back, not giving an inch. "That brown spot on your nose is not a freckle. That's shit from the attorney general's liberal ass!"

Van Brocklen balled his hands into fists, then sighed, shook his head, and got a grip on his temper. "All right, there are some among us who did, I'll admit that, but they're damn few in number. Every enforcement branch, from local to federal, has its share of hot dogs. Goddammit, Beal, we take and follow orders—"

"Yeah," Jim interrupted. "That's the same thing the gestapo members said during the war crimes trials after World War II. Just . . . taking . . . and . . . following . . . orders." The last was said very sarcastically.

"Oh, for Christ's sake!" Agent Robbins stepped in. "You can't seriously be comparing us to a bunch of Nazis!"

"I hate to be the one to tell you boys this," Jim said evenly, "but a hell of a lot of people believe just that."

Twenty-eight

One of the gay rights activists carrying a placard reading GOD LOVES HOMOSEXUALS came face-to-face with the wife of a local Baptist minister carrying a sign reading THERE IS NO PLACE IN HEAVEN FOR SODOMITES.

Alex Tarver had made himself a placard reading THANK GOD FOR AIDS, and was stomping around, scowling at the gay rights activists and making a nuisance of himself.

Some of the Aryan Brotherhood members were lurching about carrying signs, one of which read FRUITS ARE GOOD FOR ONLY ONE THING, AND THAT WILL KILL YOU.

One little girl read the sign, looked at the banana she'd been eating, and tossed what was left into a trash container.

"I'll pray for you," the Baptist minister's wife said to the gay activist.

"And I'll pray for you," the gay said.

"Why don't both of you kiss and makeup?" Vic Radford sneered as he strolled up.

The minister's wife ignored the neo-Nazi. "What could *you* possibly say to the Lord about *me?*" she questioned the activist.

"That He forgive your ignorance and prejudice."

The minister's wife's mouth dropped open. "Well! I never!"

"In that case," Vic said, "why don't you get nekked and try it?"

"You filth!" the minister's wife snarled at him.

"What the hell," Vic said. "It was just a suggestion."

One of Don's deputies walked up and said, "Move it, Vic. Right now."

"I ain't doin' nothin'!"

"Move!"

Congressman Madison stepped up onto the flatbed truck that would serve as a speaker's platform. Jesus, he thought. If I get out of this alive, it'll be a miracle.

The mayor stood smiling behind the rostrum. But his smile hid his growing nervousness. Please God, he prayed, don't let this rabble get out of hand.

The mayor tapped the microphone, and the speakers squealed in feedback. Donald "The Duck" Dumas, a local DJ, adjusted the amplifier. "Try it now, Mayor," he whispered.

"My friends," the mayor spoke into the mike, his voice booming all around the courthouse square. "I—"

"Congressman Madison is a racist!" Abudu X hollered.

"Now, now," the mayor urged.

"Impeach his lard-ass!" a Back to Africa follower shouted.

"Can you impeach the Speaker?" one of Chief Monroe's men asked the chief.

"I don't think so," he replied.

"It's an honor to have the distinguished Speaker of the House with us today," the mayor hastened on.

"Give him a bowl of grits and send him back home!" one of Abudu's crew yelled.

A local man cut his eyes. "Hey, Lumumba, or whatever your damn name is," he told the man. "I like grits. So why don't you just shut your goddamn face?"

"Why don't you go get fucked?" the local was told.

Two Arkansas State Troopers stepped in and quickly defused that potentially violent situation.

"More money for AIDS research!" a gay rights activist yelled.

"Wealth redistribution now!" a Back to Africa member shouted.

"If we give you a mule and forty acres will you shut up and go away?" a local called.

Two very nervous national guardsmen, in civilian life both minor bureaucrats on the state level, moved toward the two men.

"Get over there!" Van Brocklen ordered one of his men. "See how they handle it. Move!"

"All right, all right," one of the guardsmen said. "Let's take it easy here."

"Don't tell me to take it easy," the local told the guardsman. "I was a marine at Frozen Chosen before you were a gleam in your daddy's eyes. Go play soldier somewhere else."

It was the mayor's voice that finally brought some degree of calm to the hundreds of people gathered around the square. "Ladies and gentlemen! Is this the impression you want people to have of our community? A bunch of ill-mannered and unruly louts? Let the outside agitators show their ignorance and disrespect. But let's show the Speaker our best side."

Most of the local citizens exchanged glances and silently decided to ignore the outsiders. Congressman Madison began his speech, and much to his surprise, the majority of the crowd was polite and attentive, and he was heckled only a few times.

* * *

Stormy and Ki were about a mile from Robert Roche's rented lake property when half a dozen men suddenly stepped out from behind a clump of brush and confronted them.

"Well now," one of the men said, the words pushed past a very nasty grin. "Lookee here, boys. We don't have to go get these ladies after all. Hell, they done come to us."

Unnoticed, Ki clicked on her camera. She couldn't be sure of focus, but she would at least get the voices. The .38 Barry had loaned her was in her purse, hanging by a strap from her shoulder. No way she could get to it in a hurry.

"Get out of our way," Stormy said.

"My, my," another of the men said. "Ain't she the feisty one, boys?"

"Don't give us no trouble, Miss Stormy," another said. "You just come along nice and quiet and ever'thang will be hunky-dory."

"I'm not going anywhere with you!"

"Oh, I think you are," she was told. "Easy or hard. It's your choice."

"You're kidnapping us then, right?" Ki asked.

"Now, that's a real ugly word, missy."

"And you would damn sure be an expert on ugly," Ki came right back.

The man's face clouded with anger. He stepped forward and backhanded Ki, knocking her to the ground. Ki maintained her grip on the camera and managed to point the lens directly at her assailant for a couple of seconds. Blood leaked from one corner of her mouth.

"You bes' watch your smart-assed mouth, bitch," the man said, standing over her.

Ki kicked the man as hard as she could on the knee. He howled in pain and went to the ground, both hands holding his injured knee. Another man stepped forward, grabbed a handful of Ki's shirtfront, and popped her on the jaw with a balled fist. Ki dropped into darkness.

Stormy's hands were roughly tied behind her, and she was gagged with a bandanna and marched off.

Ki's camera was still running, the lens capturing it all. Will showed up about ten minutes later, just as Ki was crawling to her hands and knees, her mouth swollen and bloody.

"All hell's gonna break loose now," Will muttered.

Barry returned to full consciousness. He lay still for a moment, attempting to get his bearings. Then he started thinking about breaking free of his bonds. He smiled as he became his Other. The bonds fell away as hands and feet became clawed paws. He yawned and stretched for a moment, then once more assumed his human form. He heard footsteps outside on the gravel drive and crouched on the floor of the panel truck, listening as someone fumbled at the back doors.

One of the rear doors opened, and a hand appeared. Barry grabbed the wrist and jerked. The startled man was hauled into the panel truck and savagely thrown against the metal wall. Barry recognized him as one of Roche's security men. Barry reached over and smashed one hard fist against the man's jaw. The security man's eyes rolled back, and he slumped to the floor, unconscious.

Barry removed a Smith & Wesson 9mm pistol from the man's back pocket and two full twelve-round magazines loaded with hollow-nose rounds from his other back pocket. He checked the clip in the butt of the pistol. Full.

Barry tied the man's hands and feet and cautiously opened the back door to the panel truck. He could see no one. He slipped from the hot interior of the panel truck and, staying low, made his way to the rear of the expensive lake house. Pressing against the outside wall, he listened to a low murmur of voices coming from inside. He peeked through a window and saw two men sitting at a table, playing cards. Barry made his silent way to the back door and slipped into the coolness of the air-conditioned house. He stood in the archway leading to the kitchen and pointed the pistol at the two men at the table. The cocking sound caused their heads to turn, their faces paling. They kept their hands in sight and unmoving.

Barry closed the distance and put the muzzle of the 9mm to the back of one man's head. He fanned the man for weapons and found another S & W 9mm and two full magazines. A similar pistol and two full clips were taken from the second man. Barry tucked both pistols behind his waistband, and gesturing with the muzzle of his 9mm, he motioned the two men toward the open basement door.

"If you make a sound," he whispered the warning to the two men, "I promise I will kill you both. Do you understand?"

They nodded in reply.

Barry locked the basement door behind them and silently made his way toward the front of the house. He rather hoped the two men would start kicking up a fuss. The more confusion the better. But they remained silent.

The man Barry recognized as Robert Roche's personal secretary was sitting at a desk in a corner of the huge, exposed-beamed den. There was no one else in the room. Barry silently walked up behind the man and put the muzzle of the 9mm against his neck.

"Move and you die," Barry told him in a low voice.

"Don't kill me!" the man whispered, raw fear in his words. "I don't have a gun. I hate guns."

Barry noticed that the man had been writing checks, he supposed to pay any local bills. "Where's Roche?"

"Taking a nap upstairs. He's a sound sleeper."

Barry smiled as a thought sprang into his brain. "Can you write me a bank draft, partner?"

"A what? Oh! Certainly, I can. How much?"

"Oh, how about a hundred and fifty thousand dollars?"

"Is that all?"

"Yes."

"Made out to Barry Cantrell?"

"That's right. Can this draft be canceled?"

"Any personal draft can be canceled, Mr. Cantrell. But if you give me your local account number, I can make two calls, and the money will be electronically transferred to your account. And I can assure you, I will not tell Mr. Roche about the transaction."

"Why would you do that?"

"Because I hate the arrogant son of a bitch, that's why."

"He'll fire you as soon as he finds out."

"So what? By that time, I'll be long gone. I've already embezzled a million dollars from the ruthless bastard and own a nice villa in Mexico, where I plan to live out the rest of my life in luxury. He won't discover this transfer for years, if ever. I can assure you of that."

Barry chuckled. "In that case, transfer a quarter of a million dollars to this account." He gave the man the account number his lawyer in San Francisco had set up years back.

The man made two quick calls. "Done," he said, leaning back with a smile. "Now tie me up securely and hit me in the mouth. But not too hard, please."

Barry tied the man hand and foot, and then popped him on the mouth, just hard enough to bloody the man's lips. The man smiled and nodded in satisfaction.

"Where are the rest of the guards?" Barry asked.

"Prowling the grounds. You'd better hurry and get out of here. They come in frequently for cold drinks. Are you . . . are you going to kill Roche?"

"No. Just teach him a little bit of humility."

"Humility? Robert Roche? This I have to see."

"Stick around."

"I can assure you, I'm not going anywhere. Mr. Cantrell, Roche's security guards will hurt you, cripple you if they have to. The ones he has here with him are the most ruthless. They're no more than high-priced thugs."

"Thanks."

Barry moved to the back door just in time to catch one of the men he'd put in the basement attempting to slip out. He'd either had a key in his pocket, one had been hanging in the basement in case of an emergency, or he had picked the lock. No matter. Barry grabbed him by the back of the shirt and slung him down the basement steps. He bounced and tumbled down, hit the floor, and in the dim light, did not move.

"Don't worry about me," the other man said. "I ain't movin' from here, Cantrell."

"Wise decision on your part." Barry closed the door.

Barry picked up a heavy iron frying pan just as footsteps sounded on the back porch. The door opened, and Barry slammed the business end of the frying pan into the man's face, breaking the nose, pulping lips, and loosening several teeth. Barry fanned the man for weapons and found another S & W 9mm and two full magazines. He was getting overloaded with pistols. He tossed the man unceremoniously down the basement steps and closed the door. He used the frying pan again as another man entered the kitchen for a drink. He joined his buddy on the basement floor.

"There's one more, Cantrell," the only one who wasn't hurt called.

"Now, why would I believe you?"

" 'Cause we're all fired after this anyways. Maybe not right off, but as soon as we get back. You can go to the bank with that."

Barry smiled. He'd go to the bank, all right.

Barry saw the last man coming across the yard. It was the man who'd lied to him back in town. Barry made sure the basement door was wide open. When the back door opened, Barry grabbed a handful of shirt and literally picked the man up off his feet and slung him down the steps. He bounced all the way down and came to rest on his face.

Barry closed the door, locked it, and then wedged a chair back under the doorknob. He climbed up the steps to the second floor and began opening doors until he found Robert Roche, sound asleep. Barry grabbed one side of the bottom sheet and not too gently dumped the man onto the floor. Barry noticed he was wearing black silk pajamas. He jerked the billionaire to his bare feet and hauled him downstairs, not treating him kindly at all.

"I'll get you for this, Cantrell!" Roche hissed. "I'll track you to the end of the world if I have to."

"Have fun doing it. Now walk out the back door and get in that panel truck you used to haul me out here."

"What are you going to do?"

"You'll see."

"Where are my men?"

"In the basement. Move!"

Barry glanced at a wall clock. It was one-thirty. The speeches should be over and the marchers getting cranked up in high gear by now. This should work out just fine.

Standing on the back porch in his pajamas and bare feet, Roche said, "Cantrell, don't be a fool. Work with me and end all this chasing about. Sooner or later you know I'm going to get you."

"Roche, I could end it right now, you know."

"But you won't, Cantrell. For you are, among other things, an honorable man. You could no more kill me in cold blood than you could one of your dogs."

"Move, Roche. You're right, I won't kill you. You haven't driven me to that point yet. And I stress yet. But I can and will hurt you. Now shut up."

Barry drove to a spot about halfway between where the president was staying and town. He pulled off onto an old logging road, turned around, and parked facing the blacktop.

"What are you doing?" Roche asked, looking all around him. "Why are we stopping here?"

"We are going to wait for a passing parade, and then you're going to join that parade."

"In my pajamas?"

Barry grinned. "Not really."

Roche was silent for a moment then he flushed. "You dirty son of a bitch! You wouldn't do that, not to me?"

"You want to bet?"

Twenty-nine

Will helped Ki back to his truck and headed for town. Ki's mouth hurt her, but that didn't prevent the woman from cussing a blue streak.

"Did these men say why they grabbed Stormy?" Will finally managed to ask when Ki paused for a breath.

"No. But I think I've seen a couple of them before. I know I have."

"Can you remember where?"

Ki frowned as she held a now bloody handkerchief to her split lips. "Yes," she replied after a moment. "I saw two of the men out at Vic Radford's place the last time Stormy and I drove out there."

Now it was Will's turn to cuss. "That Nazi-lovin', dumb son of a bitch! I knew he was stupid, but not this stupid."

Will suddenly whipped down a gravel road and headed for his store. "We better try for the store, Ki. Call from there. It'll be faster. Don's gonna be es-cortin' all those idiots marchin' out this way."

"That's right. I didn't think about that. They'll come right by the store, won't they?"

"Unless they start fighting' 'fore they get this far."

Will slid to a halt at his store and quickly unlocked

the front door. There were half a dozen customers waiting impatiently for shiners and worms.

"Where the hell you been, Will?" one man asked. "The fish are bitin' to beat the band."

"Hep yourself, Jesse," Will told him. "And don't bother me. I got things to do."

"Well, you don't have to get uppity about it!"

Will ignored him and headed for the phone. "Hazel," he spoke to dispatch. "This is Will out to the store. Can you patch me through to Don?" A pause. "Well, hell yes, it's important, woman. You think I'd be callin' if it wasn't? Don't tell me to keep my britches on. I 'member 'bout five years ago when you was in an all-fired hurry to get 'em off."

Ki's eyes widened, and she smiled around the pain in her mouth.

"Don? This is Will, out to the store. I got Miss Ki with me. Listen, Stormy's been kidnapped. . . . That's what I said. Kidnapped. Now, you just turn that screamer on and get out here."

"Who's been kidnapped, Will?" Jesse asked, standing by the counter, his mouth hanging open.

"Go fish, Jesse," Will told him. "This ain't none of your business."

"I swear, Will. Five more years and you're gonna be the most crotchety old bastard in the county."

"Goodbye, Jesse," Will said. "And try to stay inside the boat. Don't forget, you never learned to swim."

The unrelenting heat of the late summer afternoon took some of the pep out of the marchers, but still they prodded on, and so far, without incident.

But all that was about to change.

Don Salter, upon hearing the news of Stormy's kidnapping, put on the siren and went screaming past the marchers, heading for Will's store, with several FBI agents, including Inspector Van Brocklen, right behind him.

Alex Tarver and his group had kept up a running barrage of insults directed against the gay activists and Abudu X's people, and tempers were heating up as the long line of marchers continued on toward Congressman Williams' house and President Hutton.

Alex dropped back in the line and marched alongside a man carrying a sign that read MORE MONEY FOR AIDS RESEARCH.

"That money would be better used stuffin' it down a rat hole," Alex told the marcher. He glanced at his watch. It was two-thirty in the afternoon.

"Why don't you take your ignorant mouth and go right straight to hell?" the activist told him.

"Hey," someone hollered. "There's a naked man standing in the middle of the road!"

Insults were forgotten for the moment as all eyes turned to stare at Robert Roche, standing stark naked in the middle of the blacktop, both hands covering his privates. Barry had shoved him out just seconds after Don's unit and the two FBI cars had gone rushing past his location. Barry had then pulled out and followed the police and Bureau, curious as to what was going on.

"Maybe he's really one of you fags and decided to advertise," Alex told the activist. "Why don't you get nekked and run on up there and pull his tally-whacker a time or two, and you can both get off? That'd be a real sight to see."

That did it.

The activist tossed his placard to the road and gave Alex a solid right fist to the jaw, knocking the skinhead to the blacktop. He jumped on top of the skinhead and proceeded to beat the shit out of him. Just about that time, a young boy about eleven years old, standing by the road, tossed a string of firecrackers into the line of marchers. Everybody thought they were under attack, and many of those who had guns—which was a considerable number of folks—pulled them and the fight was on.

Alex managed to get to his hands and knees, bleeding from a busted lip and a bent nose, and the activist took aim with one stout walking shoe and kicked the skinhead right in the ass, sending him rolling into a ditch, which was filled with water. Alex thrashed around in the muddy water for a moment and then reached for his gun. But it had fallen out of his pocket, and Alex couldn't find it. He decided that his contribution to the fight was over and stayed in the ditch. After all, it was a hot day and the water was cool.

Bubba Bordelon found himself facing a black man who, at least to Bubba, looked to be about seven feet tall. Two very nervous national guardsmen, both armed with M16s, were standing very close to Bubba, and the Klansman did not want to pull his pistol and get quickly filled with .223 holes. He looked at the black man, who was smiling grimly down at him.

"Aw, shit!" Bubba said, just as a huge fist exploded against his jaw. Bubba's feet left the blacktop, and he joined Alex in the ditch.

"This ain't exactly turnin' out the way we planned, is it?" Alex questioned.

Luckily, Bubba was lying half in and half out of the ditch, his face pressed against the coolness of the grassy bank. He did not reply. He was out cold.

The FBI had been closely watching the Aryan Brotherhood members and moved in on them before they could do anything. They were now lying facedown on the side of the road, their hands cuffed behind them.

Carl Radford ran through the crowd until he found

Willie Abudu X Washington, who was frantically trying to keep his people out of the growing melee.

"Now by God!" Carl shouted. "You and me gonna finish what we started a few years back." He stepped in close and gave Willie a solid left to the jaw.

But Willie was no longer a frightened boy; he had grown into a very angry man. He shook off the punch and returned it with a vengeance, rocking Carl back on his heels. Then the two went at it, cussing and flailing away under the hot Arkansas sun.

Robert Roche was dancing around on the road, the blacktop hot under his bare feet. "Will somebody give me some pants!" he shouted.

Nobody paid any attention to the billionaire, except for a little redheaded boy whose family lived along the road. The boy had just received a BB gun for his tenth birthday . . . and several very long tubes of BBs. The boy took careful aim and gave Robert Roche a BB to the butt, at close range.

"Wow!" Robert hollered, his voice lost amid the several hundred shouting, cussing, angry voices of the marchers. Robert did another little dance on the blacktop as a second BB impacted against his butt. Robert thought he was being attacked by a swarm of bees or wasps and began slapping at himself. It was quite a performance and one that would be recorded for posterity by several farm families along the way who were armed with cameras.

The fight ended when several shots were fired from within the brawling mob. The mass of protestors suddenly parted like Moses commanding the waters, and a dozen or more guardsmen, troopers, deputy sheriffs, and federal agents were knocked flat by the stampeding marchers trying to get clear of the gunfire. The only people left in the road were Robert Roche, while yelling and hopping around in his birthday suit still being butt-shot by BBs, and Carl Radford and Willie Washington, who were still duking it out, oblivious to anything else.

Thirty

The shoulder-fired rocket blew the left front tire off the president's limousine, knocking out the engine, bringing the heavy limo to a halt in the middle of the road and pinning the driver in the front seat. The second round tore off the rear door, and hot shrapnel wounded President Hutton in the leg, leaving him unable to walk. The lead Secret Service car and the car following the limo were hosed down with automatic weapons' fire, trapping the agents and wounding several.

A second team of hired terrorists hidden in the brush by the side of the road rushed the limo and looked inside.

"The bastard's still alive!" one yelled.

"Blow the door and take him!" he was ordered. "This may work out to our advantage yet."

While the Secret Service agents were pinned down, an unconscious President Hutton was yanked from the limo and dragged off into the brush.

At almost the same time, Congressman Madison's caravan was under attack. That attack killed two federal marshals, one of the Speaker's aides, and wounded a Secret Service man. The Speaker was blown out the side of the car and slid down an embankment, badly hurt, but still alive. A hitchhiker came ambling along about two minutes after the attack, just in time to look inside the car as the gas tank blew and seared him beyond recognition. But he was about the same height and weight as the Speaker.

Cliff Madison, Speaker of the House, lay some forty feet away and below the roadbed, in a pile of brush, alive, but unconscious.

When the news of the dual attack reached the officers at the scene of the recent scuffle between marchers, they dropped everything they were doing and left in a rush, a mob of reporters right behind them. The reporters had gotten some excellent footage of the brawl, and also of Robert Roche in his altogether.

Roche had been jumping around in a borrowed pair of pants and house shoes, loaned him by a farm family who lived nearby, demanding that the FBI go after Barry Cantrell and arrest him for kidnapping, assault with a deadly weapon, and a dozen other charges. No one paid any attention to him, and that just made the man angrier.

Then all the officers roared away in a scream of sirens and left Robert Roche standing by the side of the road.

In a shirt that no self-respecting bum would wear to a hobo's convention, jeans that were four inches too short in the inseam, and ladies pink fuzzy house shoes, Robert Roche turned and began the long walk back to his rented lake house. Robert Roche was not a happy man.

The scientists had pooped out about two miles from the road and could go no farther, which was just as well, for Jacques Cornet had sensed great danger ahead and had veered off, shifting into his Other and heading for the timber. The scientists had heard the faint sounds of gunfire, but to a person, they were just too tired to go on. They had lost the track of the big jaguar and were a discouraged bunch when they decided to head on back to camp. None had any idea they were about to be right in the middle of the biggest manhunt ever conducted in North Arkansas.

When the news of the kidnapping of the president and the assassination (they thought) of Congressman Madison reached those lawmen at Will's store, the FBI left immediately for the scene of the ambush. Finding Stormy, at least for the moment, was going to be left up to Sheriff Don Salter and his people.

The National Guard was ordered to escort the marchers and protestors back to town. They were not told what they were supposed to do with them once they got them there.

To say that for a time chaos reigned king in the area would be an understatement.

The van Barry was driving did not have a radio, so he had no idea what had taken place. He pulled into the parking lot of Will's store about a minute after the FBI had roared away and before the dust had even had time to settle.

"Where the hell have you been?" Don asked.

"It's a long story," Barry replied. "What's going on here?" He looked at Ki's swollen mouth. "What happened to you?"

Ki briefly explained, Barry's face turning harder with each word.

"Can you take me back to the exact spot where you were confronted by the men?"

"Sure."

"Let's go. We'll drive to where you parked your rental car, and I'll leave Roche's van there."

"What are you doing in Roche's van?" Don asked, becoming more and more confused.

"He had his men kidnap me, right after I left you

this morning. They hit me with a tranquilizer dart, and I was out for a few hours, being held at Roche's lake house."

"I see. I think. Do you want to file charges against Roche?"

"No. I've got to find Stormy."

"I'll assign a man to go with you."

"No," Barry was adamant. "I want to handle this alone."

"This thing has to be handled legally and by the book, Barry."

"You handle it legally and by the book," Barry told him. "Just stay the hell out of my way."

Before Don could object, Barry and Ki were out the door and driving away.

"I believe," Will said, "I'd concentrate on finding the president and leave Barry Cantrell alone."

"I wasn't invited to go along with the Bureau," Don replied shortly.

"It's your county, ain't it?"

Ki filled Barry in on the other attacks as she led him straight to the spot where they were attacked by the men. Barry immediately dropped to all fours and began sniffing the ground. After a moment, he stood and looked at her.

"Go back to town, Ki. See a doctor about that lip and get some rest. I'll find Stormy."

"What if they put her in a car, which they surely did, and drove off?"

"I'll still find her. Go on. Stay clear of the countryside. There are a lot of people with itchy trigger fingers searching everywhere."

Barry walked her back to her rental car and waited while she drove away. He trotted back to the ambush site, stood for a moment sniffing the air, and then moved out. Ever since moving into this area, he had been prowling the country for miles around as his Other. He knew all the little hidden places, all the caves, all the shady glens, and more importantly, he knew where the red wolf and coyote packs lived. He had visited them, and they knew him as a friend. They would know anything alien that moved in their territory. Barry would find Stormy, and after he had found her, he would find the president. He would personally deal with her kidnappers and the president's and the Speaker's attackers, and the law be damned. Then he would vanish again.

A local cop kept telling the commanding officer of the National Guard detachment that what they were doing was not legal, but the captain did it anyway. First, he put the gay activists back on their buses and told them to get gone and don't come back. Since they had made their point, they were probably ready to leave anyway, so they went without any argument. He then informed the new KKK people who had arrived that if he saw any of them hanging around the next day, he would file federal insurrection charges against them. That charge sounded really serious, so they left without incident. The Aryan Nations people who had been staying out at Vic Radford's place (those who weren't already in jail for their part in the blacktop brawl, as some members of the press were calling it) got the message without being told and left quietly. Carl Radford was cooling his heels in the small city jail, and so far his dad had made no attempt to bail him out.

That was due in no small part to the fact that the

FBI and the Secret Service had hauled Vic Radford in for questioning and were really sweating him.

"I don't know what the hell you people are talkin' about!" Vic yelled for the umpteenth time that late afternoon. "I didn't have nothin' to do with the kidnappin' of the president or the murder of Congressman Madison. Do I look stupid to you guys?"

All the agents in the room had a comeback for that line, but let it pass for the moment.

Vic took a sip of water. "I don't know anything about none of this, guys."

"Let's take it from the top," an agent said. "Again."

Vic sighed wearily.

President Hutton's leg had been tended to and crudely bandaged. They had given him nothing for the pain, and his face was shiny with sweat. He had tried to talk to his captors, but if they answered at all, it was with grunts that gave away nothing. President Dick Hutton wondered if they were going to kill him.

Stormy had been blindfolded almost immediately and had absolutely no idea where she was taken. She knew only that she had to walk for what seemed like a very long time through some very rough country. She had fallen down several times, and the men seemed to think that was very funny. Stormy did not see the humor in it.

Cliff Madison stirred and came to consciousness in a hot flash of intense pain. He thought for a moment the pain might drop him back into darkness. He resisted the urge to slip back into the relief of unconsciousness, struggling with all his might to stay alert, and won the battle. He relived those horrible few seconds of the attack over and over again. Then, mustering every ounce of strength he could gather in his torn and battered and broken body, Cliff began to inch his way out of the brush. The smell of burning rubber and scorched metal and seared human flesh still hung in the air. He began to crawl, digging his fingers into the gravel and dirt, pulling himself along with his arms and dragging his useless broken legs.

"I am going to make it," he whispered. "I am going to make it." He would repeat that phrase many times over the next few hours.

"I don't believe they got out of this area," Van Brocklen told the senior FBI officials and representatives from the U.S. Attorney General's Office who had just arrived from Washington after a very fast flight. "In less than half an hour, we had every road blocked within a fifty-mile radius of this area. Absolutely no one, *no one* has reported seeing any low-flying aircraft, fixed wing or helicopter. Within an hour, we had extended our roadblocks to a circle a hundred miles out in all directions. The governors of both Missouri and Arkansas immediately—within five minutes of our request—called out every national guardsman available to them, and there isn't a pig-path in either state that isn't covered like a blanket. We are questioning every known member of any organization who might be remotely connected to any militia or survivalist group, anyone that we know of who has ever written a letter critical of the government or has vocally espoused views critical of the government. We've pulled in half a dozen writers who live near this area who have written books or articles critical of the government . . ."

"And . . . ?" the director of the FBI asked, an impatient tone to his voice. He had personally flown in to take charge, much to the chagrin of most agents, who rightly felt that the director didn't know hog jowls from horse shit about real police work.

"Nothing," Van Brocklen said quickly and harshly.

"I am stripping every office nationwide of personnel," the director said. "In addition, I have requested authority to bring in military personnel: Navy SEALs, Army Green Berets and Rangers, Marine Force Recon, et cetera, to start a house to house search. I am considering a request to have this entire area, for a hundred miles around, placed under martial law. I believe that request will be granted within the hour."

"That's going to anger a lot of citizens," it was pointed out.

"Too bad," the director said, and walked out of the room.

Barry had immediately gone to see John Ravenna. But the immortal held up his hands and said, "I didn't do it, cousin. I was sent in here to kill both the president and the Speaker. I will openly and freely admit that to you, but this happened before I could make my move. Do you think I would be fool enough to harm your lady? Knowing that would put you on my trail for all time? Worrying me forever?" He shook his head. "And I don't think Jacques Cornet had anything to do with it. I work alone, cousin. You know that. I have never hired others to do my work for me. Never!"

"Who hired you, John?"

"I don't know. It was done through an intermediary.

A very nervous type. But I will tell you this: after he left my hotel room, I followed the careless fool back to the airport and watched him board a shuttle for Washington, D.C. Does that tell you anything, cousin?"

Barry did not reply. He turned to leave. John's voice stopped him. "I am going to disappear, Vlad. There is no point in my remaining in this area. But before I go, I want to hear you say something."

Barry faced the immortal.

"Do you think I had anything to do with the events of this day?"

Barry stared at the man for a moment, then shook his head. "No. I don't. It was too clumsy. You're an assassin, but you take pride in your work. Besides, I've had my own suspicions for several weeks. Things are not as they seem in this community."

"No, they are not. Goodbye, cousin. I hope I never see you again."

"The feeling is very mutual, John."

Barry walked out of the room.

Thirty-one

Congressman Cliff Madison was discovered just before dark by two young boys out bike riding and rubbernecking at the scene of the ambush. Moments later, Madison was air-lifted to a hospital in Little Rock where his condition was listed as serious, but not life-threatening. He was badly bruised and lacerated, both legs were broken, and he was suffering from second- and third-degree burns over part of his body.

He was interviewed briefly on the way to the hospital, but he could tell the agents nothing about the ambush. He had been knocked unconscious immediately, and all he could recall was an explosion and a flash of fire.

Not very many miles away from his own ambush site, President Hutton knew beyond any reasonable doubt who had been behind his attack. But he felt he would never get to tell his story. He was convinced his captors were going to kill him. He had seen their faces, and they could not afford to let him live. But why didn't they go ahead and do it? Why risk capture keeping him alive? That, he didn't understand.

But it would all soon become clear to the president, very soon.

* * *

As his Other, Barry ran through the gathering twilight of late summer, a gray blur in the fading light. He had stopped twice since leaving John Ravenna's lake house to "talk" with coyote packs and red wolf packs. Upon the appearance of the huge timber wolf, both species had immediately assumed the subordinate positions and were soon delighted to find that he came as a friend.

Oh, they knew where the strangers were hiding, all right, and told Barry all about it. It had long been a mystery to animal behaviorists as to whether certain species of animals really did talk to one another. And it had long been a great source of amusement to Barry why that was so difficult for those so-called learned people to accept.

After much muzzle touching, posturing, tail and ear positioning, pawing and showing of teeth and tongue, Barry resumed his trek toward where he had been told the strangers were holding the female captive . . . not in exactly those phrases, but Barry got the message.

He almost missed the place. He ran right past it without sensing it was there.

He circled around the area several times, making no sound on silent paws, until he smelled the man-scent of the guard. He bellied down on the ground and searched his surroundings, only his eyes moving. Then he spotted the rise of earth, the mound natural-looking enough, but somehow just not quite fitting in with the lay of the land.

Then it dawned on Barry: bunkers. Underground bunkers. Sure. Back in the 1960s and 1970s, when the mood of discontent was in its infancy, just beginning to sweep across America, and armed groups were forming to protest high taxes, government intervention in the lives of Americans, integration, or what have you, this area was known as a hotbed for those types of groups. Over the past thirty years, those various organizations had built probably dozens of underground bunkers. They had had years to improve the ventilation systems, dig escape tunnels, and stockpile food and water.

But where was the entrance? How deep were the bunkers? How many men and women were in there?

"Anything?" the voice cut into Barry thoughts.

"Nothing," the second male voice replied. "It's quiet out there."

"Go on down and get some supper while it's hot. Ed will relieve me in an hour."

"Ed still want to screw that bitch?"

"Sure. Bea told him maybe later, providing we could all watch. That Bea, she's something. Ed said he didn't want no audience. Said he likes to hump in private."

"But that Stormy is one fine-lookin' piece of ass. I wouldn't object to an audience."

"You're as bad as Ed. Both of you got your brains in your dick."

After a few seconds of quiet laughter, the night fell silent.

As his Other, Barry moved up to the side of the mound of earth. He could hear the sentry faintly humming an old song. So he had found the bunker; but how in the hell would he get into the thing? The small slit that ran all across the front of the mound was less than two inches wide, just wide enough to see out of. It was grass- and weed-covered top and bottom, so it was nearly impossible to detect.

On his belly, Barry circled the mound. There was no outside entrance here. Barry was certain of that. He began moving around the area, sniffing the ground, trying to pick up a scent. Nothing. Then he remembered that old shack he'd passed some few hundred yards back. Had to be. The entrance was back there; a trapdoor hidden in the floor of the tumbledown old shack. Who would think to look there?

Barry quickly made his way back to the shack and began picking up all sorts of human smells. He crawled under the shack, startling a king snake looking for supper and sending it wriggling quickly away.

Go hunt a rat somewhere else, Barry thought. These two-legged rats are mine.

But there was no trapdoor, no hidden entrance in, under, or around the old shack.

That leaves one other possibility, Barry thought: a cave.

He began quickly searching the area. This time his hunch proved out. He found the cave entrance hidden behind a thick stand of brush. The man-smell was strong. He shape-shifted and entered the mouth of the dark cave. Dark only at the entrance. Around a bend, he could see a thin shaft of light. The cave was narrow at the mouth, then opened to a comfortable standing height a few feet inside.

There was also a guard sitting on the ground just around the cave bend. Barry could see his boots. He did not appear to be very attentive. He was much less attentive after Barry suddenly stepped around the rock facing of the cave and kicked him in the head.

Barry quickly tied the man securely, using the guard's belt and bandanna. He stuffed a piece of torn-off shirt material into the man's mouth and fastened it with a piece torn from the guard's shirttail.

Barry inspected the man's weapons. A Mini-14 in .223 caliber, with several full magazines, and a Beretta 9mm pistol, with a full clip and two full spares. Then he headed deeper into the cave, his way illuminated by lanterns. The floor of the cave sloped gradually, making walking easy.

He heard footsteps coming toward him and pressed against the shadowy wall of the cave. One man walking slowly. The man spotted Barry and opened his mouth to shout a warning but Barry drove the butt of the Mini-14 into the man's stomach, doubling him over and dropping him to the rock floor of the cave. Barry balled one big hand into a fist, carefully calculated his blow, and punched the man unconscious. He tied him snugly. This man was also carrying a Mini-14 and a Beretta 9mm. Barry took the spare magazines for the rifle and tucked the spare pistol behind his belt and the clips into his pocket. He walked on toward a low murmur of voices that grew louder with each step. As quietly as possible, he jacked a round into the chamber of the Mini-14.

He had made up his mind that freeing Stormy could not be carried out with any degree of finesse. The rescue would have to be crude and very sudden. Barry paused just a few feet from the entrance to a long nature-made room, perhaps twenty-five feet square and about ten feet high, to get his bearings. He spotted Stormy, on the floor, tied hands and feet. He counted six men in the room, all of them armed. He did not recognize any of the men, but they all looked very capable. If Barry's plan worked, they would not be capable for very much longer. He could not see any woman who might be named Bea.

Barry took two small pieces of shirt he'd torn from the man he'd just trussed up and stuffed them into his ears. He took a deep breath, then stepped out from the shadows and started shooting.

The attack was so sudden and so unexpected, none of the six men in the huge cavern were able to get off a shot. Barry emptied a thirty-round magazine into the men, expecting any moment to be hit himself by a screaming ricochet as the lead bounced and screamed off the rock walls. At least two of the men who managed to get to their feet were torn by bullet fragments that howled off the rock.

The din was enormous as the sound had nowhere to go except to reverberate from rock wall to rock wall. Just as Barry was dropping the empty magazine and slipping in a fresh full one, a stocky woman came running out of a side corridor, screaming curses as she came. She had a pistol in each hand, and Barry hit the stone floor just in time to avoid getting shot as the woman was wildly pulling the triggers. Barry assumed she was the woman called Bea. Stormy stuck out her tied feet just as Bea reached her prone position.

Bea's boots got all tangled up in Stormy's feet, and the woman went headfirst, flailing her arms and stumbling across the body-littered cave floor. She came to a very abrupt halt as her head impacted against the far wall with a sickening thud. Bea sank to her knees and did not move. Barry assumed she was still alive though blood was pouring from her face.

Barry jumped to his boots and ran to Stormy, ripping the bonds from her wrists and ankles. "Let's get out of here," he said, his voice strangely far away due to the ringing in his head from the gunfire. He helped Stormy rub some feeling back into her ankles. "Can you stand?"

She nodded and rose to her feet. Just as they reached the entrance to the huge natural room, Stormy turned her head, glancing behind her, and yelled, "Behind us!"

Barry dropped to one knee and brought up the Mini-14, triggering off three fast rounds at the man who had suddenly appeared amid the blood and the gore and the bodies. The sentry, he supposed. His timing was really lousy. The front of the man's camo shirt blossomed wetly with blood, and he stumbled back against the stone wall and slid down, coming to rest on his behind, his eyes wide open in death. His sentry duties had come to an end . . . permanently.

"Are there any more?" Barry asked, his hearing still somewhat impaired.

"These were all I saw. What the hell group is this?"

"A very dangerous one, I'm thinking. And one that has been hard underground for a long, long time. Come on. Let's get out of here and get some fresh air. This place stinks."

As they walked away, the underground bunker complex as silent as the death it contained beneath their feet, Barry said, "I'll lead you to a road just ahead about a mile or so. Call the sheriff's office and tell them you escaped. Tell them you wandered in the woods for hours. It was dark, you were lost and stumbled up on a gravel road. We'll be at the road in about half an hour. Show them the rope burns on your wrists and ankles and tell them you're exhausted; you need some rest. Go on out to the house and lock the doors."

"You know more than you're telling me, Barry."

"Yes. But I promise that you will have the full story when it's over."

"And it will be over soon?"

"Tomorrow, I would imagine. I can't envision it lasting much longer."

They walked through the thick brush and timber in silence for a few moments, Barry skillfully leading the way. "You know who is behind all this, don't you, Barry?"

"I've suspected for a long time."

"You want to give me a hint?"

"You can have the whole story tomorrow." Then he told her about the attacks on the president and the Speaker of the House.

She was so stunned she stopped in the darkness and stared at him.

"Do you know where the president is being held?"

"No. But I'm sure it's in some underground complex much like the one where you were held. I'd bet this area is honeycombed with them. Not just this area, Stormy. In areas all over America where the terrain is suitable for such work."

"Then you believe this group is just a small part of a much larger nationwide organization."

"Yes. There have been whispers about a group such as this for years. I never knew whether to believe the rumors or not. Now I believe them."

"Why did they kidnap me?"

"I'm not sure. I don't know if they're responsible for the attacks on Hutton and Madison. I would think not."

"Then . . . who?"

"It goes much higher up, Stormy. All the way back to Washington."

"I have to ask again: why did they grab me?"

"My guess is for publicity. At first I don't believe they meant to harm you in any way. But extremists within the group went too far and it all got out of hand. Maybe they jumped the gun. Maybe they acted on their own without orders. Maybe this is a breakaway from the original group. We'll know by this time tomorrow." He paused and put out a hand to stop Stormy. "See those lights up there, to the north?" He smiled in the darkness. "Your left, Stormy. To your left."

"Oh. Yes, I see them."

"That's a roadblock. The government has this area sealed off tight. The gravel road is about a quarter of a mile straight ahead. You can't miss it. You'll run right into it. When you get to the road, turn left . . ." He smiled and ignored the dirty look that got him. "As soon as you get on the gravel, start yelling and waving your arms. I'll see you tomorrow." He put his arms around her and pulled her close, touching his lips to hers for a few seconds. Then he pushed her away. "Now, go. You haven't seen me."

Before she could reply, he was gone, leaving her with only a slight breeze whispering through the leaves of the trees. She stood for a moment, staring into the darkness. Just as she turned to go, a long, wavering primitive call of the wild cut the night.

Stormy smiled and began walking toward the road.

Thirty-two

Victor Radford took that last step over the edge early that evening. After the Bureau had finally released him, he drove straight home and poured a stiff drink, then another, then another. Then he loaded up his guns and called the motel where the federal agents were maintaining phone banks. He proceeded to give them a good cussing, tracing their ancestry back to the caves and beyond. He ended with admitting he was a white supremacist, he hated every Jew and black man who ever lived and ever would live, swore his life's work from that moment forward was overthrowing the government of the United States, swore his only true leader was Adolf Hitler, the greatest man who ever lived, and swore on the word of Jesus Christ to kill any federal agent who set foot on his property.

He tried to close with, "Come and get me you god damn no-good federal assholes! And come shootin'!"

"You don't know what you're saying, Radford," an FBI agent tried to reason with the man. "You're drunk."

"Fuck you!" Vic screamed. "I know exactly what I'm sayin'. I got automatic weapons buried all over this county. I got one in my hands right now. And want to kill me some federal pukes. Come on and get me, you assholes! I'm waiting on you bastards!" He hung up.

"Make damn sure nothing happens to that interrogation tape," the senior agent said to the others. Van Brocklen was out in the field. "I want to be able to show we didn't lean on this nut."

"What happens now?"

"Hopefully, he'll go to bed and sleep it off."

The phone rang again. Vic Radford. "I'm callin' the press, you assholes!" he shouted. "I'm tellin' them what a bunch of cowardly pricks you are. You hear me?"

"Go to bed, Mr. Radford," the agent said wearily. "Sleep it off. Please?"

Then Vic said the magic words. "I know who kidnapped the president, you nitwits! And I know where he is!" He hung up.

The motel room was quiet, all the agents staring at the now silent speaker.

"Now we have no choice in the matter," a Secret Service man said.

"None whatsoever," the senior FBI man agreed. "Let's go."

"He doesn't know anything," Van Brocklen said, arriving at the scene and taking command. "This is a publicity stunt. Nothing more."

"Well, if that's true, it's a hell of a stunt!" the director flared. The director was wearing body armor from his ankles to his neck and a Kevlar helmet and throat protector. Some agents at the scene thought he looked like an idiot. Others just thought he *was* an idiot and let it go at that. The director was not well liked. "The man is putting his life on the line."

"Radford is not stable," Van Brocklen argued.

"Of course he isn't!" the director snapped. "The man worships Hitler, doesn't he? Get him out of there so we can find the president."

Van Brocklen sighed. He knew beyond any reasonable doubt that Radford had no knowledge of the president's whereabouts. He'd already received word from several reliable informants that the attacks on the Speaker and the president had originally been plotted from outside this area, and was fairly certain the orders for at least one of the attacks had come from Washington, D.C.

"Did you hear me, Inspector?" the director pressed.

"I hear you," Van Brocklen replied. Then took a chance of blowing his whole career. "But you're making a mistake, sir."

"I take full responsibility for this. Do it!"

"In writing," Van Brocklen said.

"What!" the director's reply was almost a shout.

"I want this order in writing."

"By God, Van Brocklen! You're relieved. Go on back to the search parties. I'm taking over here."

"Yes, sir. With pleasure." Van Brocklen muttered the last two words.

The director whirled on the inspector. "What was that last bit?"

"Nothing, sir. Nothing at all."

"I'll see you when this is over, Inspector."

"Yes, sir."

Van Brocklen walked quickly to his car and drove away. Just as he was driving off, he heard over his radio that Stormy Knight, of the Coyote Network, had just been found. He headed for the location.

"Sir." An agent hesitantly approached the director. "We just got word that there are at least seven people in that house with Radford, including two women."

"All members of Radford's group?"

"As far as we know, sir."

"Flush them out. Use tear gas."

"They have gas masks, sir."

"Did you hear me?"

"Yes, sir."

"Then do it!"

"Yes, sir." Oh, Lord, the agent thought, walking away. Not another Waco. Please, not that.

The agent looked toward the blacktop road. The press had gathered and were filming. The agent sighed. "Here we go again," he muttered.

"Miss Knight," Van Brocklen said. They were sitting in Will's store, having a soft drink. "May I speak bluntly and off the record? One adult to another?"

"Go right ahead, Inspector," Stormy said, meeting his direct gaze.

"You wanna cut the bullshit and tell us what really happened?"

Stormy smiled. "Why, I just did, Inspector."

"You just slipped away without being seen?"

"Well . . . something like that."

"And you didn't have any help in getting away?"

"Now, Inspector, I didn't say that."

"Cantrell," Van Brocklen said. "Or whatever his name is. Has to be. All right, Miss Knight. Let's go. You lead us to where you were held."

"Well, I'll try. But I'm awfully tired."

Van Brocklen smiled. "Of course you are. And I've taken that into consideration. We'll use four-wheelers."

"You can use one of my four-wheelers, Ki," Will said to the camera-person. "And since you don't know the country, I'll ride along on another so's you won't get lost. I think I know the spot."

Van Brocklen lost his smile. "You're just a real nice fellow, aren't you, Mr. Will?"

"I do try," the man replied.

The agents surrounding the Radford compound had no choice but to return the fire coming from the house. And under newly rewritten federal guidelines, they were perfectly justified in doing so; no one in their right mind would argue that. Tear gas had done nothing to drive the occupants out, and the agents were fighting for their lives. The firefight was brief but very intense. In a matter of only a few minutes, the house was shot to splinters and bits, and those inside were dead, dying, or badly wounded.

Tillman Morris, who had been one of the first to join Vic in his last stand, had been shot twice in the chest and was not long for this earth. "Vic was just a-shittin' ya'll . . . 'bout knowin' where . . . the president is," he gasped, as a medic worked frantically to keep him alive. "But I betcha I know who did. It was . . . it was . . ." If Tillman did know, he took that knowledge with him. Tillman closed his eyes and went goose-stepping off into that Great Aryan Nation he had long envisioned.

The director had never seen a man die violently before. He was a lawyer, not a cop. He trotted off into the darkness to barf. He did not hear an experienced field agent mutter, "Our fearless leader. I hope he pukes on his shoes."

The house went up in flames, and no trace was found of Victor Radford. But the sounds of exploding ammo went on all night long, punctuated occasionally by a grenade going off, blowing sparks in all directions and causing little fires to flare up out of the ashes.

"Vic ain't dead," Tom Devers proclaimed from his

hospital bed. "He'll pop up again. You'll see. Heil Hitler!"

"Oh, screw you!" one tired FBI man muttered.

Leroy Jim Bob "Bubba" Bordelon maintained a low profile after the attacks on President Hutton and Congressman Madison, and told his group to do the same. "I don't want them damn feds all over me," Bubba said. " 'Sides, I got my hands full keepin' them damn scientists off my place. They're camped right at my fence line. Damn crazy people."

"We must not think of giving up," Dr. Dekerlegand told the tired and discouraged group as they sat around the dying embers of the camp fire. After pooping out chasing Jacques Cornet earlier in the day, the group had twice gotten lost in the hills and ravines, and several were suffering from cuts and bruises after taking tumbles. They still knew nothing about the attacks on the president and the Speaker or the massive manhunt going on all around them.

But all that was about to change. Abruptly.

One National Guard unit leader from South Arkansas, who was about as much at home in the mountains as a polar bear in the Gobi Desert, had seen the dying camp fire of the scientists. He and his men were slowly circling the camp, weapons at the ready, though they were totally, completely, and utterly lost.

Two of the young assistants had slipped away from the main body and were engaged in a bit of slap and tickle before retiring for the evening. They were trying to be as quiet as possible, but they were young and the gettin' was really gettin' good. Their moans and groans weren't carrying far, just far enough.

"Sarge, I hear sounds of torture," a young guardsman radioed. "It's really bad, too."

"All right," the young squad leader whispered into his walkie-talkie. "On my signal we go in. Don't fire unless you're sure of your target. That might be the president of the United States in there." He felt very hot breath on his neck and frowned. "Goddammit, Jenkins," he hissed. "You're too close to me. Back off, man."

About fifteen feet away, PFC Jenkins cut his eyes. "You talkin' to me, Bob?" he whispered.

The squad leader froze against the ground. If Bob was way over there to his left, who the hell was that breathin' down his neck?

Or . . . what was it?

Bob slowly turned his head and looked into the glowing eyes of what had to be the biggest damned leopard in the world. Actually, it was a long-extinct species of jaguar, but to Bob's mind, now was not the time to be making distinctions.

The jaguar slowly opened his mouth and yawned. Bob had never seen so many teeth in all his life. Then the jaguar screamed. A split second later Bob screamed, and a half second later he was up and running. He suddenly remembered he had an M16 with a full magazine of live ammunition. Bob stopped, turned, and split the night with gunfire. He didn't hit anything except warm night air, for the jaguar had jumped to one side and trotted off into cover as soon as Bob screamed.

The scientists all jumped to their feet at the sound of the animal's scream—they knew exactly what had screamed—but they didn't stay on their feet long. The national guardsmen all thought those around the dying camp fire had opened fire on them, since the gunfire was coming from very close to the camp, and they

began firing. The young assistant on top of the other
young assistant plumbed depths he had never before
achieved, and his partner let out a satisfied wail that
only added to the confusion.

By this time, Jacques Cornet was loping along a half
a mile away, smiling an animal smile at the fun he'd
just had.

Not too far away, Bubba Bordelon jumped to his feet
at the sound of gunfire and grabbed his shotgun. He'd
been camped out near his fence line so he could keep
an eye on the nutty scientists. He thought the feds
were attacking him, and he was going to make a last
stand. He stopped at his fence and uncorked a full
tube of twelve-gauge shotgun rounds, just as fast as he
could pump.

The guardsmen returned the fire, and the night was
ripped apart by wild gunfire that seemed to go on forever, but really lasted only a few seconds.

"Come out with your hands up!" an eighteen-year-
old private yelled toward the camp, his voice very
shaky.

"My God!" Dr. Biegelsack shouted. "What have we
done?"

"And bring the president with you!" Bob shouted,
trying to jam home a full magazine with trembling fingers.

"Oh, shit!" Bubba muttered, and decided to get the
hell gone from this area. He beat it back to his house
just as fast as he could travel through the night.

Acting without orders from his squad leader, the
radio operator frantically called for a helicopter, telling communications on the other end they had
found the president of the United States and were
all engaged in a very heavy firefight with an unknown
adversary.

Within ten minutes, a SWAT team from the Arkansas

State Police had rappeled in, an assault team from the
FBI had done the same, a team of heavily armed and
very menacing-looking Navy SEALs was on the ground
A hysterical Dr. Gladys Dortch had gone blundering
around in the very dark and moonless night, looking
for the recently dug latrine, tripped, and plunged
headfirst into the grassy ditch with the two young and
very sweaty and naked assistants, who could not find
their clothes, gotten all tangled up with the freshly
sated flesh, and was screaming in a voice that would
crack brass that she had fallen into the clutches of
what she assumed to be two of the missing links in the
chain of humanity. Meanwhile, the young squad leader
was trying to explain what had happened to an unbe
lieving and totally unsympathetic commanding officer

"It is my belief," the captain of this contingent of
National Guard said to Bob, "that your career in the
Arkansas National Guard is over."

"So who gives a big rat's ass?" Bob told the CO, who
fifty weeks out of the year was the manager of a men's
clothing store. "I'm tellin' you that I seen a goddamn
tiger! And if you don't believe that, then you can just
kiss my ass, you son of a bitch, right up to the cherry
red where it ain't never been sunburned or blistered!"

One minute later, the manager of the men's clothing
store and the mechanic at a Ford dealership were
duking it out.

All in all, it was a very confusing night in North
Arkansas. And the night was still young.

Thirty-three

The woman called Bea was still alive, but unconscious, suffering from a broken nose and jaw and a fractured skull. The sentry Barry had trussed up in the cave was defiant and would give only his name, serial number, and old military rank.

"Get him out of here!" Van Brocklen said, then turned to face Stormy.

"It's all coming back to me now," Stormy said. "I was so traumatized by everything. You see, I was blindfolded. I didn't see who it was who rescued me."

"Right," the inspector said, very drily. "I'm sure that's what happened."

Will stood off to one side, smiling.

Van Brocklen glared at the man. "You find all this amusing, Mr. Will?"

"Shore do," the older man replied.

"You have a very strange sense of humor, sir."

"That's what my wife used to tell me."

Van Brocklen shook his head. Twice he had told Will to stay out of the cave. Twice Will had smiled and ignored him.

"Must be half a million rounds of ammunition stored down here," a Secret Service man said, walking up. "Cases of everything from grenades to MREs to you name it, it's here."

"They were preparing for war," an FBI man said.

"Just make shore you guys are on the right side when it kicks off," Mr. Will said. "And it's gonna kick off, bet on that."

"Problem is," Van Brocklen muttered under his breath, "he's probably right."

Only Will heard him. The older man cut his eyes, smiled, and whispered, "You better believe I am, sonny."

Barry squatted in the timber, trying to decide what best to do. With the help of a few of his four-legged friends of the forest, he had located the underground bunker complex where they told him a man was taken against his will earlier that day. They showed him one of the many entrances and exits, and then vanished into the night.

Barry finally decided that the best thing for him to do was nothing at all, except alert the FBI and let them handle it. He shape-shifted and began his run through the woods. His friends had also told him where he would find a lot of strangers—told him with no small amount of animal humor in their eyes and position of their ears and tails. Barry knew exactly where his friends meant. Animals, especially wolves, coyotes, dogs, and cats, had a fine sense of humor. But it was awfully difficult for most non-animal lovers to see it. Even many dog and cat owners often failed to recognize it.

Barry knelt above the bunker entrance he and Stormy had left only hours before and waited. Mr. Will finally came out and stood for a moment, smoking a cigarette.

"Mr. Will," Barry whispered. "Tell Van Brocklen I want to see him. Make sure no one else hears you."

The older man nodded and stepped back into the darkness of the cave. A moment later, Inspector Van Brocklen stepped out, looking all around him.

A scratching sound above and behind him turned the FBI man around. He sucked in his breath at the sight before him. The biggest timber wolf he had ever seen stood above him, the yellow eyes glowing in the night. Van Brocklen didn't know much about wild animals, having been city born and bred, but he had seen enough wildlife documentaries to know better than to reach for a gun. He remained motionless, but his heart was beating so fast he thought it might explode.

Then, suddenly, the wolf was gone and Barry Cantrell was standing where the wolf had been, smiling at him. "Eight and a half miles due west of here, Inspector, there is a small valley. A tumbledown old house sits in the center of the valley. Part of a native rock fence is still standing. I'm sure Mr. Will knows where it is. That entire area is honeycombed with underground bunkers. President Hutton is being held there. How you get him out is up to you."

Van Brocklen's mouth opened and closed silently a couple of times. He finally found his voice. "How did you . . . I mean . . . you were a *wolf!* How . . . ?"

But Barry was gone, melting silently into the night.

John Ravenna rented a car at the airport and drove to a motel in the suburbs, not far from Senator Madalaine Bowman's home in Northern Virginia. After checking in, John stood by his rental car for a moment, parked in front of the motel room, and then shifted into his Other.

Thirty minutes later, he was standing in his human form in Senator Bowman's bedroom. He smiled, then shifted. As his Other, he growled once, and Madalaine opened her eyes. Her nose wrinkled at the strong animal smell, and she sat up in bed. She had only a second to form a scream in her throat that never made it past her lips before the huge spotted hyena leaped. Within two minutes' time, the bedroom walls were splattered with blood and gore. The sounds of bones cracking under the force of powerful jaws filled the death house. Then . . . silence.

Two more U.S. senators would die that night, under the most horrible of circumstances. Hard-nosed investigators from the Virginia State Police and seasoned agents from the FBI would, to a person, be sickened at the carnage. None of them had ever seen anything like it in their long careers.

"It would appear," an FBI spokesperson would later read from a carefully worded statement, "that after the victims were killed, the flesh was torn from the bones by some sort of animal with very powerful jaws, and then . . . eaten."

"Motive?" a reporter asked.

The agent shook her head. "We don't have one as yet."

The firefight at the underground bunkers that night in North Arkansas was over very quickly. To a person, those holding President Hutton captive committed suicide rather than be taken alive, but for reasons that would be forever unknown, they spared the life of President Hutton.

He was treated at the scene by emergency medical services personnel and then flown to Little Rock for surgery on his injured leg.

A very weary Van Brocklen and Chet Robbins were back at the motel complex a couple of hours before dawn. Both of them wanted no more than a long, hot soapy shower and a few hours sleep. They were stopped by the sight of a wolf peering around the corner of the building at them.

"That's him," Van Brocklen said.

"I don't believe it!" Chet said.

Barry shifted.

"Son of a bitch!" the Secret Service man whispered, as both men stepped closer to the corner of the building.

"President Hutton is all right, Barry," Van Brocklen said.

"I know. Friends of mine told me."

"Friends of yours?" Chet questioned.

"Please don't ask who," Van Brocklen said.

"What friends?" Chet blurted.

"Friends in the forest," Barry replied.

"You had to ask," Van Brocklen muttered.

"If you're interested, we can wrap this all up tomorrow morning," Barry said. "Meet me on that side street behind Nellie's Cafe at nine o'clock. Inspector, I expect you to keep your word about trying to get the government off my back."

"I said I'd try, Barry, and I will. I'll do everything within my power. But don't expect me to work miracles. I'm just a minor cog in a great big bureaucratic wheel."

"I'll see you in the morning."

Chet started to speak, then closed his mouth. Barry was gone. He shook his head and said, "This is the strangest case I have ever worked."

"And it isn't over yet," FBI added.

"You just had to add that, didn't you?"

Thirty-four

"Won't Inspector Van Brocklen object to my being along?" Stormy asked.

"Probably," Barry replied. "But you will at least be able to get film of them taking the man away. That is if they have proof enough to do that. I really don't know what they have."

She had watched Barry pack his few belongings and then muscle the camper shell onto the bed of the pickup and bolt it down. He had laid a thin mattress on the bed of the truck for the dogs to lie on.

"Do you know where you're going?" she asked, as they sat on the front porch of the house, sipping coffee in the relative coolness of morning.

"Yes. I'll let you know as soon as I'm settled in." He smiled. "And I promise one of the first things I'll do is get a telephone."

"Promises, promises," she teased him, then her smile faded. "Do you think Inspector Van Brocklen has enough stroke to do any good, Barry?"

"No. But he'll try. And while he's doing that, I might gain a little time."

"How about Robert Roche?"

"He's the one that worries me more than the gov

ernment. After what I did to him, he'll never quit chasing me." Barry smiled. "But it was worth it."

Ki pulled in, and the three of them walked through the house, checking to see if Barry had missed anything. He was leaving his furniture, including the television and satellite dish. When Barry left a location, he broke clean.

"The president and the Speaker are going to be all right," Ki brought them up to date. "They've both scheduled press conferences for later today."

"That will be either a very interesting event," Barry said, "or a very boring one. What is the mood in town?"

"Relief that it's all over," Ki replied. "But I get the funny feeling that some people around the county know a hell of a lot more than they're saying."

"Sure they do," Barry said. "And certainly not just in this area. Lots of unrest around the nation. Militia groups springing up all over the place. But the government doesn't seem all that interested in addressing the problems these millions of people point out. At least the party in power doesn't seem interested. It's just the same ol' political Potomac Two-Step, day after day. When the Republicans point out that government needs to be downsized, programs need to be cut, departments cut back or done away with completely, they're vilified by democratic left-wing extremists as advocating children starving, old people left to die, et cetera, et cetera. Any thinking person knows all that is a crock of shit. Both parties spend far too much time conducting witch-hunts against the other, instead of addressing the problems facing this nation . . ."

Barry noticed that Stormy had clicked on her small cassette recorder and was getting his words on tape.

He did not object. She would probably use it as an anonymous "man on the street" interview.

"We've been all through this several times," Barry continued. "You both know how I feel. I've seen governments rise and fall, and most of the time it's because those in power did not listen to the people. But"—he held up a finger—"it's not necessarily those in the majority that should be listened to; it's those who can do the most damage. The left-wingers in this country know this, and that's why they're so intent on disarming the American public. But all they're doing is making criminals out of thousands of heretofore law-abiding gun-owning citizens and setting the stage for dozens or perhaps hundreds of resistance groups to form. And these democratic left-wing extremists are so naive they don't, or can't, understand why Americans won't just willingly and happily hand over their guns, agree to more government control of their lives, and consent to higher personal taxes and a never-ending national debt so the left-wingers can fund more unworkable and unpopular social programs. The balloon has to pop one of these days, and in my opinion that day is not far away."

"Do you think the majority of Americans support an armed revolution?" Stormy asked.

Barry shook his head. "No. But when it comes down to the nut-cutting, many will hold their noses and champion the revolution as the lesser of two evils. It all depends on how the revolutionaries put it all together." He paused for a moment, then said, "Don't forget, I've seen it happen before. Americans won't support racist or hate groups, but many will support groups attempting to return to a more common-sense-based form of government. A government where the law-abiding have more rights than the criminals. Where a citizen can protect his or her property without fear of arrest, prosecution, or civil lawsuit should the criminal get hurt or killed. Where the tax system is more evenly established and millionaires pay their share. Americans have advocated a flat tax rate for years, yet Congress won't do a damn thing toward setting that up. And the fault lies on the shoulders of both political parties. Neither wants to give an inch on their favorite programs. So . . . many Americans have decided that if elected government officials won't get this mess straightened out, they, as citizens, are going to have to do it themselves. And more than one great American leader has stated that the citizens have the constitutional right to do that. Hell, revolution has happened all over the world at one time or another. Why should America be immune?"

"You're convinced of some sort of civil uprising, aren't you, Barry?" Ki asked.

"Yes. And sooner than later."

The four of them walked into the office to face the man, sitting behind his desk, a pistol in front of him. Van Brocklen had asked Stormy to wait outside.

"I know you didn't put it together," he said, looking at Van Brocklen. "You people are too goddamn stupid." He cut his eyes to Barry. "You did, didn't you?"

"That's right. Almost from the very first."

"How?"

Barry smiled. "Let's just say you were careless."

"I don't believe that. Let's just say you got lucky."

"Whatever it was, you're finished."

The man smiled, his eyes drifting to the pistol on his desk. "I might be, but the movement isn't."

"You're probably right about that," Van Brocklen said. "But why would you people plot to grab the president and the Speaker?"

"We didn't. Even if we did, you think I'd admit it? But I have . . . ah . . . shall we say people highly placed in and around Washington. Planted so deep you'll never find them. They told me late last night the plot to kill Hutton and Madison came from the halls of Congress." He grinned. "How about them apples, boys?"

Neither Van Brocklen nor Chet Robbins replied to that. They already knew it. They also had been informed early that morning of the bizarre deaths of three very prominent senators.

The man behind the desk grinned up at those standing before him. "Aren't you forgetting something, boys? Aren't you going to read me my rights?" Then his grin changed to a laugh. "Oh, I see. You don't have enough proof to arrest me, do you? Well . . . you must be close or you wouldn't have chanced coming to see me." He looked at the serious expressions on the faces of the feds. "No? Then . . . I don't understand."

"We're not here to arrest you," Chet said. "Just to tell you that you're all finished in this area. You've had a lot of people fooled for a long time, including us, I have to admit that. But no more. You're through."

The man behind the desk looked first at the two federal agents, then at Barry, then at the man standing beside the immortal. "Well, I'll just be damned. It was you, wasn't it?"

"I talked to Barry about you late last night," the man said. "We agreed it had to be you."

"I always figured you for the dumb sort. Guess I was wrong."

"We're open for a deal," Chet said, a hopeful note to his words.

The man shook his head. "No way. No deals. Why

should I? You just admitted you don't have enough on me to arrest."

"You know the answer to that," Van Brocklen said.

"Sure. The IRS is going to be all over me now. You guys are going to start investigating me, word will quietly leak out about it, and that will finish me in politics. Am I getting warm?"

"Your words, not ours," Van Brocklen was quick to speak.

Jim Beal sighed audibly and said, "Man, you're the sheriff. The most powerful man in the county. You had it made. Why get mixed up with Vic Radford and Bubba and the others?"

Sheriff Don Salter leaned back in his chair and smiled. "Who says I was?"

"The deal Chet mentioned is still open, Don," Van Brocklen said. "We could use a man like you in this area. You know it's only a matter of time before we close in on you. We're going to sweat Bubba and a few of the others. We'll lean on them so hard they'll think they've been hit by a truck. One of them will break. You know what happens to cops in prison, Don."

Don's grin didn't fade. "You'll never put me in prison. The movement's too big for that to happen. I'll just go underground and help run operations from there."

"I'd start sweating Vic Radford first," Barry spoke to no one in particular. "He's the weak link and he's still alive." He looked directly at Don. "The Bureau found the tunnel under his house, Don."

"We'll get him, Don," Chet said. "His kind can't keep their mouths shut. You know that. That's why you planted that automatic weapon in Vic's house and blew up your own jail trying to kill him. Barry told us about you not knowing he had made bail that evening."

Don's grin faded just a bit. "Prove it!"

"Oh, we will," Van Brocklen told him. "In time, we will."

"You want to work with us, Don?" Chet asked.

"Turn against my own people?" the sheriff replied. "No way. Movements like mine are the only thing that's going to keep America strong. We've got to knock the Jews out of power and slap the niggers back down where they belong and we can keep an eye on them. You boys know damn well crime didn't start to skyrocket until the nigger civil rights bill became law and we couldn't roust them. Niggers have virtually destroyed this nation and you know it. They're nothing but savages. Work with you? No way. Go to hell. And get out of my office. You boys got nothin' on me."

Outside the sheriff's office, Jim Beal said, "Your bluff didn't work."

"It was no bluff, Mr. Beal," Chet replied. "He'll be under arrest by noon. We have federal arrest warrants on the way now. We just would rather have had him working for us, that's all."

"Am I free to go?"

"You were never being detained, Mr. Beal," Van Brocklen said. "We don't like militias, but you haven't broken any laws. We think your philosophy is all cockeyed, but you're not a suspect in any plot to subvert the government. Thank you for your cooperation."

As Jim Beal walked away, Barry said, "Don will never be taken alive. You both know that."

"Yes," Chet replied with no change of expression. "We know."

As if to punctuate that remark, the sharp crack of a pistol came from inside the sheriff's office.

Barry met the eyes of both federal men. "If I was a suspicious type, I'd think you boys planned it this way."

Something moved behind Van Brocklen's eyes. "You'll play hell proving it."

Thirty-five

Barry parked on the side of the winding mountain road, got out of his truck, and looked down at the town he would soon put behind him. Pete and Repeat showed no inclination to leave the comfortable bed of the truck. Barry stared at the picturesque scene for a moment. Really, the town was no different from dozens, perhaps hundreds, of other small communities scattered throughout America. It was quietly being torn apart by philosophical differences about what was best for the nation.

He heard a whisper of sound behind him and turned to face Jacques Cornet.

"Leaving, Vlad?" the man asked.

"Yes. And so should you."

"Oh, I am."

"What in the hell ever prompted you to come here, Jacques?"

"John Ravenna."

"But you didn't confront him. And what would have been the end result if you had? Both of you maimed and torn . . . and for what? You both would have been healed in twenty-four hours."

The Frenchman shrugged his shoulders expressively. "No matter. I have much work to do in this nation."

"Oh, Jacques! Give it up and go home. Why stick your nose into the internal affairs of a nation in which you have no interest?"

"Because France is hopeless, that's why!"

Barry chuckled. "Well, I won't argue that with you."

"Why do you suppose John killed the politicians? And we both know he did."

Barry shook his head. "Who knows why John does anything?"

"True. Vlad, John would work with us if for no other reason than the adventure of it. Just think, the three of us could change the course of this nation. I've given up on France, but there is still hope for America."

Barry shook his head. "No way, Jacques."

"But this is your adopted country!"

"It's going to have to work out its own problems without my help."

For a moment, the French immortal looked reflective. Then he sighed. "Perhaps you're right. I might go down to Central America and organize against the hunters and poachers."

"I'm sure the environmentalists would love you for it."

"I'll think about it."

Several rental trucks rattled by, the occupants waving at the two men standing by the side of the road. The scientists and their assistants, off on yet another adventure.

"I had fun with them," Jacques said.

"I'm sure you did." Barry's reply was decidedly dry.

Jacques smiled. "I have an idea, Vlad."

"I can't wait to hear this."

"Why don't you tell your Mr. Roche about me? Let him chase me for a while. I can promise him a much more exciting time of it."

"I don't know that I want to wish you on him Jacques."

The Frenchman nodded, and his expression turned serious. "You know how we French feel about liberty and freedom, Vlad."

"Yes. So?"

"When the time comes for this country's second revolution, I shall be on the side of the libertarians. felt you should be advised of that."

"You think I won't be, Jacques?"

"I don't know, Vlad. Sometimes you're very difficul to predict."

"You're not."

"Thank you. Well, I won't keep you. I, ah, jus wanted you to know that, ah, any hard feelings I migh have held toward you are, ah, no more. Au revoir Vlad."

Before Barry could reply, Jacques stepped off th shoulder of the road, trotted into the timber, and wa out of sight.

Barry looked back at the town, Norman Rockwellish in the sunlight. "Very interesting little town," he mut tered. "I wonder if the next one will be as interesting.

He got into his truck and stared at the winding road for a moment. He sighed, thinking of the long journe ahead of him. He pulled out and headed northeast. A few moments later, when he had settled into th rhythm of the road, he began to relax.

Stormy and Ki had interviewed several people abou the suicide of Sheriff Don Salter, then packed it uj and pulled out for the Memphis airport. Barry and Stormy had said their goodbyes earlier.

Barry had met with Van Brocklen and Chet Robbin one more time before pulling out.

"Any way I can reach you?" the Bureau man ha asked.

"I'll get in touch with you," Barry told him. "It'll be a couple of months, at least." He stared into the eyes of both federal men. "Why did Don eat a pistol?" he asked.

"I've been thinking about that," the Secret Service man replied. "I think the organization Don was a part of—whatever it is—is so hard underground, and so committed to their beliefs, the members would rather take their own lives than be taken prisoner and risk giving anything away."

"They're that dedicated?"

"I think so," Van Brocklen said. "And I think they've been around for a long time."

"Then . . . the people who grabbed the president were part of Don's group?"

"Maybe," Chet picked it up. "But I think not. I think they took their orders from a group in Washington. The people who attacked the Speaker . . . well, that's another story."

"Victor Radford's people?"

"No," Van Brocklen said with a strange smile. "Jim Beal's people."

"Jim!"

"Oh, yeah. That's a smart man, Barry. I think he was Don's boss for this cell . . . maybe for the entire state or region. We'll probably never be able to prove it. But I'll go to my grave believing it."

Barry glanced at Chet. "That's your thinking, too?"

"Yes. The strangest thing is, in his own way—and Van and I are in agreement on this point—Jim Beal is a nice guy. He loves America, doesn't want to see any harm come to minorities, but he is firmly convinced that they are inferior to the white race. He's a man fighting his own personal demons. We think Don engineered and pulled the kidnapping without Jim's permission—with some breakaway members, and those members probably not from this cell or region. When the kidnapping attempt failed, and this now becomes pure guesswork, he knew Jim Beal would nail him. Rather than disgrace the movement, he took his own life. Something silently passed between the two men while we were in the sheriff's office, some hidden signal. Don got the message and knew it was over for him. So he ended it then and there."

"And left you people with a very cold trail."

"Yes," Van Brocklen said. "Hell, Barry, we know we've got people with racist or subversive or militia or survivalist ties within our organization. You can't turn around in D.C. without bumping into one of them. We know that. Hell, we know who some of them are! Not many, but a few of them."

"The military is full of those types of people," Chet continued. "If, or I should say when, this second revolution starts, the military really can't be counted on to do much. They're going to be busy fighting among their own ranks . . . at least for a time, and God only knows who'll win. And all this organization wasn't done overnight. It took a long time and some very careful groundwork. This thing is much, much bigger than most people think."

"Members of Congress know how big it is?" Barry asked.

"Some of them," Van Brocklen said. "They're the ones who are really concerned about it. Others refuse to admit we've got a real problem growing in this nation. Still others realize we've got a problem, but think it will work itself out."

"It's gone too far for the latter to happen," Barry said flatly.

"Of course it has," Chet said. "We know that. But the liberals in Washington still cling to the notion that disarming the American public is the way to go. They can't see, can't or won't understand that type of action only adds to the problem."

"Then they're idiots!"

"The term is liberal," Van Brocklen said sourly.

"Barry, do you have any idea how many cells of militia, survivalist, or groups, some armed, some not, of alternate political philosophy there are in the United States?"

"I have no idea."

"As of right now, ten thousand eight hundred and ninety-nine that we know of. That is approximately two hundred and twenty groups per state. Many of them have only five or six members and they're completely harmless, but others can field five or six hundred heavily armed members."

"And to say that many, if not most, of these groups are very unhappy with the direction the government has been heading for the past three or four decades would be the understatement of the century," Van Brocklen said. "Pissed off, would be a better way of describing their mood."

"And dangerous," Barry added.

"Oh, hell, yes!" the Secret Service man said quickly. "There are some out there who would make Jim Beal and Don Salter look like choir boys. This nation is facing a rough and rocky ride. And how it will eventually turn out is anybody's guess. Guys like Van and I are in complete sympathy with that little Dutch boy with his finger in the hole in the dike. He just doesn't have a long enough reach or enough fingers to keep up with the new holes that keep breaking through."

"Barry," Van Brocklen said. "Put some distance behind you, and when you get there, keep your head down."

Barry thought he knew what the Bureau man was

trying to tell him: the government was coming after him. They wanted him for research.

"All right," Barry said, then shook hands with both men. He watched them walk away.

Now as he drove steadily northeast, Barry wondered if he would ever be able to put enough distance between himself and those chasing him. Maybe not, he thought. But he figured Maine was a pretty good start.